SQUEAMISH PRESS

For her... Wherever she is.

ONCE UPON A TIME ON THE INTERNET...

facebook

Timeline

About

Photos

Friends

"Greetings, my friend. We are all interested in the future, for that is where you and I are going to spend the rest of our lives. You are interested in the future. You are interested in the unknown... the mysterious. The unexplainable. That is why you are here. And now, for the first time, we are bringing to you, the full story of what happened on that fateful day. We are bringing you all the evidence, based only on the secret testimony, of the miserable souls, who survived this terrifying ordeal. My friend, we cannot keep this secret any longer... "

-- *Plan 9 From Outer Space*

PART ONE

THE BOOGEYMEN: ORIGINS

"Some people never go crazy. What truly horrible lives they must live."

-- Charles Bukowski

"Hello! Hooray! Let the show begin, I've been ready.
Hello! Hooray! Let the lights grow dim, I've been ready.
Ready as this audience that's coming here to dream.
Loving every second, every moment, every scream... "

-- Alice Cooper

EARLY MAN
He fucked her in the ass first, Oprah.
TMI?
Oops. Are we out of order here? Sorry. My bad.
Take it away, Warfield...

WARFIELD
"Any chance you can look like that?" I joked to my wife Nikki, as I pointed to the sexy bikini girl on the cover of Maxim magazine.

Nikki responded by pointing to a muscular stud gracing the cover of Men's Health magazine. "Well, maybe if you could look like that. He doesn't drink his six-pack." I smiled. Fair enough. I didn't marry Nikki for her snark, but it came with the package, anyway.

As she pushed our shopping cart away from the newsstand, she got a phone call from her mother. She told me to meet her at the registers with the cart. She needed a few small items from the next aisle.

I watched her go as she walked off. She'd always been lean and athletic, and was busting her ass to lose the remaining baby fat she'd accrued during pregnancy. I wished she'd kept her hair long, but she preferred it neat and short and I'd stopped nagging her about it. We'd been college sweethearts back in Colorado and married six years. I'd had my share of girlfriends in high school yet nothing serious. Nikki was my golden ticket.

But she was pretty irritated when she found me back at the newsstand moments later, thumbing through an issue of Stuff magazine. The good Kardashian was preening for the cameras. "If you play your cards right, maybe I'll get you a subscription for Christmas," she said. After returning the magazine to the shelf, she caught me off-guard with a quick kiss. Occasionally, marriage held some surprises.

We picked up our two-year-old daughter, Page, from my in-laws' house. Children really do change your life. It's an old cliché, but that doesn't make it any less true. Parents now, custodians of a child, Nikki and I were more nearly business partners than anything else. Still, Nikki had her needs and I had my wants. Her needs might include something as tame as a surprise kiss in the supermarket, but my wants were another story altogether. These are distinctions worth noting. I know that now.

Problem was, since the baby was born, rarely did Nikki's needs and my wants meet up. Marriage can be a robotic, rewind-and-play existence, a series of limiting routines, but a guy like me didn't mind much. At the end of the day, marriage may have just been the lesser of two evils. I wanted a family and now I had one. It was what it was.

For Nikki, it was all about scented soaps and carpet swatches. Plans and Pilates. New restaurants and outlet stores. And, of course, now our baby. That doesn't sound so sexy, but I loved her very much and was grateful. Even when deathly bored to tears I remained grateful, but far less so when her Wasp parents moved nearby after Page was born.

Hailing from hardy Republican stock, their blood was so blue they probably would've been impervious to a vampire attack. Her father and I engaged in mostly innocuous political discussions. He probably thought Deepak Chopra was the name of the 20th hijacker. He'd taunt me about the "inconvenient truth" of Global Warming. He wanted to know if they were now calling it 'climate change,' because when we weren't looking the weather got suddenly chillier? When will they make up their minds? "Yeah, some of 'your best friends' are stem cells, right?'" I'd parry back.

What I found more disagreeable than her parents' politics were their constant visits to our house. Naturally, they were thrilled to have a granddaughter. I wasn't an asshole, and understood and appreciated their excitement at being grandparents. But it quickly grew exasperating when I'd come home from work, wanting nothing more than a beer, dinner, and a little "SportsCenter," and her folks would be there, fresh off the golf course and three whiskeys deep.

I was Assistant Director of New Business Development for a software firm twenty miles north of Phoenix. It wasn't a bad job, defined as one good enough that Nikki didn't have to work, but I was pretty bored with the whole corporate soldier gig. There were days I would've been happier selling iced tea and fish tackle in, say, Hawaii.

I was eating lunch at my desk one Friday afternoon, and reading an AOL story headlined" *Families sue MySpace after Daughters Abused.*"

Associated Press
NEW YORK -- Four families have sued News Corp. and its MySpace social-networking site after their underage daughters were sexually abused by adults they met on the site, lawyers for the families said Thursday.

Something similar happened to the daughter of one of my salesmen about a year earlier. At our company Christmas party, Ricky Wender displayed photos of his teenage kids to me. Pointing to the picture of George, he said, "As long as he gets laid." Pointing to the picture of Erin: "And she doesn't." We toasted to that, but Ricky wasn't toasting anyone three months later when Erin met a boy on the Internet who she deemed both cute and 19. An online courtship began. Pictures and flirtations were exchanged. After school one day, Erin took a bus to meet the boy and disappeared for 24 hours.

The Wenders prayed their immediate worst fears wouldn't be confirmed. Fortunately the police returned Erin, safe and unharmed. The "boy" she thought she'd been corresponding online with was some 50-year-old creep who attempted to sexually assault her. The Wenders had dodged a really scary bullet.

Nikki called just before I left the office and asked if I'd pick up a few bags of ice on my way home. Maybe a good bottle of wine. When I pulled into the parking lot of Scrappy's Liquor Locker, there were two pretty high school girls chatting in a blue pickup truck beside me. When they noticed me, they hopped out of it, revealing themselves: tanned and toned and wearing not much more than cutoff shorts and flip-flops. The brunette had a belly button ring serving sentry over her ridiculously flat stomach.

"Excuse me," she said. "Can you buy us a liter of Sky vodka?"

"Sorry, girls. Can't do that." I headed into the liquor store, where I bought five bags of ice and a bottle of Malbec. Upon my return to my car, the girls were making out by the truck. Really going at it, too, thrusting their tongues in each other's mouths.

When the brunette caught me ogling them, she flashed me a beautiful, naked tit.

She might have been a better salesman than Ricky Wender, because a few minutes later I was back inside Scrappy's buying a bottle of Sky vodka. It wasn't the wisest of ideas: stupid, in fact, and obviously illegal. Once back outside, I ensured the coast was clear before handing the bag of booze to the brunette. Like a good father figure, I warned them not to drink and drive. They told me not to worry; they were going straight to a pool party. The brunette blew me a kiss as they drove off, leaving me feeling a bit foolish. They'd definitely hit their mark with me.

But fueled by this little flirtation, I decided to follow them. Like a bad father figure, if I'd just contributed to the delinquency of minors, I'd follow through on some more diversion. Stupid ideas have a way of gathering momentum.

This one led me to Tanglewood Drive, which was lined with cars and Jeeps. After pulling over, I watched the two girls trek towards the house party with their vodka. I fixed on the brunette, her ass and legs and little curves. I imagined what she'd be like at the party in four or five hours. She'd be in the pool, shitfaced and sloppy in her bikini. Splashing and flirting, and maybe even topless. A strong swimmer.

The stage was hers. She'd be exposed there beneath the glow of floodlights, the music booming out, the boys bellowing catcalls down at her, raising their beers high. Some kind of horny Greek Chorus and each wanting to fuck her until her teeth hurt. She was so almost-naked, so shiny and tipsy, it was driving them mental. She was captivating. She was their captive, and they her captive audience.

One boy in attendance would quietly lust after her more than the rest of them. He'd be pretty shy, so no catcalls for him. He'd just be hanging out, sipping his beer like a gentleman, wearing a blousy T-shirt and Adidas sneakers. Maybe a small colony of pimples settled on the side of his neck. But he'd be watching her. iPhone at the ready, maybe he'd shoot a photo of her.

That picture would keep him busy tonight when he turned out the lights to go to sleep. The resolution would be amazing. Thank you, Steve Jobs. Loved your work. He would fixate on that photo – Drunk Pool Girl, backlit by the dark sky and the desert mountains rimming the distant horizon like broken teeth. He would punish his prick, euthanizing that erection like an ailing loved one. He would hit his mark.

But that would come later, and at the present moment his erection would be in the wings, building with excitement and threatening to reveal itself from behind the curtain. He'd watch her do the drunken backstroke, giggling and thrashing and having the time of her life. He'd wonder what was in her naughty heart, knowing only what's in his. And he'd fantasize privately about the things he'd love to do with her. Some of them maybe a little weird or dark or even dangerous. So many achy, unbroken desires.

In twelve years, that boy would be me.

I was awash in rivulets of salty perspiration, the fever building. It should've been a shameful fool's errand, but felt strangely liberating. Maybe this little daytime adventure was a little wake-up call in my head: *Hey, your life isn't over yet. It doesn't HAVE to be so routine and boring. You don't have to be in the background all the time. There's fun to be had. You gotta just know where to find it. So bear down. Focus. Go for it.*

I removed my prick. And went after it right there in my car on Tanglewood Drive. Nikki railed at me with snarling hostility when I returned to the house about fifty minutes later than expected. To make matters worse, water was pooling all over the kitchen table because all the ice had completely melted. I was in trouble.

"Jesus. How did it melt so fast?" she asked.

"It's hot out there, Nikki. I'm sorry. But ice melts. We live in the desert."

"And that's my fault? Really?" She never wanted to live in Arizona, and whenever presented with a chance, she loved to remind me.

"I didn't say that. And there was a ton of traffic."

"A ton, huh?"

Sometimes I felt more like a witness under withering cross-examination than a husband. Her moods could sure swing, and she was capable of launching into villainess overdrive faster than ice melts in a desert.

Her parents arrived shortly thereafter and for once I was glad to see them. As a temporary diversion or distraction they could be convenient. They opened the wine, and then Nikki and her mother went into the kitchen to compare carpet swatches. Nikki wanted to re-carpet the baby's room and who was I to argue? Doesn't every self-respecting two-year-old desire the finest in Berber rugs?

In bed that night, I was feeling a little amorous. It had been too long. Once upon a time, Nikki would e-mail me racy photos of herself while I was at work; now all I got were baby pictures. Sometimes Nikki was in the background. Tonight I was hoping to get her back in the foreground. But she wasn't having it.

She glanced at me. "What's gotten into you tonight?"

"Nothing. Why?"

"Well, you're not getting into me tonight."

She fired up her iPad, and that was the end of that. Her patience had a shorter fuse since the baby was born, and nothing throws a sex drive into screeching reverse like a colicky two-year-old. She was finally weaning the baby off breastfeeding, and I was hoping to make up for lost time. A few months earlier, I had suggested she get breast augmentation, just a minor upgrade, nothing too dramatic. She reminded me I was still too young to have a mid-life crisis. But you're not, I joked. She punched my shoulder and we had a laugh about it.

After some further discussion, she began to actually entertain the idea. I think she was even excited about it. The idea of something new never gets old. I'm a salesman, so I knew that better than anyone. But her new breasts were on hold, too. They were also in the background.

Unable to fall asleep, I crawled out of bed sometime later. I was pretty wound up. When I couldn't sleep, I'd often grab a beer and play online games in my office, solitaire mostly, until my eyes got heavy and it was time to shut her down for the night.

I grabbed a beer from the fridge and checked on Page in her crib. She was a beautiful child, with great blue eyes, chubby cheeks, and thin wisps of blonde hair haphazardly springing out of her little scalp. Before putting her down, Nikki and I had read her "Humpty Dumpty":

> *"Humpty Dumpty sat on a wall*
> *Humpty Dumpty had a great fall*

All the King's horses and all the King's men
Couldn't put Humpty together again."

It probably wasn't possible for babies to have nightmares, but that nursery rhyme sure sounded like a downer to me. Humpty Dumpty basically just dies. He falls apart and crumbles to pieces. No one can help him. The End. Not sure a two-year-old needed to learn this. But Nikki was officially in charge of nursery rhymes, so I knew better than to voice my protest.

I went into my office and actually locked the door. No solitaire tonight. I logged onto some free porn sites instead. Ignoring the webcam opportunities to "Video Chat With Strangers," I started surfing some videos: "SQUIRT COLLECTION." "THE COCK WHISPERER." "HI DEF CUM SWAMP." It was quite the porn-ado, but I chose to weather it, ultimately logging onto a site called Whoregasm.com.

I rubbed one out to a clip called "Black Poles in White Holes." The black guy was hung like a skyscraper and practically pounding the spray tan off a blonde girl. Between the three of us, it was a toss-up as to who was enjoying it the most.

Before finally logging off for the night, I checked Facebook. I saw that I had a strange "Friend Request" from someone calling himself "Early Man." The name didn't immediately register and his profile picture certainly didn't foster any recognition: it was someone wearing a rubber Frankenstein mask, flashing a peace sign, and holding a beer.

I had no clue who this guy was until I read the Personal Message he had added. What rang a distant bell were the words "CAMP HIDEAWAY!" Was this Early Man from Camp Hideaway? It was, indeed.

Sitting in the dark with a small puddle of goo in my lap and my wife and daughter asleep in other rooms, I accepted Early Man as a friend. I'd check him out. See what he was up to these days. Wasn't that what Facebook was all about? What was to lose?

And along came a spider...

EARLY MAN

It was after my sixth Jack and Coke that I considered following the leggy Shot Girl home. That's just how I roll. Got a fetish for hot chicks, that's all. Sue me. This one was Restraining Order Hot. Oof! A big, rangy bundle of sexy you'd blow up an animal shelter for. The kind of girl you don't Google Earth but Google Sky, because you're convinced she's from another planet.

I could've eaten her alive.

Yeah, I lived in Los Angeles. The Dream Factory. So many ageless wonders. JonBenét Ramsey would've loved it there. And there's a simple reason why that alternative universe is the second biggest city in the U.S.: the beautiful, bangin' gals. Which is probably the same reason it's also the country's serial murder capital.

Perchance to dream? ☺

I took a piss in the Jackal Bar bathroom and forgot I ever laid eyes on The Shot Girl. That's also how I roll. An old zombie movie poster hung on the wall above the toilet: *Revival of the Dead.* It was Rated R "For Creature Violence." Howdy, fellas.

I read the scramble of graffiti scrawled inside the stall, like so much pig-drunk poetry: "For every smart, funny, beautiful girl, there's a guy sick of fucking her."

I wanna BE that guy.

And thanks to the Internet, it's easier to become that guy. I remember, in a galaxy far far away, the very first time I passed a cafe sign advertising "INTERNET CAFE." How exciting, I thought: a cafe with Internet service. What'll they think of next? But that's how desperate we were for access to anywhere else but here.

But today I'm as much of a "Web detective" as the next guy. A devoted student of the game. An online junkie and sucker for instant gratification. The Internet is The Great Equalizer, the ultimate candy store. It can be your closest friend, most trusted ally, and dependable mistress. Your only truly faithful audience. Where else but online can you find such nakedly unconditional love? Anyone with a throbbing hard-on and a mouse can find it.

Cuntdump.com, anyone?

Cyberspace is a global playground and all-inclusive vacation package; we're just living in it. It's another alternative universe, our brave new world. And it allows many of us to make up for lost time. Enabling and fostering anonymity when desired, it might as well be outer space. We're all essentially the same when trolling through, our identities merging and colliding, our performances seeking validation or, at the least, recognition.

A little fantasy role-playing never hurt anyone, and if free will costs an arm and a leg, then color me one fun-lovin' double amputee. It's all out there, unabridged for your reading pleasure and hideous detachment. There are even torture websites, featuring all kinds of criminal acts played out on the computer screen. Check out my latest discovery: STRANGULATION, ASPHYX Women hunted. Uncut reality series Internet only TV series. CLICK HERE.

So I clicked there. Didn't you? When in Rome...

You gotta love Rome.

Like cyborgs, we trawl and traverse, interacting and interfacing, courtesy of the same technology that helped play a part in our creation. In the fabled words of Dr. Henry Frankenstein, in describing his monster: *"Look! It's moving. It's alive. It's alive... It's alive, it's moving, it's alive, it's alive, it's alive, it's alive, IT'S ALIVE!"*

That would be us. ☺

The Internet is a research tool, moving on with blinding, nonjudgmental, merciless speed. It takes no prisoners. That's your job. It's the propagator of unadulterated, unvarnished, unexpurgated, and unabridged truths and animal fictions. It doesn't discriminate, having broken down almost all boundaries and unearthing very different portals to troll though. There are virtual porn displays, which the Supreme Court actually ruled legal. And clubs that exist online for child molesters, and websites that tell predators how to abuse kids, where to find them, and how to get away with these acts.

Perchance to e-stalk?

Think I'm over the top, do you? Well, I think not. I think you've just raised the bar too high. Lower it, and we will get along just fabulous. We all have bad scenes inside our heads, so don't pretend you don't have a little monster in your blood.

FYI: Ashleymadison.com is a website that actually promotes infidelity. Its slogan is "Life is short. Have an affair."

And *I'm* the irresponsible one?

I didn't think so. The Internet both alienates and connects, an online democracy where everyone gets to cast a vote. Some win, some lose, but everyone plays. It's why the bummed-out eunuch chooses to live directly above The Cock Factory: no one wants to feel left out. Endless cyber-venues are available for your good and bad decisions. You can re-invent and "radicalize" yourself online with a heady self-made makeover. You can become a global imposter, a curious tourist, eagering for beaver, navigating ad infinitum. It's called "social networking," even for the anti-social. *Leatherface*book!

We are the generation lost in cyberspace. Instead of being the Voice of one's Generation, we're reduced to just another voice, a blip in the blogosphere, a meek cry in the dark. Yet it's often less the age of the information superhighway than the Too Much Information one. No longer are we Generation X or Y, but TMI. Check it out: why would I ever possibly need to "follow" Subway on Twitter?

Anyone?

But if cyberspace was an online underworld and Facebook the most powerful and influential of The Five Families, I was Don Corleone. MySpace was Fredo.

So come scratch my surface.

Let's be friends, shall we?

The inscription on The Statue of Liberty reads, in part:
"Give me your tired, your poor,
Your huddled masses
Yearning to breathe free,
The wretched refuse
Of your teeming shore.
Send these, the homeless,
The tempest-tossed, to me
I lift my lamp beside
The golden door."

But it might as well be the slogan advertising the infinitely boundless pleasures of the Internet.

Come as you are.

FYI: there are 29,000 registered sex offenders on MySpace.com.

And then there are the lazy ones, like me.

Who forgot to register. ☺

SPECIAL ED

"There was a guy who climbed Mount Everest and successfully
reached the summit but lost his limbs and his nose in the process,
due to frostbite. So isn't that like, cheating?"

That was the quote I'd written in my Facebook profile.
No reason, really, just thought it was interesting to ponder. When
is a hero really a hero? I didn't know.

I lived in Seattle, about ten miles away from Lake
Sammamish State Park. Ted Bundy Country if you're scoring at
home. LOL. I worked graveyard shift security at the local
morgue. Midnight to eight. Morbid, you're probably thinking but
it wasn't so bad and Wall Street wasn't exactly beckoning. LOL.
At least it was quiet and I got to surf the Internet like crazy.

I was single but constantly looking. I got a lot of those
junk mail flyers in the mail, advertising dating services.
"Someone wants to meet you!" But no one really wanted to meet
me. It was fraud. I should've sued for false advertising! Either
that, or killed the mailman. LOL.

My social life was quieter than Helen Keller at a Metallica
concert. LOL. I preferred the Internet. That was my lifestyle
choice. I'm much cooler online. LOL. I had Twitter and
Instagram accounts but rarely ever used them. Only on special
occasions, which were very few. Like this one:
#SeekingMoreSpecialOccasions.

Yeah, the Internet could get frustrating. I once got this e-
mail:
I want to meet a guy, 19/f with pics Seattle, WA   Stacey
<stacey@contact-45.com> to me More options Wanna chat and
see my pics? Send me a text message.
Stacey19newbie. I am new in town, 19/f Seattle, WA
Send me text, look for stacey19newbie.

So I clicked to see her "pics," but 50 other nude girls
popped up because it was just an ad for a porno Website.
Irritating! More fraud! I never learned. I was a total sucker,
always clicking on someone's "new pics," even if she was never
there. Maybe this is the real reason porn supposedly leads to
violent behavior: just trying to access it can cause blind rage!

LOL. By the way: who needs 'torture porn' when there's simply porn? Talk about having A.D.D.! LOL.

I once discovered an actual online matchmaking agency for "the learning disabled." What's the sales pitch? "COME MEET REALLY DUMB CHICKS AND DUDES!" But I guess it's maybe true what they say: there's a lid for every pot.

But imagine the ads in that Personals section:
SEEKING HOT BI-POLAR GIRL! (After all, who doesn't love "promiscuous sex and impetuous travel"? Sounds like a great vacation!)
SEEKING RETARDED CHICK WITH BIG RACK! (Just not TOO retarded.)
SEEKING GIRLS WHO PLAY WITH CRAYONS - AND HAVE A TOUCH OF PALSY!
WAS COMATOSE, BUT STILL CUTE!
SEEKING CUTE GUYS WITH HEAD TRAUMA!
LOATHES NPR AND PBS – BUT FANCIES MUD SLIDES AND ANAL PLAY!
LOVES ORAL SEX – AND HATES JEOPARDY!

LOL. But seriously, it was a jungle out there. Even the Personals were impersonal. More about me: since what I called "The Rita Disaster," I had become a strict vegetarian. No meat, chicken, turkey, or fish for me. I refused to eat anything with a face. But I ate a ton of pizza, just not the "four-cheese" kind. When did "Extra Cheese" become not enough cheese? Who needs four cheeses? The suicidal pizza fans? It's enough cheese! Isn't it? Who are you people!? LOL.

Anyway, so no, I wasn't thin. For ten minutes during high school they thought I might even have an "eating disorder," which confused me because I was overweight and thought only anorexic/bulimic folks had eating disorders. So many mixed messages!

I wasn't a pretty picture, to be honest. Bald, too, I should add. Self-inflicted, though. I shaved it myself. Self-image comes in handy because you never know when hope might land in your lucky lap. Someday, somehow, Special Ed might find himself real love, or at least something so cool that passes for it.

Occasionally I'd sort of almost "meet" pretty girls in line at the supermarket. They'd be buying shampoo and bottled water and *Us Weekly*. Sometimes I made small talk if I felt there was an opening. ("Cool shampoo," I'd say, which was super lame since I was balder than an egg).

One day I tried a different tactic. A really pretty girl was ahead of me in line, buying milk and cigarettes and batteries. She looked like she'd just come from the gym because she was wearing a T-shirt and sweatpants, her long, black hair tied back in a bun. And who doesn't marvel at the girl who goes right from the treadmill at the gym to the cigarettes at the supermarket? That's an open mind for you. LOL.

Instead of attempting to make small talk, I listened closely as she told the cashier her Club Card Number: her phone number. I discreetly programmed the digits into my cell phone. Savvy, no? Later that night, I scrolled through my cell contacts and stopped at the name of the supermarket fancy I'd programmed for her: "IT GIRL." I dialed her number, juiced with nervous excitement, but when she answered, I realized I didn't know her name. Which wasn't so savvy. So I hung up on her. I admit: my game needed work. LOL.

A year earlier, I'd joined the Pacific Northwest's competitive eating circuit. There are about 100 weekend events each year throughout the country but I only participated in local contests. I became a "gurgitator," which in layman's terms means binge eater.

I was still a novice and never won any money but I had met some nice gurgitators along the way. The key to our training was gorging on food and guzzling up to three gallons of water a day. The water kept our innards stretched in preparation for the 10-minute eat-offs, when we cram massive quantities of meatballs, hot dogs, crab cakes, tiramisu, or whatever the contest food was for that particular event.

Some of the power-eaters really got into the theater of the thing. Some painted their faces, hid behind masks or greased their hair into these bizarre sculptures. More important, though, was to have silly fun and meet new friends. Eating contests might be serious sport for others but for me they were another form of social networking. And I won't lie: the real reason I joined the circuit was to meet girls.

I met a Russian one named "Rita the Eater" at a hot dog-eating contest in Springfield, Oregon. She was compact and muscular with long, lank black hair, funky roach clips for earrings, and tattoos covering her body: skulls, demons, and KFC's Colonel Sanders himself. I thought that was pretty cool, until I realized the Colonel's fist was jammed up a chicken's ass. "FINGER-LICKIN' GOOD!" read the thought bubble above his head. Crazytown.

It was a brutally humid day. Rita and I were positioned beside each other behind a long row of tables, facing the cheering crowd as we slammed hot dogs into our heads. Rita was a southpaw but deftly used a two-fisted technique to gobble the wieners.

But the guy on my other side, who called himself "Hannibal Shapiro," appeared to be winning the contest in the early going. A real character, this one; his oversized black T-shirt read "WORD OF THE DAY: SWALLOW." He had his own cheering contingent right up in the front row, as if he was the Michael Jordan of gurgitators. Every guy in his fan base wore the same T-shirt as their gluttonous superhero. (And I thought I needed a girlfriend. LOL).

"Eat, Hannibal, eat!" his fan club chanted. "Swallow, Hannibal, swallow!" But midway through the contest, things went stinky sour for Hannibal. His rapid consumption ceased because he'd started to cramp up with killer sharp abdominal pains. Grimacing in agony, his legs went rubbery. His troubled fans went quiet, reduced to murmuring concerns as they shifted uneasily in the blazing swelter.

I asked Mr. Shapiro if he was okay but a moment later he exploded, simultaneously puking and losing his bowels. (I took that as a "no.") In one Herculean expulsion of stomach and sphincter, Hannibal Shapiro became Hannibal the Massive Bodily Emission and collapsed into his own gooey slop. On the circuit, these gastrointestinal gaffes are called "reversals of fortune." If Nike had been sponsoring the event, the slogan could've been "JUST SPEW IT." LOL.

The crowd went berserk but Hannibal's fan club fell into a stunned, dazed silence, their fallen hero a mess unto himself. The contestants took a moment to register our nausea before resuming our consumptions, hell-bent on taking advantage of Hannibal's setback and winning the contest money.

With around two minutes remaining in the contest, I saw Rita's cheeks swell to bloated, beet-red proportions. She was puffed up like an old jazz musician and started to perspire heavily, bathed in thickening sweat, lathering her entire body like a fragrance... or a hot dog casing. Then it was she who collapsed onto the staging area. (A local tabloid would later dub the event as the "Hurricane Katrina of Competitive Eating Contests.")

Our fellow gurgitators ignored her plight but not yours truly. I came to her aid and cradled her in my arms, attempting to keep her conscious. Too late, she was already out. Yet I couldn't help but smell the scent of her perspiration: hot dogs!

An ambulance transported Rita to the local hospital. After her stomach had been pumped she awoke to see me sitting in her room. I was her personal fan club.

"My little hero," she said. She seemed grateful to see me.

"It was nothing," I said.

She told me what had stricken her during the contest. She had fallen victim to "meat sweats," which are apparently occupational hazards for seasoned gurgitators like Rita. Meat sweats occur when people eat so much, they start to literally excrete sweat that smells like the food they'd just consumed. Crazytown!

Rita gave me her contact information. She wanted to stay in touch, saying she owed me one. "I have a healthy appetite for other things besides food," she teased. We began a super cool online relationship over the next few months, and it wasn't long before Rita sank her choppers into old Special Ed's tender heart. She told me she "really liked my core." I wasn't sure what that meant but it sounded fantastic. This was too much for fun. Ultimately, we made a plan for her to come to Seattle for a weekend. I was nervous because I didn't have many visitors.

She arrived at my apartment on a Friday afternoon, wearing tight jeans, green sneakers, and a black "The Lord of the Rings" T-shirt: Gollum's face sniveled from it above the words "MY PRECIOUS!" She looked super lovely. We talked for a while, and I made her laugh a couple of times. We were having a good time but at one point, she got super serious.

"Can I ask you a question?" she asked.

"Sure."

"What do you want?" I could tell this was like, some big philosophical girly question or something. I knew I had to answer as honest as I could because I truly believe that someday, honest men will rule this world. And then things will get interesting.

"How about a blowjob and a club sandwich?" I said. It was a joke, of course, but she didn't betray either a smile or a laugh and I thought I was in big, fat trouble. But I was thrilled to learn that I wasn't because a moment later, she did smile! And then suggested we eat ourselves sick and drink meat sweat off our bodies. Crazytown!

I mean, why not try everything once? I'd do it for giggles, anyway. A guy like me needed giggles. We decided the fare would be $100 worth of boneless Balderama Brothers' Buffalo wings. We set a timer for the standard ten minutes and began pounding chicken wings into our cakeholes. Using her two-fisted technique, she consumed much faster than me. When we were all finished, she asked if I had a sauna. A sauna? Of course not. I didn't even have HBO. LOL.

But she demanded a sauna, and pretty girls get what they want, right? So we took a cab over to the local YMCA. Rita was holding up much better than me. I was thisclose to deucing myself like crazy. My insides felt like a gory, unsolved crime scene, and a wholesale purge from front and back was the only way it was gonna get solved. The stuff you eat for love, huh?

Fortunately, we were all alone in the YMCA sauna, she in her bikini briefs and me in my boxer shorts. We sat in silence and sweated together. I was growing dizzy, hoping I wouldn't suffer the same gastrointestinal fate as Hannibal Shapiro.

"Do you smell it?" she asked, foisting her moist cheek close to my face.

I took a sniff of it. "A little bit, I guess."

"Lick it, hero. Taste it. Come on. Make all gone."

So I lapped up the perspiration from her face. And yup, she did taste like chicken. LOL. Her meat sweat tasted like Balderama Brothers' Buffalo wings. She became aroused, touching herself, and sipped at my meat sweat like a fine wine. She grabbed my arm, sank her teeth into the juicy bicep, and literally drank from it.

#MeatSweats. LOL.

Crazytown!

Then she started to fondle my dink.

Craziertown! She jerked me off, and I came in an instant, the blast so powerful it would've blinded a midget. Rita just laughed. I was slightly embarrassed, to be honest, but the truth is I've always been a short-timer, a premature ejaculator. Not a whole lot of fun if you're scoring at home.

In bed that night, Rita started talking about Russian history: epidemics and famines and the civil war. In 1921, a lengthy drought and deadly famine plagued the region, devastating agriculture and the economy. Five million people died of starvation. Desperate citizens were forced to survive any way they could, leaving them little choice but to summon up their basest instincts. It was a Natural Selection kind of scene. Survival of the Fittest. (If not the thinnest. LOL.)

Whenever a slightly overweight person was seen on the street, everyone knew he was a cannibal. It was a calling card or a "tell" that he'd been feasting on human flesh to feed his hunger. Cannibalism was common among those who managed to survive.

"If you are what you eat, I could be you by tomorrow," Rita joked. We never had real sex but I didn't mind, because we kissed a lot, and that's what I liked best of all.

The next morning I awoke with searing abdominal pains, flatulent as a billy goat and feeling like I was going to give birth. And much to my stunned surprise and disappointment, Rita wasn't there. No note, no voice message. Nothing was stolen, either. She'd made all gone with me! I couldn't believe it. Was she some kind of serial meat sweat drinker? Human food poisoning?

Over the next few days and weeks I was unable to communicate with her, either by e-mail or phone. She'd changed her contact information. Was she hiding from me? I was staggered with fury. She had vaporized from my life as fast as she'd materialized into it. She ate and ran?! Who are you people?! My only consolation was this: Rita would die someday. And then we'd be even.

I plunged into a weird, dark place in subsequent months. On yet another lonely morning at dawn, I returned home from work and set the microwave timer to ten minutes. I cranked up the thermostat to 90 and nearly inhaled two boxes of macaroni and cheese, singeing the roof of my mouth in the process - *youch!* - to the point where I almost lodged my head in the oven just to alleviate the pain.

I sat and sweated and wondered if vultures in the desert ever experienced meat sweats after devouring carrion. Food for thought. But mostly I thought about Rita. I glanced at the new name for her I had programmed into my cell: "SHIT GIRL." Before vanishing from my life, she'd told me about drought and famine and Natural Selection. I could sympathize with all three.

Later that night I received a Friend Request on Facebook from someone wearing a Frankenstein mask, holding a beer and flashing a peace sign. His name was Early Man, and I instantly remembered who he was. Crazytown! We'd gone to overnight camp in Maine at Camp Hideaway. We were bunkmates and best friends for almost three straight summers, and those guys were the first real friends I ever had.

I immediately accepted the request. He e-mailed me back right away and we went back and forth for a while. He offered me instant solace about Rita, saying she sounded like *"cautionary tail. It's a sisterhood. You picked a pretty poison, is all. It happens."* He wasn't wrong. *"Girl like that needs a setback. Fuck her and move on."*

He didn't mince words but the way I was feeling, I couldn't disagree. He said he was *"hoping to spread some seed in Canard Beach in March, because 'March ain't the only thing that's in like a lion, and out like a lamb!'"*

Even as I considered his entreaty, I kept thinking about Rita. And I licked at my arm, seeking meat sweat but finding nothing. Just me. Pathetic me.

Wondering when a hero was really a hero.

PART TWO

MUTUAL FRIENDS

"Hello darkness, my old friend. I've come to talk to you again… "

-- Simon and Garfunkel

EARLYMAN@AOL.COM
To WARFIELD@GMAIL.COM
Date 1/10/13

Subject: "THE BOOGEYMEN!"

Hey, stranger. Hope all is well in your universe. How's life? It's Early Man from Camp Hideaway.

WARFIELD@GMAIL.COM
To EARLYMAN@AOL.COM

Hey, man. What a surprise. Life is good. Can't complain. You?

EARLYMAN@AOL.COM
To WARFIELD@GMAIL.COM

You can't complain at all?

WARFIELD@GMAIL.COM
To EARLYMAN@AOL.COM

Well, maybe I overshot that a little. Haha. Yourself?

EARLYMAN@AOL.COM
To WARFIELD@GMAIL.COM

I'm swell. Ever go back to camp for Old-Timers weekend?

WARFIELD@GMAIL.COM
To EARLYMAN@AOL.COM

No. Never went back. I'm in Phoenix now. What about you?

EARLYMAN@AOL.COM COM
To WARFIELD@GMAIL.COM

Nope. Me, neither. I'm in LA. On Disability. Back problems. Was Assistant Managing an Ace Hardware store. You can IMAGINE the girls I pull! ☺

Hey, think our camp ghost stories would still scare the shit out of everyone?

WARFIELD@GMAIL.COM
To EARLYMAN@AOL.COM

Haha. Probably not so much.

EARLYMAN@AOL.COM
To WARFIELD@GMAIL.COM

You ever hear from Special Ed at all?

WARFIELD@GMAIL.COM
To EARLYMAN@AOL.COM

No. I haven't heard from anyone since camp, 100 years ago.

EARLYMAN@AOL.COM
To WARFIELD@GMAIL.COM

Perfect! I'm searching for an audience. Looking to host a party. Come as you are. "Two's company, three's a crowd, but four's a party."

WARFIELD@GMAIL.COM
To EARLYMAN@AOL.COM

What do you mean?

EARLYMAN@AOL.COM
To WARFIELD@GMAIL.COM

Let's "create an Event!" What do you say we get The Boogeymen back together again?

WARFIELD@GMAIL.COM
To EARLYMAN@AOL.COM

I don't know if I could swing that. I got a lot going on here. A new baby girl. It's kind of crazy.

EARLYMAN@AOL.COM
To WARFIELD@GMAIL.COM

Congrats!! Good for you. Sounds like you could use a little vacation, though, no? A vacation away from the "crazy."

WARFIELD@GMAIL.COM
To EARLYMAN@AOL.COM

Thanks on the congrats, man. But no thanks on the vacation. What do you have in mind, anyway?

EARLYMAN@AOL.COM
To WARFIELD@GMAIL.COM

Ah, so you're thinking about taking the bait? Allow me to be your Adventure Captain! I'm thinking Canard Beach, Florida. Anytime in March or early April. 'Tis the season!

WARFIELD@GMAIL.COM
To EARLYMAN@AOL.COM

What season??

EARLYMAN@AOL.COM
To WARFIELD@GMAIL.COM

Spring Break season! What do you say, Warfield? You deserve YOUR MTV! We all do.

WARFIELD@GMAIL.COM
To EARLYMAN@AOL.COM

SPRING BREAK? Aren't we a little old for that?

EARLYMAN@AOL.COM
To WARFIELD@GMAIL.COM

Come on! What's old is NEW again! Cold beer, hot chicks, and old camp friends! What's wrong with any of that? This is your life. It's not rehearsal! Think about it, okay? I'm gonna see if I can find Special Ed on Facebook. I bet he'll be down for it.

WARFIELD@GMAIL.COM
To EARLYMAN@AOL.COM

Let me know how you make out. Good luck. And good to hear from you, Early Man.

EARLYMAN@AOL.COM
To SPECIALED@AOL.COM
Date 1/14/13

Subject: "THE BOOGEYMEN!"

Hey, stranger. How's life treatin' you?
It's Early Man from Camp Hideaway.

SPECIALED@AOL.COM
To EARLYMAN@AOL.COM

Crazytown! How are you, Early Man? I don't believe it's you. Nice profile pic. LOL.

EARLYMAN@AOL.COM
To SPECIALED@AOL.COM

Things are great. Hangin' in, you know. I see you live in Seattle. Not married, either?

SPECIALED@AOL.COM
To EARLYMAN@AOL.COM

Not I said the fly. LOL. I'm still getting over this
Russian girl I really liked. It ended super badly.

EARLYMAN@AOL.COM
To SPECIALED@AOL.COM

Sorry to hear. What was her name?

SPECIALED@AOL.COM
To EARLYMAN@AOL.COM

Rita.

EARLYMAN@AOL.COM
To SPECIALED@AOL.COM

Sounds like a cunt.

SPECIALED@AOL.COM
To EARLYMAN@AOL.COM

LOL!

EARLYMAN@AOL.COM
To SPECIALED@AOL.COM

I'm craving a vacation. Sounds like you are, too. I was
thinking a little Camp Hideaway reunion might be just
what the doctor ordered.

SPECIALED@AOL.COM
To EARLYMAN@AOL.COM

For real?

EARLYMAN@AOL.COM
To SPECIALED@AOL.COM

Sure. What's wrong with craving a little succor from old camp friends?

SPECIALED@AOL.COM
To EARLYMAN@AOL.COM

Hold on. I'm Googling the definition of "succor." LOL.

EARLYMAN@AOL.COM
To SPECIALED@AOL.COM

It'll be a Boogeymen reunion!

SPECIALED@AOL.COM
To EARLYMAN@AOL.COM

LOL! "The Boogeymen." I remember that nickname. We were awesome. LOL.

EARLYMAN@AOL.COM
To SPECIALED@AOL.COM

You're big into this LOL thing, aren't you?

SPECIALED@AOL.COM
To EARLYMAN@AOL.COM

LOL!

EARLYMAN@AOL.COM
To SPECIALED@AOL.COM

I found Warfield on Facebook, too. He wants to go to
Canard Beach, Florida, sometime in either March or
April. He just doesn't know it yet. 'Tis the season! So
what do you say?

SPECIALED@AOL.COM
To EARLYMAN@AOL.COM

I'm confused. Baseball season?

EARLYMAN@AOL.COM
To SPECIALED@AOL.COM

SPRING BREAK season, you silly bastard!

SPECIALED@AOL.COM
To EARLYMAN@AOL.COM

LOL! That does sound fun. I'd be up for that, for sure.
Something different.

EARLYMAN@AOL.COM
To WARFIELD@GMAIL.COM,
SPECIALED@AOL.COM
Date 1/21/13

SUBJECT: "PLAN 9 FROM CYBERSPACE."

"Far better it is to dare mighty things, to dare glorious triumphs, even though checkered by failure, than to take rank with the poor spirits who neither enjoy much nor suffer much, because they live in the gray twilight that knows not victory nor victory."

-- Theodore Roosevelt

Teddy makes a point, does he not? We're gonna smash our guitars in Canard Beach! But before we figure out target dates, we gotta get the head of the snake aboard this party train – DOC HOLIDAY! The leader of the pack, right? We can't go without him. The more the merrier. Safety in numbers. It'll be a "Boogeymen" reunion!!

I'll check Facebook to see if he's there. Until then, don't forget to ask yourselves this question:

What are strangers, but friends waiting to happen?

PART THREE

DOC HOLIDAY

"It is impossible to say how first the idea entered my brain; but once conceived, it haunted me day and night."

-- Edgar Allan Poe

DOC HOLIDAY

"Goodbye friend, it's hard to die/With all the birds singing in the sky/Now that the spring is in the air/Pretty girls are everywhere/Think of me and I'll be there..."

English teachers are fond of the old cliché "write what you know." But another cliché, "those who can't do, teach" may be an even more accurate one.

I taught English at Wilton Community College, 20 miles west of Boston. Creative Writing and American Literature. And in my Creative Writing classes, I sometimes found myself telling my students to "write what you know." (If nothing else, it was more encouraging than telling them "those who can't do, teach.")

I had a decent apartment just outside of Boston, and that's where I was on that frigid night in mid-January. Sitting at my desk, grading overwritten homework assignments with a red pen and picking at leftover Chinese food. Mrs. Dubin's TV was blasting from the apartment next door. Nice enough old lady, but deafer than a bowl of porridge.

In my Creative Writing class a week earlier, I had imparted to my students the 'Gothic Elements in the Short Story.' *"Through a dream landscape, a girl flees in terror and is alone amid crumbling castles, antique dungeons, and ghosts. She nearly escapes her terrible persecutors, who seek her out of lust and greed, but is caught; escapes again and is caught; escapes once more and is caught. Finally she may break free altogether and be married to the virtuous lover who has all along worked to save her."*

The class assignment was to incorporate these themes and elements into a short story. It should've been a fun, creative exercise, but these results were poor. George Bernard Shaw famously said that "youth is wasted on the young," and tonight there was no arguing with him. Yet another old literary cliché a teacher tells his students is "kill your darlings," which are the favorite anecdotes a storyteller often forces into the text, shoehorning them in at all costs, even though he knows the passages don't belong. My students had way too many darlings. A mass murder was in order.

When I was finished with the last story – the biggest red-ink massacre of them all – I went online and read the breaking news of the day. There's always something. ("IT'S OKAY TO START EATING BAGELS AGAIN.") But this much is probably true: you can find everything you ever wanted to know on Wikipedia, except for two things: the cure for cancer. And why she never loved you.

A day earlier, I heard that Camden Miller had just gotten married in Connecticut. Whenever Camden was on the brain, she was an easy trigger, so I logged onto the Boston Globe website and read the news: CAMDEN MADISON MILLER & TUCKER ANDREW BATES WEDDING ANNOUNCEMENT. There was a smiling photo of my old carpool crush, and the husband. Resplendent in wedding gear, they were perched at the pretty, sun-dappled ocean's edge. And in case anyone was wondering, the handsome couple had "honeymooned in Hawaii and resided in New Haven, CT." And did I "want to sign their wedding Guest Book?" Not really.

I clicked onto Facebook moments later. I was more of a tourist and only had about 300 "friends. " I couldn't remember the last time I'd actually written a Status Update, and even my profile picture was the sleepy factory setting: the slightly disheveled, faceless white silhouette on the light blue background.

But tonight I learned that my old best friends, Reese and Lansky, were respectively "checked in" at a restaurant named Jimbo's Chophouse in Chicago and an art opening in Taos, New Mexico. That "Facebook Places" feature was strange to me. Why do I care that you've "checked in" at, say, Starbucks? You're getting coffee. So what? Not sure how I can help you with that.

I hadn't spoken to those guys in a while. They sure liked to "check in," just not so much with me anymore. Both were happily married – Lansky maybe a little less so - and living out of state. The three of us had sort of lost touch. It happens sometimes.

I guess I was still preoccupied with exhuming the past, which Facebook is nothing if not forgiving of, because I then did a "CAMDEN MILLER" search. I discovered that the old high school heartbreak was nowhere to be found. She was a ghost in the social networking machine. The Girl Next Door eventually goes away. Everyone knows that. But sometimes she completely disappears. She vanishes. And not everyone knows why.

Camden and I had been neighbors since grade school, yet lived in decidedly parallel universes. But life was good when you were young, both your parents were alive, and your neighbor was the sweetest, most beautiful girl in the whole world. When you've lusted for her friendship as much as you've lusted for the rest of her, well, that might even be love. (I once expressed this sentiment to Lansky, who replied, "Or... it *might* mean you're a massive homosexual.")

This baby obsession of mine was supposed to be fleeting and transitory, if not painfully debilitating. The Girl Next Door is like a mother's breast milk; it's incipient nourishment. You drink it because you don't know any better. Eventually this crush dissipates and subsides, vanishing from your system only to be replaced by new avenues for your desires, opportunities, entertainments, and adventures.

Every boy in the neighborhood had climbed aboard her bandwagon at one time or another. Eventually these suitors fell off, after crashing and burning in their attempts to woo her. They moved on. Those were normal and natural expectations and progressions – you catch another ride. But I remained on Camden's bandwagon, white-knuckling for dear life, even as it spiraled dangerously out of control. I couldn't shake her. She always messed me up.

Yet that was a different era altogether, before my crush kicked into poisonous bloom in high school. That's when other boys came into her life, boys who lusted after far more than her friendship. Boys who wanted to put their fingers and tongues and puds inside her special places. And it was before I also joined those boys in these desires, if for no other reason than a stubborn attempt to level the playing field.

In ninth grade, I finally asked her out twice. But she politely rejected me, saying she wanted to remain "just friends." Reese and Lansky constantly reminded me that I was "punting out of my coverage" with Camden. But there's an "inspirational" Peanuts cartoon strip that features Lucy holding down the football for Charlie Brown to kick. She was smiling, but he stood there, looking painfully uncertain and pensive, stricken, really - as if thinking Should I stay or should I go? You couldn't blame him. He'd been burned before. Yet the caption read "NEVER EVER EVER GIVE UP!"

But why did he constantly try to kick the football when she always pulled it away at the last minute? He had to know what to expect from these Hellish play dates every time. He knew the drill: he'd run up to the football, poised to boot it, but she'd snatch it away at the last minute. Again. And he'd land flat on his ass. Again. She was the most predictable girl he knew, always toying, teasing, and fucking with his weird, round head.

He could've been farting around at the mall with Linus, trying to score steadier, more reliable girls, but he wasn't interested. He was too preoccupied, and maybe even obsessed, with trying to kick that damn football. Why? Was he a total schmuck? A glutton for punishment or masochist? Did he have OCD? ADD? Or was he just secretly in love with her? The answer seems pretty obvious.

I was Charlie Brown to Camden's Lucy. She'd never held the football that was her heart down long enough for me to make a serious advance. But I kept coming back for more. (Yeah, I know the purists would insist that Charlie's true love was The Little Red-Haired Girl, but I'm calling bullshit on that. I bet she was just his beard.)

Camden was the girl who keeps you up nights, your thoughts pinballing every which way in a restless trajectory of profound, heartsick dread. *Does she like me? Or hate me? What will I say to her in school tomorrow? Will she talk to me? If so, will she be faking it? How will I know, either way?* Once her spell had been cast, she became another ally in insomnia's merciless arsenal. My only companions were the achy, noxious discomfort and quiet parasitic fester. The vexatious shame, as distinct and recognizable as an orangutan in a party hat.

Camden Miller always kept me up nights.

You know the girl.

EARLYMAN@AOL.COM
To SPECIALED@AOL.COM,
WARFIELD@GMAIL.COM
Subject: DOC HOLIDAY

Hey. Just Facebooked Doc Holiday with a personal message. No response yet, but I'll let you know when I hear back. We're close, guys. "Two's company, three's a crowd, but four's a party." ☺ Why not make new wine from old grapes?

The Boogeymen could be baaaack very soon.

Stay tuned…

DOC HOLIDAY

I replied to a Facebook Private Message from Alexis, who I'd met in a bar called The Beer Trap a few months earlier. New in town from Texas and starting a job with an advertising agency, she was a pretty blonde with a pointy chin.

She liked horses, theme parks, biking, hiking, microbrew, and, of course, her beloved University of Texas Longhorns. She was amused by my dismissal of the whole "We Have 5 Million Beers On Tap" trend. Sure, it's cool to have some options, but I didn't require such a sales pitch to get excited. You don't need to have five million beers on tap to induce me into drinking at your bar, as I'm pretty sure I can't drink even one million beers during the course of a night.

I never cared *where* beer was brewed, or *how* it was brewed, or *when* it was brewed. I didn't need to hear its résumé, nor its oral history. Alexis called me a curmudgeon, but I countered that the opposite was true: I was so easy I'd drink camel piss as long as it got me drunk. I just didn't give a shit where the camel hailed from.

We flirted until Last Call and had gotten along well. We connected rather quickly, and I think I could've liked her. Over the next couple of weeks the flirtation continued, mostly through e-mails and texts. She always signed off with XOXO. But when I finally mustered the courage to ask her out on a proper date, she said she had a boyfriend. XOXO.

Sometimes you just get there a little too late.

Before logging off and crashing for the night, I noticed I had a new Facebook Friend Request. A bizarre one from a guy calling himself "Early Man." His profile picture featured him wearing a rubber Frankenstein mask, raising a can of Budweiser and flashing a peace sign. He'd added a Private Message: he was *"searching for an audience. Looking to host a party. Come as you are."*

I wasn't sure who this person was until two words caught my eye, fueling a spark of nostalgia and recognition: "THE BOOGEYMEN!"

Could it be… Early Man? Those guys? I had created that Boogeymen nickname for myself and three others at Camp Hideaway in Cornish, Maine. But that was over twenty years ago.

I probably shouldn't have been surprised, since Facebook holds no real surprises anymore. I confirmed Early Man as a friend, but had no plans to respond to his message until another time. But not thirty seconds after I pressed the "CONFIRM" button, he sent me another one. That was a trifle creepy. Someone clearly had too much time on his hands. Either him or me.

He informed me of his Spring Break adventure plan, calling it "Plan 9 from Cyberspace." A Camp Hideaway reunion in Canard Beach, Florida. He said he'd already enlisted Warfield and Special Ed to partake in a little fun in the sun, sometime in March. Warfield and Special Ed. Crazy. I hadn't thought of those guys in a lifetime.

I still didn't plan to respond to him until a later time, so even surprised myself when I replied moments later. Spring Break? I asked. We were 34 years-old. Was he high?

He replied: *"YES! But who cares? The sun, the beach, the girls — all of them nature's candy and none of them discriminating. It'll be summer camp for grownups! Fantasy camp. It'll be like EAT, PRAY, LOVE! ☺."* He also said something about how a vacation in Canard Beach had to be "better than the shit-garden you're watering."

He was right about that last part, so I wrote back that I'd think about it, and then logged off. Of course, I really wouldn't consider such a thing. I hadn't seen nor heard from these guys in over 20 years. We'd spent three and a half summers together in Maine. Period.

But Early Man was determined and wouldn't go gently. The next day he e-mailed me again, beseeching me, really: *"Dude, you got lyrics from 'Seasons in the Sun' on your Facebook profile?! Sounds like SOMEONE needs to get laid! So*

*let's go woo some wool!" Come on, Doc Holiday — "Idleness is
the holiday of fools," right?"*

Couldn't they just go to Canard Beach without me, I
asked. Early Man pleaded for me not to hold their vacation
hostage. He wanted all of us Boogeymen, or none of us at
all. *"Don't hijack my adventure plan. Don't be The Lone Stranger.
Safety in numbers."*

Like I said: someone clearly had too much time on his
hands. Either him or me. "No offense, but I usually don't vacation
with strangers," I wrote back. *"Come on! What are strangers, but
friends waiting to happen?"* he replied.

Actually, I knew the opposite was true: that friends were
often strangers waiting to happen. Time's a funny thing. His
online proselytizing had become more than a trifle annoying, but
maybe it was growing on me. I told him I'd think about it a little
more and this time, I really did. I suppose his parting e-mail
resonated:"This is your life. It's not rehearsal."

He had a point. Truth was, I could've used the change of
scenery to air out my brain a little. Yeah, something like Club
Med obviously sounded more age-appropriate, but Early Man
convinced me of the virtues of Canard Beach: cheap, easy, and
convenient.

About a week later, I e-mailed him and asked what dates
in March he had in mind. The only window I had was between the
14th and 21st, which was my students' Spring Break week.
"Perfect!" he responded.*"This viral marketing is a success. Hell,
everyone's doing it."* Both Warfield and Special Ed were good
with my dates, apparently much more flexible than I. So we
hatched a plan and arrangements were made. This was a crazy
lark, but I'd gotten a wild hair across my ass.

If Reese and Lansky only knew what I was up to, they'd
think I was desperate to be going on Spring Break with three old
summer camp friends. But the Terminally Single Dude Agenda
doesn't discriminate and knows no boundaries. I guess I'd been
lonely for so long, I didn't even know what it was like to feel
lonely.

Safe to say there was no chance I'd be "checking in" at
Canard Beach. I was pretty sure no one deemed me important
enough as to want to know my whereabouts every sixteen

minutes. But who knows, maybe Canard Beach would be fun. I'd just try and make the best of it.

So it was official: after a twenty-year dry spell, "The Boogeymen" were going on vacation together. Four disparate worlds were about to collide in Canard Beach, Florida. "Two's company, three's a crowd, but four's a party!" Early Man wrote to us once the plan was finalized. "Doc Holiday is looking for a holiday," I replied to the other Boogeymen in my final "acceptance" e-mail.

But this is a story about a girl...

PART FOUR

THE OLD COLLEGE TRY

"Hey there Little Riding Hood.
You sure are lookin' good.
You're everything a big bad wolf would want… "

-- Sam the Sham and The Pharaohs

EARLY MAN

Two nights before "Plan 9 from Cyberspace" was set to descend in Canard Beach, I e-mailed my lesbian sister, Jenna, and told her I'd be unable to attend the "Tolerance" fund-raiser she was co-hosting the following weekend. Jenna was fifty shades of creepy, and a tireless devotee of fancy liberal causes. For example: "renewable energy" made her downright dewy.

Look, I'm all for people helping people, but if you can't even clear up your own pimples, what makes you think you can save the environment? She was all about rescuing endangered rhinos and whatnot, and once shared this link on Facebook: "NAVY TO DEAFEN 15,900 WHALES AND DOLPHNS AND KILL 1,800 MORE."

Who gives a shit, right? Like that was *my* problem? But those fucking sea creatures got the best press. When she wasn't attending "leadership breakfasts," Jenna was always signing online petitions and forwarding them to her contacts. Domestic Violence Awareness Month. Alzheimer's Awareness Month. Tumor Awareness Month. Even AIDS Awareness month. (Because apparently Polio was no longer in vogue).

I wasn't sure if she was altruistic or narcissistic, and maybe it's the same thing if you really think about it, because either way, get over yourself, no? If there was a 13th month on the calendar that celebrated "National *Self*-Awareness," its name would've been Jenna.

Naturally, she was a big fan of LGBT, the Mafia of lesbian, gay, bisexual, and transgender people created to support depressed oddballs who are either bullied and/or whose friends have committed suicide. They have a nifty slogan: "It gets better." Ha! Nice try. And if it doesn't get better, you're literally gonna kill yourself just because someone's giving you shit about your sexuality? Really? Seems a little dramatic, no? Toughen up, right? Otherwise, aren't you just letting the terrorists win?

FYI: no one ever bullies a HOT lesbian. ☺

I had no problem with Jenna being gay, just didn't need all the constant reminders. I GET it: *you eat a boatload of pussy. I'm jealous, okay? Now leave me alone.* But she wouldn't, because she was so proud to be "out." I told her I was straight and not so proud, so why should she be any different? Being "out" was fine, but being annoying is an entirely different animal. So dial it down a notch. Everything in moderation, right?

Don't get me wrong: I fucking Heart equality. As long as they've got the courtesy to cut down down on the parades and keep their dicks outta my face, I don't care who marries whom or what they do in the privacy of their homes. I think that's a fair trade.

Before hopping on a plane for Canard Beach on the night before the other Boogeymen were scheduled to arrive, I e-mailed them something I found online. I figured they'd get a silly kick out of it. A little message from Ground Control:

Spring Break Risk Factors

* Know where you are going before you start. Use the Internet to research the city, state or country that you're traveling to and know both the good and the bad about your destination. If another language is spoken at your location, learn a few phrases like "I need the police" or "I need a doctor" or just "Help me."

* Insure that someone at home has all of your travel and contact information, including a copy of your passport, the front and back of your credit cards and identification cards, and information as to where you are staying and who you'll be staying with. If this data changes, find an Internet kiosk and send the new information along so that you can be found should the need arise.

* There is always safety in numbers. Don't travel alone and try to travel in threes. The idea of three is the hope that no matter how crazy you and the situation get, out of three friends one can be counted on to be the voice of

reason. You should always be within eyesight of each other. And don't accept any offer to leave with a person you've just met.

* Avoid using stairwells or elevators by yourself. Don't tell any "new friend" where you are staying. Remember not all "taxis" are really taxis and insure that you're taking a safe mode of travel every time you go out at night.

* Drink from only sealed containers or get your drinks directly from the bartender. And don't leave your drink unattended - you don't know what someone could put into it. Date-rape drugs - often called 'forget me pills,' 'roofies,' 'wolfies', etc. - are many and varied.

* Know your limitations, set boundaries, and stay with your wingmen. Predators look for the lost, the weak, and the inebriated. You don't want to look like a zebra or gazelle that's been separated from her herd our surroundings, or be too forward to strangers.

Just a thought: imagine if they advertised date-rape drugs on TV.
Side effects *may* include bruised ego and sore vagina...

DOC HOLIDAY
Since 9/11, I never felt truly safe on an airplane. I had trust issues. Buckled within my seat belt among all those strangers made me feel like defenseless cattle. I never liked to fly even prior to the terrorist attacks, so consequently, "Terminals" and "Departures" were two words I never liked seeing at an airport. How subliminal could they get? When it came to air travel, the War on Terror was inside my head. I know it's a little crazy and more than a little neurotic, but I'm just not so sure we belong up there. At least not until there's free pizza, Ambien, protective gear, and Air Marshals on every plane.

So I was a trifle nervous as I sat on my flight, nibbling on an Egg McMuffin and attempting to read some essays from my American Literature class. We had just finished reading *The Catcher in the Rye,* and I had assigned my students to interpret what the last two lines of the book meant to them: *"Don't ever tell anybody anything. If you do, you start missing everybody."*

I had unfortunately forgotten to bring my old Camp Hideaway scrapbook, after unearthing it from a collection of old junk boxed in my bedroom closet. I couldn't remember the last time I'd looked at it. I made some small talk with the pregnant woman seated beside me, who said she was having a baby boy. She dozed off about an hour into the flight. As I braced myself for any forthcoming turbulence, I closed my own eyes. Maybe I could squeeze in a little nap.

As I drifted off, I imagined the woman's baby boy lying awake in a bassinet, beneath harsh, bright fluorescent lights. He's in a hospital Maternity Ward. Two days old. A chubby little wonder, but clueless; just a pink vessel of humanity with no idea of what's in store for him. And then he spots her, the chick infant in the bassinet directly beside him. Say her name is Camden. She's adorable, bouncing baby fun. A precious morsel, a marble-eyed delight. She's cooing quietly and her poo smells like juniper berries. He wants to beat the rest of the infant fuckers to the poaching punch, so he issues her a sidelong baby glance, hoping she notices. And she does! And he baby smiles, thinking, Hey, this shit's EASY! And cuts right to the chase.

"So what's your story, neighbor?" he asks.

"Attached," she replies.

Because sometimes you just get there a little too late.

"Got it," he says.

"Sorry," she says.

"You gonna be on Facebook?" he asks.

"No comment," she says.

She baby smiles. He baby shrugs. Suddenly he's not in baby Kansas anymore. And even at this most nascent stage of his existence, he already hates lousy metaphors, but allows himself this one: conversing with Camden is like test-driving a car he knows he'll never be able to afford to buy. But thanks for the ride.

But he had to give it a shot, and though he was unable to close the baby deal, he'd like her to promise that she'll forever stay "out of his stadium." But she wouldn't know what the Hell he's talking about, so he'd be forced to clarify: he needs early assurance that she'll never again crush his heart like a grape. It's a preemptive strike integral to his future arsenal.

But he never utters another word. Content and complacent with cooing and pooing and waiting for his parents to take him home forever. Not a week-old but life is already a battle cry. And he's out of bullets.

Someday, they both might regret that he didn't ask her to make that promise.

WARFIELD

I flew out of Phoenix early on Friday morning. Nikki didn't like when I occasionally traveled for business, but appreciated its necessity. There's some old expression that says, "You marry in haste, but repent in leisure." I never thought it applied to me until I found myself lying to Nikki about going to Miami on business, and not to Canard Beach on leisure. The only thing she hated more than her husband traveling was her husband lying. And this lie was extra advanced, so I'd need to be extra careful.

I kicked back in my window seat and stared out at the sky. It always felt good to get away. Sipping my oily coffee, I tried to envision what my old camp friends were like these days. "The Boogeymen." This was sure going to be interesting.

SPECIAL ED

I landed in Fort Lauderdale around noon. I was super excited to meet the guys in Canard Beach. I hailed a taxi and headed that way. I looked forward to some "succor." LOL. I was always sad when camp ended every August, especially that last summer. But today was a new beginning and maybe both Early Man and Teddy Roosevelt were right. It is better to "dare mighty things," because life is short. It's not forever, unless you're lucky enough to be a vampire. LOL. Canard Beach, here we come!

DOC HOLIDAY

Early Man, Special Ed, Warfield, and myself were best friends during those summers up in Maine. We were inseparable, our bond sealed by the ghost stories we'd recount to our bunkmates.

We used to scare them good. "Three-Fingered Willy," "Hatchet Harry," and "Wheelchair Mary" were some of the tales we spun. I dubbed us "The Boogeymen."

Early Man's ghost stories were always the scariest and goriest. In fact, after he spun a particularly twisted tale one night, one of our bunkmates – a homesick little nebbish named Gilbert Adelson – was so horrified that he tried running away from camp the next day. After he was safely retrieved, our camp Program Director forced Early Man to confront the traumatized runaway and concede that the killer in his ghost story was not due to return to Camp Hideaway and seek out a boy named "Gilbert" to cannibalize, and then repurpose into a hearty soup. Early Man was not a happy camper to say the least, but he reluctantly complied. He admitted to Adelson that he hadn't been telling the truth: it wasn't soup, but stew. Ha-ha.

But Adelson didn't get the joke, nearly fouled his Underoos, and attempted to run away from camp again. The beleaguered Program Director was finally able to get Early Man to concede to Adelson that he had fabricated the entire ghost story.

Warfield was the only good athlete among us. Conversely, Special Ed was somewhat of a weirdo, and maybe the most uncoordinated kid in the annals of American sporting youth. None too bright, either. During a softball game during our second summer, he hit a ground ball to the shortstop yet inexplicably started running to third base instead of first. He would never live that down. For less athletically inclined campers like Special Ed, sports were more frightening than any ghost story.

He was oddly accessorized, always wearing black dress socks, which Early Man derided as "Bar Mitzvah" socks, along with waist-high gym shorts and white Jack Purcell sneakers. Warfield used to ask him why he was so "aggressively dressed."

During the one-hour Rest Periods after lunch every day, I'd write letters to Camden at her summer camp. It was a bittersweet lull in the day's whirlwind activities. The other Boogeymen often asked to whom I was writing all those letters. "No one," I said. But I was already smitten with Camden. Maybe our quiet neighborhood carpools to grammar school were the origins of blame, the seedlings of doom, which would unravel and blossom over the course of years to come.

This driving rotation was certainly convenient and pragmatic for our parents, but maybe it had exposed me to Camden too early. She'd look all pretty and adorable, running her Bonne Bell lip gloss across her mouth... the same one I was dying to kiss someday.

Like so many friendships that form or coalesce at places such as overnight camp or vacation destinations, the Boogeymen's fell by the wayside after our last crazy summer together. We were 12 years old. We never spoke again.

EARLY MAN

My first order of business in Canard Beach on Thursday night was buying beer. I also bought a few trashy celebrity magazines "for men." They're selling sex, so I was buying it. I'm pretty sure that's the point. I had arrived in town packing the heavy artillery. My trail mix included a treat for every occasion: uppers, downers, weed, a little coke, and some Ecstasy. Better living through chemistry – that's no lie.

You can never be too prepared when you vacation.

DOC HOLIDAY

After landing in Fort Lauderdale in late afternoon, I emerged from the airport into a stupefying, remorseless Florida sunshine, shielding my eyes like a logy vampire forced out into dawn's early light. I threw on my shades and jumped in a cab. The plan was to meet the guys at a diner across the street from the motel called The Dove's Nest.

"The Island Oasis in Canard Beach, please," I told my cabbie as we sped away from the terminal. Early Man had sold us on the place because it was the cheapest deal he could find. He'd paid for two rooms and we were to reimburse him upon our arrival.

The main boulevard in Canard Beach was dotted with bars, clubs, motels, fast-food chains, restaurants, and other attendant fixins: looming billboards preaching sunscreen, strip clubs, and beer. Neon signs advertised Wet T-Shirt and Hot Body contests, and All-You-Can-Eat buffets. According to a McDonald's sign, the McRib was back in spooky vogue. (Thank God it was "okay to start eating bagels again.")

My taxi was immediately trapped within a vortex of gnarled, bumper-to-bumper traffic, bustling with countless Spring Breakers just arriving into town. A fresh, new breed of students with various out-of-state license plates and college bumper stickers denoting their origins: OHIO STATE, ITHACA COLLEGE, URI, etc. Nothing of the sort was affixed to the back of my taxi, of course, which made me feel a little old and more than a little creepy. I was already having second thoughts about this excursion.

We passed an outdoor bar called Barnacles, which was center-punched by a swimming pool and flanked by tented cabanas. The cabbie remarked that Barnacles was one of "the hotter spots" in town.

The further I traveled into the belly of the Canard Beach beast, my vision was assailed with attractive college girls parading down the strip: bared skin and big boobs beneath tiny crop tops, Daisy Dukes, and bikini bottoms; long hair, oversized shades, and ankle jewelry. Tramp stamp tattoos lurked above a few thong bikini bottoms. One girl wore a T-shirt that read "I HEART SPRNG BREAK."

A Greyhound party bus pulled up alongside us, a traveling bacchanal crammed with boozing college kids raging and dancing and grabassing. Two sloppy-drunk girls in bikinis splashed their friends' boobs with beer. One of them stumbled into her window seat, giggly and breathless and toying with her bikini top.

When she saw me leering up at her, my face not literally pressed up against the window but still close enough to appear creepy, I was embarrassed. But she flashed me a loopy smile. And as if to officially indoctrinate me into this depraved Spring Break realm, she pressed her soggy pumpkins against the window and waved. It felt like a welcome greeting, so I waved back to them. Um, thanks.

Oh, boy. Check your inhibitions at the campus exits. There were clearly no mysterious agendas here. Some things never changed and Spring Break was one of them. You probably wouldn't find an ulterior motive for twenty miles. Boys and girls were here to get fucked up and hook up. I began to grow slightly emboldened, and even excited by the prospect of spending a few days in Canard Beach.

Maybe this wasn't such a bad idea, after all.

EARLY MAN

And introducing . . . from rainy Seattle, Washington . . . a short, bald ogre and morgue employee, with a body fit for cancer. Give it up for Special Ed. Cue the applause.

And introducing . . . from the sweltering desert of Phoenix, Arizona, a husky software salesman . . . Give it up for Warfield. Cue the applause.

And introducing... from Los Angeles, California, a reliable narrator, subversive motherfucker, and Adventure Captain... an Internet visionary and dashing gentleman. Give it up for yours truly, Early Man. Cue the applause.

A Camp Hideaway reunion was on the books. Two of my three old camp pals were getting reacquainted in a window booth at The Dove's Nest across the street.

WARFIELD

Special Ed was short, round, and repulsive. Pretty much like I remembered him.

SPECIAL ED

Warfield seemed like a bit of a dullard. I didn't care. We were gonna have fun.

EARLY MAN

I watched them through binoculars from across the street in Room 211 at The Island Oasis. Mission control. The social experiment had begun. Our rock 'n roll Spring Break would be commencing shortly. Doc Holiday was the final piece of the puzzle. Fitting that he was the last to arrive, since he'd been the last one to join our party. Come as you are.

The head of the snake is necessary to take a bite out of any good apple.

DOC HOLIDAY

My taxi dropped me off at The Island Oasis motel, a low-slung, two-story concrete building that had seen better days. Some oasis, I thought. The cheesy neon sign advertised the requisite "We

Have Cable and Air Conditioner." As if that's really such a big deal anymore. The place looked dead, too. I didn't see a soul. It looked like we'd almost have the whole place to ourselves. The "real" college kids were probably staying in hotels on the main strip.

I headed for The Dove's Nest across the street, located within a little strip mall beside a CVS and a Starbucks. The sign in the window announced that it was open 24 hours. Once I was inside, a voice called out to me: "Over here!"

It was Special Ed, sitting at a corner booth. I crossed over to him. He was bald, with small chunks of shrapnel for eyes, as if debris from a detonated bomb had lodged in his grille and he'd decided to just go with the look. Warfield was seated across from him.

"Hey, guys," I said, planting myself in the booth beside Special Ed.

"Hey, man," Warfield said, extending his hand. I gave it a firm shake, but despite the overture he didn't appear so friendly. He was constantly checking his cell phone for messages. He was fairly handsome, in that soap-opera-actor-after-a-car-accident kind of way. You could easily have pictured him rockin' an eyepatch, elbow cast, and 14 stitches. He seemed like someone who spent equal amounts of time at both the gym and over the barbecue grill. A frat boy tamed by time and marriage; he'd gone a trifle soft, but not too soft.

"Doc Holiday… in the flesh again!" Special Ed said, slapping my back.

"That's me," I said. "Doc Holiday is lookin' for a holiday."

"I hear that," Warfield muttered, poring over a menu. Special Ed slid one over to me and I started to peruse it. I noted that The Dove's Nest boasted an "award-winning Tuna Melt." Apparently I'd missed that awards show.

A giddy voice alerted us: "And introducing . . . from varying locales… three brothers from a different mother… The Boogeymen!"

It was Early Man. Approaching our table, smiling wide, wearing tennis sneakers, ripped bluejeans, and a white T-shirt reading VAGINATERIAN. Captain Subtle, he was not. Even behind his big, oversized mirrored shades, he looked sun-cooked and sinister. Whenever I saw someone driving a car that had a bunch of dents bashed into the bodywork, I'd instinctively wonder: *what the Hell? Drive much?* It was easy to ascertain that Early Man had bong water on the brain. And you wouldn't want him behind the wheel.

But we all exchanged awkward handshakes and hellos. It was certainly weird seeing these guys again after so many years. But there we were, strangers in a strange land.

"I don't recognize you without your Frankenstein mask," I said to Early Man.

"That's the idea," he said. "Old friends with new minds. That's what it's all about." He grinned and reached for a high-five. I lazily reciprocated. "Welcome to the candy store," he gushed as he plopped down into the booth. He pointed to the yellow Livestrong bracelet on my wrist. "Heard those things cause cancer," he said.

"Not funny," I said.

"Lighten up," he said. "You're on Spring Break." He grabbed hold of Warfield's hand and beamed. "No wedding ring? Thattaboy! Way to start your mancation!" Warfield wasn't amused and jerked his hand away.

WARFIELD

I had removed my wedding ring after deplaning in Miami. The little gold noose that had me buckled in for safety. In sickness and in health. It wasn't a big deal, really. There was nothing diabolical about it. But all these years later, Early Man was still clearly a massive pain in the balls. But then he moved onto Special Ed.

SPECIAL ED

"You still got the old sour stomach, you gassy bastard?" he asked me. Crazytown! I couldn't believe he remembered. Back at Camp Hideaway, the food sucked moosedick and my little stomach voided a good deal of it during our summers there.

DOC HOLIDAY

After checking in, Special Ed and I unpacked our bags in Room 209. Early Man and Warfield were sharing Room 211 across the hall. Our room smelled like stir-fried ass, and stale from old cigarette smoke. Two dirty plastic chairs and a small round table were displayed on a small patio overlooking the parking lot.

I turned on the air conditioner, which barely worked. Other than that, the place was the Four Seasons, minus a couple of seasons. For all I knew, Early Man's travel agent was Satan.

"So much for 'we have air conditioner,'" I groaned.

"We should sue for false advertising," Special Ed snickered. "But we're only about a mile from the strip. And I bet they have a Continental breakfast."

"Whatever. Ever woken up in time for one of those in your life?"

"Not really," he said with a chuckle. "But this is cool, huh?"

"Don't vacation much?"

"No."

"Actually, me, neither."

"Hey, good seeing you again."

"You, too."

I clicked on the TV, and after surfing for a moment found what I was looking for: an NCAA hoop game. It was March Madness and I was pretty happy with how my brackets looked this year. My Final Four picks were UCLA-Memphis State and North Carolina-Kentucky, with North Carolina beating UCLA in the title game.

"We're gonna have fun," Special Ed said, as he emptied his duffel bag onto his bed. I noticed he was wearing tall white socks with his flip-flops. It was tactile TMI, and I should've instantly known there was something horribly wrong with him.

SPECIAL ED

Something was a little sad about Doc Holiday. I don't know what it was, but he seemed a little uneasy being in Canard Beach with us. I saw him looking at my feet, which I was thought was odd. Maybe he was just tired. But we'd cheer him up!

WARFIELD

We started out the night in the room Early Man and I were sharing, drinking beers and shooting the shit about Camp Hideaway.

"Here's to old friends and young girls," Early Man said, raising his beer in a toast. We drank to that. Doc Holiday told us he forgot to bring his camp scrapbook, and we agreed that would've been fun to look through. Early Man wore a white "HOMELAND SECURITY" T-shirt, which I thought was weird. Then again, he was the guy whose idea it was to go on Spring Break at age 34. And we were the ones who agreed to join him.

EARLY MAN

Special Ed was wearing a green hospital scrub jersey. Yeah, he was *that* fuckin' guy. The same festive douchebag who wears a Santa Claus hat every day and night during the holiday season. "Are you a doctor?" I chided him. "Or an asshole?" We all had a laugh over that. Even Warfield piled on. Pointing to Special Ed's faggy footwear and scrub attire, he asked, "Why you so aggressively dressed?" Special Ed giggled and attempted to fist bump Warfield. He hesitated, but hit him back. The boys were back in town!

SPECIAL ED

I asked the guys if they remembered PlayTown in Portland, Maine. That place was super fantastic. Biggest and best amusement park I'd ever been to. Those trips to PlayTown every July 4th were the highlights of every Camp Hideaway summer.

DOC HOLIDAY

I remembered PlayTown. It was the land of Roller-Coasters, corn dogs, funnel cakes, arcade games, and ample bouts of nausea and indigestion. It's funny what you remember sometimes and what you don't, but I recall our trip to PlayTown during our last summer.

We were late for the bus heading back to camp, because we had eagerly crowded ourselves into one of those $2-for-a-strip-of-photos booths. The kind that features an array of fantastical backgrounds depicted around the camera lens. Sugared-up and excitable, we argued over which background to choose.

Special Ed was farting up a rotten storm. He'd brought his own "background" into the booth with us. Forced to tolerate his lactose intolerance, we smiled for the camera.

WARFIELD

I removed some more beers from the mini-fridge and doled them out to the guys. Early Man removed a big baggie of pot. "'Tis kind," he said, sniffing the dope. "Stinky-dinky fun. Called 'Jerry's Kids' weed. Know why?"

"Why?" Special Ed asked.

"'Cuz it makes ya all retarded and twisted," Early Man explained.

"Neato," Doc Holiday said.

"None for me," I said.

"We all have our poisons," Early Man said, removing a medicine bottle.

"What's that?" I asked.

"Viagra," he beamed proudly. "Breakfast of champions." Special Ed giggled.

"Aren't you sorta putting the cart before the horse?" Doc Holiday asked.

Early Man grinned. "We'll fuck the horse, too." Special Ed snorted laughter.

DOC HOLIDAY

Special Ed was an easy audience, all right. He was drinking the Kool-Aid. Early Man sparked a joint and actually convinced Warfield to take a few pokes from it. "Live a little," he said. "Do it for Jerry's Kids." All of us proceeded to get really stoned, and I was very baked almost immediately. We sat slurping our beers for what seemed like a long time, higher than Hell, and Warfield looking like he was literally *in* it, trapped and silently howling behind the gates.

WARFIELD

I hated Facebook.

DOC HOLIDAY

It grew a trifle claustrophobic with these "aliens" from cyberspace; more summer camp disorientation, than reorientation. I wasn't sure if it was as uncomfortable for the others, but

Warfield appeared to be an uneasy kindred spirit, pacing the room and checking his iPhone for messages. He was clearly unsettled with our whole deal.

"You okay?" I asked him.

"I haven't smoked dope in about 15 years," he said, explaining the near-suicidal look on his face. "Was that stuff laced?"

WARFIELD

Early Man laughed and said that people always ask the same question when they're way too stoned: "was that stuff laced?" But that wasn't exactly reassuring.

SPECIAL ED

I threw out a question to the gang: "Hey, what was that girl's name?"

"What girl?" Warfield asked.

"The Camp Wildwood one," I said.

"Shit. Remember that?" Early Man said.

"I don't remember her name," Warfield said.

"It's on the tip of my tongue," I said. "But I swallowed it!"

DOC HOLIDAY

And suddenly I was much too stoned. Jesus. How could anyone forget her name?

SPECIAL ED

Betty. It was Betty. Betty something. "I think it was Betty," I said. Early Man suggested we Google it, and popped open his laptop computer.

WARFIELD

It wasn't Betty. Bianca, I think her name was Bianca. Yet I was far too high on pot to want to prolong such a depressing topic of conversation. I kept Bianca to myself.

EARLY MAN
"It was Barbara!" I said. That was it. Barbara. And I think her last name began with a J. Barbara J. "That was the name of the dead chick," I said.

DOC HOLIDAY
Nothing like old camp friends getting back together again, huh?

SPECIAL ED
LOL!

DOC HOLIDAY
In July of our last summer in Maine, Camp Hideaway hosted what was essentially a prepubescent singles mixer with the Camp Wildwood girls from across the lake. These events were billed as "Socials," but they were more like "Antisocials."

    The affair was held in our gym or "rec hall." A rather unremarkable event, but a personal rite of passage: the very first time I ever asked a girl to dance. She was as tall and blonde as she was awkward. We had the latter trait in common, so we sort of just listlessly shuffled our feet to a Cheap Trick song. I think it was "The Dream Police." We didn't exchange a single word until I finally broke the ice: "Um, those Teenage Mutant Ninja Turtles are pretty cool, huh?" She just shrugged. Maybe talking turtles freaked her out. I'm pretty sure I was too preoccupied with thoughts of Camden, anyway. I wondered whom she might be presently dancing with at her summer camp social in Cape Cod.

    Early Man, Special Ed, and Warfield didn't dance with any girls. They were either too shy or too scared, choosing instead to sit together in the bleachers, sipping fruit punch and tapping their sneakers to the music. I joined them after my dance and we agreed to sneak back to the bunk. We tore open big bags of potato chips and pretzels and watched *Night of the Living Dead* on our C.I.T.'s TV. Foraging and snacking quietly in the darkness beneath those long wooden rafters, we were engrossed. The movie was much more frightening than any ghost story we'd ever told. Maybe the only things scarier than girls were zombies.

    The hero of the movie was a strong, noble black guy, and

just watching him gamely trying to fend off the ravenous undead, I couldn't help but think of Camden again. Did *she* like black boys?

Most kids dread the first day of school, but I was already pining for the Sunday night of Labor Day Weekend. I'd be home with my parents, maybe eating pizza or Chinese food, and watching the Muscular Dystrophy telethon on TV. The days would've grown shorter, darkness falling earlier and earlier as if portending a certain doom. There'd be a fresh, new nip in the air and the shrill, relentless chorus of Back To School Sales would be summoned like white noise, playing on both radio and TV, like danger music advertising the end of summer.

Those folks really wanted you to get back to school. But not before rubbing it in and broadcasting the MDA telethon on the day before classes started. *"Welcome back to school! Now here's Darby, this year's woefully ghoulish poster child. Flail and snivel and wave to the camera, Darby. Attaboy! One more time now."*

Jesus. Not sure about you, but never the kind of pep rally I had in mind. And was the telethon a Ponzi scheme? I mean, who even had this disease other than the 14 kids capable of reading the cue cards that were paraded before the cameras every year? Muscular dystrophy seemed not unlike leprosy, but with a better publicist. Personally, I'd rather pledge elsewhere.

But school would begin the following day, which meant I would again get to see Camden on a consistent basis. (Preferably without her new black boyfriend.)

Yet for now, I watched the movie with my friends. Chief McClellan was issuing some reporters his zombie State of the Union.

"Yeah, they're dead," he said. *"They're all messed up."*
And he was right.

SPECIAL ED

Doc Holiday was the winner. "Her name was Bethany Joseph," he said. "Bethany Joseph." He was right! Warfield and Early Man agreed: that was her name.

DOC HOLIDAY

Bethany Joseph was found dead at Camp Hideaway the morning after our Social. Much to the shrieking horror of a cluster of passing campers, the handyman's addled son was seen hefting her severed torso across the volleyball court, spilling meaty streaks of gore onto the pavement. Coloring in between the lines, as it were.

The Camp Wildwood girl had been bisected. Cut in half. And the handyman's son was blubbering incoherently, as if he'd discovered buried treasure yet was unable to elucidate his excitement. We'd always heard that he had a steel plate in his head, though we didn't know what that meant. Our C.I.T. once confided to us that he was "almost retarded." We sort of knew what that meant. Folksy and dutiful, if not the most reliable narrator, the handyman's son was immediately arrested.

Police cars flooded the campgrounds for two days straight. The murder obviously stamped a bleak finality on our summer. It was a horrifying time, and we were traumatized to pieces; Hellish nightmares were born. (Gilbert Adelson, for one, would never be the same.)

We had to call our parents and make arrangements for them to pick us up. A few days later we were spirited home, Post-Traumatic-Stress-Disorders doubtless seeded within our little brains. The Boogeymen never got to tell another ghost story again.

Sometimes truth is stranger than fiction.

WARFIELD

"Google the retard!" Special Ed said much too excitedly. "What was his name?"

DOC HOLIDAY

For a guy with such a good memory, he couldn't remember dick.

EARLY MAN

I was confused as to what "retard" Special Ed was referring to, until he clarified for us: the mental midget who killed Bethany Joseph. "No idea what his name was," I said. Warfield said he had no recollection, either.

DOC HOLIDAY
I couldn't believe they didn't remember this name, either.

SPECIAL ED
Doc Holiday reminded us of the killer's name: Toby Danforth.
Early Man wanted to Google the story just to be sure. We had
obviously been too young back then to remember any gory
details.

EARLY MAN
According to the old story I Googled from *The Cornish Tattler,*
Danforth was charged with one count of murder, one count of
unlawful disposition of human remains… yet two counts of
"illegally moving a body." As if it's not enough of a crime that he
killed a girl, they also charged him with a moving violation? And
why two counts? One for each piece? Would it have been legal to
move her body if she weren't in two pieces? Why all the fanfare?

"The body was released to the victim's family after an
autopsy. The results of that examination and the cause of death
were sealed by the county attorney's office, and police would not
reveal details about the cause of death."

Wasn't the "cause of death" a little obvious? The girl was
split in two. Is this rocket science? And why "seal the results?"
What else do we need to know? The autopsy report revealed that
Danforth stabbed her 42 times, to ensure he did it proper. Imagine
that. 42 times?

That takes some serious energy.

WARFIELD
Are we having fun yet?

EARLY MAN
You gotta wonder why they even bother to count the stab wounds.
Who really benefits? The Guinness Book of World Records?
Point is you've got a very dead girl, so why not simply notify her
next of kin and be done with it? Why bring a statistician to the
party?

DOC HOLIDAY

Early Man said the report also cited that, in the process of stabbing her, Danforth managed to tear his rotator cuff. The import of this fact was lost on me, other than it's the only thing he and Sandy Koufax would ever have in common.

WARFIELD

Early Man Googled Bethany Joseph's obituary next. Great. What an aphrodisiac. Fortunately, Doc Holiday had grown as annoyed and impatient as I had. He tossed out a question of his own: "Guys, can we please go look at *living* girls?"

DOC HOLIDAY

I suggested we try out the action at Barnacles and the others were game. "Time to take a test drive!" Early Man announced. "Let's kick this sleeping dog."

We decided to walk rather than take Warfield's rental car. It was a beautiful night, with a sweet, comfortable tropical breeze. The streets were filled with buzzing college girls, sun-kissed and excitable.

"Check out the ass traffic," Early Man declared with building excitement. "Let's whore about!"

SPECIAL ED

"It's Pussy Palooza," I said. "LOL!" The guys gaped at me like I was sick in the head. Maybe sometimes I might be.

DOC HOLIDAY

I hated when guys who never got any "pussy" threw that word around so casually. They should've been penalized. Imagine if there was a Pussy Police Department. Every time someone gratuitously threw around that word, the PPD would materialize and taser the offender on the spot. ZAP! The offender would drop like a homesick brick. But it would be a deterrent: he'd know never to use the word pussy again so brazenly, until or unless he was enjoying a steady diet of it. And if he chose to be a repeat offender or recidivist, ZAP! Down he'd go again. Special Ed seemed like that kind of guy. One of the fries at the bottom of the bag.

WARFIELD

We passed a vast parking lot in the process of getting a concert venue makeover. Workers were unloading portable toilets, lights, and equipment from off of trucks. Early Man hollered at a passel of pretty girls crossing the street: "For those about to rock, we salute you!"

EARLY MAN

I was gripped with the fever. The place was alive with pure pleasure, and I felt as if I'd been dipped inside it. It was like arriving in New York City after being gone awhile, that fabled "energy" overwhelming you, intoxicating you with its infinite possibilities and promises. You know you're in a very special place.

Canard Beach was no different, a candyland of honey-limbed biscuit. Balls-deep with ravening hunters and gatherers. Raucous, drunken, carefree. Higher education as Neanderthal Society. So many wonderful cock-starved creatures of opportunity. Spring Break was *on.*

The Boogeymen were going mental tonight.

DOC HOLIDAY

As we bustled across the street toward Barnacles, I still wondered what the Hell I was doing in Canard Beach, and was curious as to whether the others harbored similar stoned thoughts. Early Man was all business and purpose, wild-eyed and chain-smoking, his covetous head on a swivel. Special Ed tagged along, creepy, giddy, and dutiful, rubbing at his bald scalp. Warfield was aloof, quiet, and cranky. He'd already melted six or seven beers back at the motel.

We were the most unusual of suspects, like some kind of collective Alice, plunging ass-over-elbows into the Rabbit Hole. And if Early Man was Harry Potter, we were his little band of magical dingbats.

"Come on, guys. Get into character," Early Man practically decreed.

SPECIAL ED
And so we did.

DOC HOLIDAY
"I'm in grad school," I lied to the pretty, sandy-blonde girl at the bar inside Barnacles. It was a preemptive strike, because in her mind I probably seemed older than a pharaoh. After all, I didn't go to school, I taught at one.

She was hazel-eyed and engaging with legs that were long and tan, nicely complementing her pink Polo shirt, blue shorts, and flip-flops. If I had to guess, I'd say she was 20 years old and at least three Cosmos older. She was a senior at North Carolina State. The Girl Next Door. If you're so lucky. Her name was Jill Cassady.

"I'm at Boston University," I lied again. "Law school." Attempting to imply that I wasn't on Spring Break, I explained that I was in town en route to play golf in Palm Beach. Jill expressed zero interest in my golf game, but was eager to attend a Red Sox one. She'd never been to Boston and was dying to check it out. "Is now a good time?" I joked. She smiled into her red drink.

EARLY MAN
The place was wall-to-wall wool. Target practice. The Boogeymen were back in business. A beautiful Muslim chick at the end of the bar wore skimpy shorts with the word JUICY stitched across her ass. A guy like me sees that, he reads between the lines and just assumes she *wants* it there. Is that wrong?

I pointed her out to Warfield and Special Ed. It woulda been nice to pour a little ivory into her ebony. She was High Alert material, had all the candy. You'd LIKE her on Facebook. Blind guys would've hit on her, and even their Seeing-Eye dogs may've taken a run. If I'm not allowed to "objectify" that, I may as well not draw breath here on God's green Earth.

Then again, maybe she was a "disappeared" suspect in the War on Terror. (FYI: if you don't want me to religiously profile you, please ask your cousins to try and stop killing us). And imagine falling hard for a smokin' Muslim girl, only to discover she's a suicide bomber? On second thought: consider the minimal commitment. Maybe that's the perfect girl! ☺

SPECIAL ED

That pretty Muslim girl had bangs, which have always been a mystery to me.

"Why do girls think bangs are sexy?" I asked the guys.

"No one knows," Early Man said. Warfield even smiled at that.

DOC HOLIDAY

The other Boogeymen were keeping to themselves at the bar, uncomfortably nursing their drinks. They weren't chatting up any girls and looked most certainly out of place. Like understudies for a family portrait.

WARFIELD

Unlike the college kids in here, we needed fake I.D.s that made us look younger. When the Muslim-looking girl came crossing in our direction, Early Man kind of got right in her face. He grinned and said, "I'm the reincarnation of John Holmes. You interested?" She just sneered at him. You couldn't blame her. "Hey, no offense," he said, and pointed to his "Homeland Security" T-shirt. The girl shook her head and skulked off. Special Ed erupted in laughter. I just ordered another beer. I had a pretty good feeling this was going to be a long night. These guys were rotten.

DOC HOLIDAY

"I should go back," Jill said, gesturing to her friends.

"Have I tuned you out already?"

She smiled and shook her head. "No. Not at all."

"Okay. Well, nice meeting you. Have fun."

"You, too." But as she departed to join up with her friends, she turned back and waved at me. I returned the overture, and I guess I looked pretty enchanted with her because Early Man was at my side a moment later. He joined my gaze.

"Sometimes even Maseratis have to sit in traffic," he said.

"What do you mean?" I asked. Early Man just grinned and nipped at his drink, eyeballing the dance floor. He pointed to a really drunk girl who had stumbled harmlessly to the ground during her attempt to dirty-dance with a boy.

"I need a girl who falls down," he said, almost wistfully. He was plenty odd for everyone. He slapped me on the back and headed back to the other guys.

I gazed over at Jill. Some obnoxious frat dude with a buzz cut was hitting on her. She was trying to rebuff him, but he persisted before a few of her girlfriends deftly intervened and whisked her away. As they did, her eyes met mine again and she smiled thinly, as if this was just an occupational hazard. She was hotter than train smoke, so often had to deal with similar boozy predations. That kind of attention came with the territory, it was business as usual. Even the giraffe at the zoo grows accustomed to people always gawping skywards at him.

But I was surprised when she crossed towards me, slithering through the roistering throng, nearly spilling her drink; the jarring techno beat seemingly guiding her advance. She arrived at my side with a smile, as if we were old friends. It was pretty cool. She vanquished the rest of her drink a little too fast, chasing it with a cute little wince.

"You okay?" I asked.

"Some asshole from Ohio State wouldn't leave me alone."

"No shortage of them in here. Do you want another drink?"

"Yeah. That'd be great. Thanks. Another Cosmo."

That cocktail led to a few more. She seemed comfortable around me, occasionally waving to her friends; a tacit signal that she was okay. She was talking to a good guy, no matter his age or false pedigree. She was safe with me. I learned she was from Virginia and had no boyfriend to speak of, just "having fun, you know." There was an ex-boyfriend back at school, and they were still "best friends." In fact, he was still trying to get back together with her. And why wouldn't he? She was pretty damn adorable.

Jill pointed out her best friend to me, a rather moon-faced, heavy-legged girl named Ashley. She was hammered out of her skull and crashed at a table with another friend. I noticed she wore a bunch of black rubber bracelets around both her wrists. Jill told me Ashley was a lesbian, but a "pretty one," as if that made all the difference. (And I guess she had a point, since apparently unattractive lesbians – like unintelligent nerds - are good for nobody).

I spotted the other Boogeymen leering at me from their seats at the bar. The Gang That Couldn't Puke Straight. Warfield seemed less interested in my progress, checking his cell phone for messages when not feasting his eyes on the young co-eds bustling about on the dance floor. I raised my beer toward these unlikely wingmen: Cheers, fellas. They raised their drinks in a sleepy toast, and suddenly we didn't appear so united in our delusions of debauchery. If they were Native-American Indians, their names would've been "Dances Alone."

But to be fair, mine would've been "Dances Poorly," because moments later Jill dragged me onto the dance floor, her Cosmo keeping precarious rhythm within her glass. But despite my poor dancing skills and general discomfit at being in Canard Beach, I was having a lot of fun with her. This was going better than I expected. Our old friend George Bernard Shaw might have said that "youth was wasted on the young," but tonight I had to argue with him. Poor guy had obviously never been on Spring Break.

SPECIAL ED

Doc Holiday still couldn't dance worth a lick. LOL. Early Man pointed to the pretty Muslim girl again. "Check out the smokin' hot terrorist," he said, adding something about how the 9/11 terrorists definitely weren't "morning people." He started talking about The Koran, calling it 'Slaughtering Americans for Dummies.' He said he was "surprised Oprah never pimped that one for her Book Club."

EARLY MAN

"Naturally, it would be the glossy, picture-book edition, too," I explained. "Family-friendly. The cover would display leering visages of the 19 hijackers, like some kind of sinister site map from Hell. Between the covers, horrific images of 9/11, searing and indelible: desperate, flailing bodies plunging out of those blazing towers; shots of the towers collapsing, Goliath castrated in his own bedroom. New York-*style* terrorism at its most spectacular: frenzied Big Apple residents, agape, slack-jawed in mounting horror, fleeing those rapidly-moving giant dead mushroom clouds, as if they had nefarious minds of their own, low-lying, noodling around corners and blocks, hovering over buildings, into alcoves, sifting into cracks and eyes and lungs and pores, bleeding into the firmament, seemingly following the panicked denizens, suddenly refugees in their own living room, fueled as much by intractable anti-American hatred as simple laws of gravity. Mortified reaction shots of harried bystanders, hands clapped over mouths, weeping and wide-eyed, dizzy with incalculable notions of creeping dread, some of it already baked-in, this fresh new Hell. Lastly, the remains of the day, Ground Zero itself, in all its ghoulish, murderous quietude. New York City has just been fucked in the ass without a condom. "America Under Attack!" the 24/7 reality show (also available in Hi-Def) — all of it a harrowing reminder that someone had tossed a poisonous worm into our apple, infecting us all, now and forever. Over 2700 natives voted off the island in the blink of an eye. Wake-up call. The City That Never Sleeps, caught sleeping."

WARFIELD
Jesus Christ. Early Man was either one bad dog, or that weed was definitely laced.

DOC HOLIDAY
After the song ended, Jill surprised me with a kiss on the cheek. She was drunker than I imagined, but the only thing stronger than her buzz might have been her fragrance.

We repaired to an empty cabana and planted down onto a couch by the flickering candlelight. It was cozy stuff. She kicked off her flip-flops and wiggled her toes, the way sexy girls often do. The ones who insist they hate their feet but grow up to be toe models.

"Cool feet," I said, instantly wishing I could've retracted it. Cool feet? What a douche.

Then the Asshole from Ohio came into the cabana, clearly on the prowl for Jill and about as subtle as Ebola.

"Yo," he said, a limited vocabulary predator. And I thought "cool feet" was lame.

"You, what?" she said, annoyed at this enormous jackass. Ditto for me.

"Come on. How 'bout a dance?" he said, never

acknowleding my presence.

"No thanks. Again," she said, trying to be civil.

"Come on. Let's dance. I wanna see you jam out with your clam out, " he jeered.

"Hey!" I said, rising to my feet and trying to defend my hot new friend. Two of his Ohio State boys suddenly appeared behind him, red-eyed and red-faced. Unsteady buffoons in their long Tommy Bahama shirts, cargo shorts, and garish I'm-Pretending-To-Be-African-American Nikes. The Dingbat Mafia. These were the kids who always refer to each other as "Yo!" and "G!" and "Dawg!" because they weren't satisfied enough with being white, from Long Island, spoiled, shitfaced, and on Spring Break.

They were itching for trouble, any kind of physical interaction at all, for that's what many boy do when the female attention isn't flowing their way, but the booze is.

Either that, or they decapitate their neighbor's snowman...

But more on that later.

WARFIELD

From across the bar, I noticed Doc Holiday was having a problem inside that cabana.

DOC HOLIDAY

Glowering meaty confidence, Asshole From Ohio got right into my face, the stench of beer and shitty cologne preceding his advance. He was bigger and stronger than me; all I had on him was age, which was almost as embarrassing as being smaller and weaker. He shoved me hard, sending me crashing down onto a couch. Jesus! Jill was going to witness her aged suitor getting his ass kicked.

But just as I righted myself and attempted to do clumsy battle, they were there, like a three-headed monster: The Boogeymen! Warfield smashed his fist into Asshole From Ohio's head. Expletives were exchanged between his boys, but my boys exchanged punches. And this much was true: The Gang That Couldn't Puke Straight could sure punch straight. It was awesome.

EARLY MAN
FYI: you always protect the head of the snake.

DOC HOLIDAY
In a rapid, merciless assault, the Assholes From Ohio were rendered dazed and moaning; two of them were on the ground. Warfield did the most damage, throwing probably only four total punches but landing them effectively. "Long live The Boogeymen!" Special Ed cried over the fallen kids. Warfield shot him a frosty look, and I thought he was going to punch him next.

I was a pretty shaken and rattled. Bar fights were like cinemas showing Van Damme movies: you never found me in one. Warfield's eyes were peeled for security goons who might've been onto us and suggested we get out of there. We all concurred and fled out a rear exit and into the parking lot.

Early Man turned to me and grinned. "Safety in numbers, right?"

"You guys arright?" I asked. "I owe you one."

"Not at all. Those idiots should die in a fire," Early Man said.

"Or get cancer in the ass!" Special Ed bellowed. We all just stared at him. He shrugged. He was always shrugging.

Jill emerged from the rear exit and trotted over to us. "You guys okay?"

"Yeah," I answered for all of us. I was surprised to see her. "Are you?"

"I'll be a lot better once I leave this place."

"Where's Ashley?" I asked.

"She's a mess. She wanted to go back to the hotel bar."

"Is she hot?" Special Ed asked.

We glared at him again. He shrugged, swiping moisture from his glistening pate.

"Can we go somewhere?" Jill asked me, and only me.

"Uh, yeah. Let's go somewhere."

"Aren't you gonna introduce us?" Early Man asked me. I complied, introducing them as "my old camp friends." The guys, disordered and shiny-eyed with drink, murmured hellos.

Jill grabbed my hand and turned to me. "Can we go?"

"Sure," I said. "We're gonna go, guys. Talk tomorrow. Thanks again."

"Go where?" Special Ed asked, looking disappointed.

"He's off to see The Wizard," Early Man said behind a little smirk.

"Hey, there's plenty of fish in the ocean," I said.

"So says the dude who hooked the beautiful marlin," Early Man said. He removed his cell phone and made Jill and I pose together for an awkward photo. After we examined the result, she turned to the guys. "Well, nice meeting everyone."

SPECIAL ED

We watched Doc Holiday shuffle away with that pretty girl, like Spring Break's Homecoming King and Queen. Warfield and I must've looked super jealous or something because Early Man attempted to boost our spirits.

"There's plenty of sand on this beach, if you know what I mean," he said. "Let's go smash our guitars somewhere else." But Warfield and I remained fixed at the two new lovebirds receding down the strip. "You guys know the running of the bulls in Pamplona?" Early Man asked. Warfield and I nodded. "But did you know those same bulls who stampede in the streets are later killed in the ring that night?"

"What's your point?" Warfield asked.

"Amusement comes at a price," Early Man said.

WARFIELD

I didn't know what he meant by that, but I was calling it a night. Early Man tried to convince me to join them at the Tarantula Club, apparently some after-hours place. I wasn't interested in finding any more "sand on this beach." It was late, I was cocked, and I'd just punched the shit out of three college kids. That wasn't exactly the behavior of a married guy who needed to keep a low profile in Canard Beach. I was heading back to the motel and cutting my losses.

DOC HOLIDAY

Jill and I walked the strip together, shuffling through the detritus of candy wrappers, beer cans, crushed cigarette boxes, and soiled nightclub flyers stamped with hundreds of footprints. We passed a shuttered storefront with a splash of graffiti spray-painted on it: "I'M CREEPIN' WHILE YOU'RE SLEEPIN." Accompanied by a green, four-eyed phallus-shaped ghoul with a dangerously lascivious smile, it may as well have been a rendering of Spring Break's official mascot.

When Jill grabbed my hand and squeezed it maybe a little too hard, I had a feeling this wacky Spring Break adventure was going to be worth it, after all. She even kind of reminded me of a young Camden. They shared the same cute, unremarkable nose and olive coloring. There was also the similar dimpled smile, lean, rangy trunk, and pert bosom.

Back in high school, I used to wish there was a way I could literally clone Camden, in the hopes that maybe her duplicate would dig me. Yet if that didn't happen and her clone wasn't interested either, I'd be in twice the lovesick trouble. And that's good for nobody. But Jill was like Camden 1.0, and I hoped to have better luck with this edition.

"Your old camp friends are a little weird," Jill said.

"Aren't they all?"

She giggled. "Is the bald one a doctor?"

Special Ed's hospital scrubs must've misled her. "No. He's just playing one in Canard Beach."

She chuckled, a bit unsteady now, the Cosmos' cumulative effect starting to wallop her pretty good. She removed her cell phone. Complaining that her battery was dying, she left a message with Ashley, saying "maybe she'd meet up later." She threw me an impish smile. "So, law school, huh?"

"Yeah. Law school," I said, but for a spooky moment I thought she saw right through me: I was no law student, but some creepy 34 year-old preying on young, vulnerable, Cosmo-swilling college girls on Spring Break.

"What's so funny?" I asked, wanting reassurance this wasn't the case.

"Nothing," she said, kissing my cheek again.

Yeah, this was turning out better than I expected. It was all working for me: my lies and half-lies. It was my night, that's all. It was just my night. Sometimes it's like shooting fish in a barrel. Other times there's either no fish, or your gun is empty.

You know how it is.

WARFIELD

Back in my motel room, I plunked down on a patio chair with a fresh beer. I knew I had to check in with Nikki back in Phoenix; she'd left me a few messages. She hated it when I left her drunk voicemails after business dinners. "Don't drunk-dial me," she'd say. "I'm your wife."

So I drunk-texted her, instead. "Hey, hon. Checking in. Dinner and drinks with the guys from Oracle. Call you tomorrow. Love ya."

But I felt lousy about lying again. I had a baby girl at home now, which meant I had to think of a lot more than just myself. I needed to be that much more focused and responsible. The days of white lies and petty obfuscations should have already ended. Instead, I was in Florida during Spring Break with three old camp friends? But this was the last big lie, I told myself. At least I'd never cheated on Nikki before. I wasn't that guy. Diversion is one thing, perversion quite another.

EARLY MAN

A neon sign hanging behind the bar inside the Tarantula Club read "I HAVE SEEN THE ENEMY AND IT IS DAYLIGHT." The place was every shade of shady, but the real enemy were the chicks. It was a sanctuary where erections went to die. Special Ed and I sat at the bar, knocking back tequila shots and nursing beers.

"These girls are 35 years-old," he assessed with disappointment, as if that classified them as officially mummified. I was surprised to hear him complain, because jerking-off was probably his idea of a vacation.

"Dude, they're our age," I said. "Stop facial profiling."

He giggled. "Crazytown."

"We'll do better tomorrow," I assured him. "And younger. Have a little faith. Even diabetics know where to find the candy."

He started to fumble with his phone, snorting exasperation. "My service sucks here," he said. "T-Mobile. It's the worst." I shrugged and drained a tequila shot. "But I can't switch," he continued, "cuz I'll break my contract and have to pay a termination fee penalty." I just stared at him. He was some piece of joy, all right. "What?" he said.

"Is this conversation boring the fuck outta you, as much as it is me?"

"Sorry."
"It's okay."

DOC HOLIDAY

We weren't in my room long before I was removing Jill's top and her bra.

"I don't usually do this," she assured me.

"Me neither," I assured her back.

"Sorry to hear that."

"Back at ya."

We were on my bed moments later, kissing and muscling through it all, her breasts jouncing onto my chest. She unzipped my pants and went well, dirty south. That's as gory as I'd like to keep the details. When it was over, she toyed with her phone, perhaps thinking to check back in with her friends. I'd never been too comfortable in those "post-mortem" silences. Most guys like to cut and run, but I never felt like running. I just didn't feel like talking. And if the girl wanted to cuddle, I wanted a taxi. Reese used to call these moments "time to punt."

But with Jill, I found myself volunteering information, hoping I wasn't oversharing, or worse, boring her senseless. But we had connected quickly at Barnacles and now I was telling her about the origins of 'Plan 9 from Cyberspace.' And why I had nicknamed us "The Boogeymen" way back when at Camp Hideaway.

"Will you tell me a ghost story?" she said.

"I thought you'd never ask."

I really didn't travel to Canard Beach to hook up with a college girl, and it was a safe bet she didn't come to town to do the same with a 34-year-old liar. Yet here we were. She was graduating in a few months, and as long as she was still single she'd be "in play" or "open for business," to use a couple of Reese's old terminologies. We'd had a great time together and maybe there were more good times in store for us this week. There was no crime in that. But I didn't want to feel like an imposter any longer.

"I was lying to you earlier," I said. "I'm sorry."

"What do you mean?"

"I'm not in law school in Boston. I'm an English teacher."

"Well, I'm a student. Does that mean we're breaking the

law?" She giggled and kissed me. Oh boy, that was a relief. Jill had a good little sense of humor. Not many girls made me laugh, but a few had made me cry. I made a comment about how lousy the room was. She and Ashley were staying at a decent hotel on the strip called Beachfront Property. "You should see if they've got any rooms available," she said.

"Should I?"

"If I'm you, it makes good geographical sense." It seemed like a good idea and now I was pretty sure we had more good times in store for us. Her hotel was most likely booked solid, but I'd inquire, anyway. I told her I'd look into it tomorrow.

"You'll let me know how you make out?" she asked.

"You'll be the first to know." She chuckled. I asked her if she was hungry. The Dove's Nest across the street was open all night. But she appeared uncertain, maybe even troubled.

"What is it?" I asked. "Are you okay?"

"Yeah. I'm fine. But maybe I should go."

But before we could discuss this much further, she drifted off to sleep. When her cell rang moments later, it startled me, its ringtone as jarring as it was unrecognizable. Snatching up her cell, I glanced at the screen: Ashley was calling. I debated a moment before shutting off the phone. Only to realize that wasn't too smart, and maybe a bit selfish. Ashley was probably just worried: her friend had left a bar with a stranger, and now someone had killed her phone after three rings. I could certainly understand her cause for concern. But I didn't want to wake Jill.

SPECIAL ED

I staggered into our room around 2:30 a.m, brain-scorched like crazytown with tequila. Doc Holiday and the Jill girl were asleep in his bed, partially covered beneath the blankets. I quietly got undressed and climbed into my bed. I gazed over at It Girl. She was Crazytown, I tell you. Crazytown.

DOC HOLIDAY

I woke up, achy and leaden with a bruising hangover. The nightstand clock read 8:13 a.m. Jill wasn't in my bed. I sat up and blinked out the mossy cobwebs, realizing her clothes and purse were gone, also. She must've decided to split, after all. That was disappointing, but she was entitled. I'd reconnect with her later.

When I cocooned myself back within the blankets, I felt something hard leaning against my arm: Jill's cell phone. I'd make a plan to return it to her. I went back to sleep.

EARLY MAN

He fucked her in the ass first, Oprah. Take it away, Warfield. He was eating dessert first. Nothing like cutting to the chase. He had gotten a mighty second wind, fueled by the hit of Ecstasy I supplied him with. It was on.

Special Ed was across the street getting coffee for the team. It was around 8:30 a.m now. After returning to the room about six hours earlier, I found Warfield on the patio outside, mumbling something about a stupid text message he'd sent his wife. But you'd never know that rascal ever walked down the aisle at all, if you'd seen how he was pummeling our Fair Princess from behind.

The knock on our door had come around 3 a.m. I hopped out of bed and peered through the peephole. Special Ed had the girl manacled to the spot, his hand clapped over her mouth, her eyes wide with panic. This leering bald demon smiled into the peephole. "Crazytown," he hushed, just loud enough for me to hear.

So I opened the door, because it sounded like a nice place to live for a while.

PART FIVE

THREE PEOPLE LIKE THIS

"There she stood in the doorway;
I heard the mission bell
And I was thinking to myself,
'This could be Heaven or this could be Hell.'"

-- The Eagles

SPECIAL ED

I waited in line to buy coffees and snacks in the Starbucks across from the motel. A sign behind the counter read HOMEMADE BROWNIES MADE FROM SCRATCH! Sorry, not impressed. I don't get "scratch." Never did, really. You? What's the big deal? So someone actually made the brownies *themselves.* Who gives a shit? LOL.

After buying my treats I headed back toward the motel, wondering what was now going down in Room 211. I had taken it upon myself to make it personal with someone.

It happened in the middle of the night when I saw her get up to pee. A bit woozy in her bra and bikini underwear, she slinked through the darkness. I caught a glimpse of her ass crack, just a slash of it, really. But wow! So I climbed out of bed and waited outside the door. I could smell the tangy scent of her perfume, fruity and fun. When the door opened and she emerged, she slightly flinched at the sight of me.

"Oh, hi," she whispered shyly, trying to remain quiet. She was embarrassed and re-covered her private place with both hands. Her hair was a tangled mess, falling down over her face, and her nipples were visible through her bra. Standing guard. Like the size of fighter pilots' thumbs. Good tits, too. Not huge but solid. Perky fun.

Special Ed likes perky fun.

"Hi," I said, falling in mad love with her in about six seconds. Super pretty girls were like ghosts to me: they didn't exist in my world.

"Sorry," she said, forcing a weary smile. I loved that she was apologizing for some reason, as if I'd somehow earned or merited an apology. It felt strangely empowering. Just what she was "sorry" for, I couldn't tell you. Unless she was sorry for being so hot, yet forever unattainable despite standing only a foot away.

Which made two of us.

She glanced at her watch, rolled her eyes, and cracked an adorably sheepish smile. "I think my business is done here."

"Okay."

"I'm gonna call a cab downstairs." She glanced over at Doc Holiday, looking dubious. She clearly didn't want to wake him. "Tell him I'll call him tomorrow?"

"I will. Definitely." Bringing sexy back, this one. Big-time. This was a girl with a huge fan base.

"Thanks." And as she went to gather up her clothes, I wondered how many people loved her. Truly loved her. Back home, back at school, out there in the world… how many were there?

She hiked up her shorts and pulled her pink Polo shirt over her head. And if she was uncomfortable because I was watching her dress, she didn't betray anything. You had to be impressed with this perfumed little princess, despite the fact she had chosen to eat and run. She was almost like another girl on the Internet who says she 'really wants to meet me.' But who really doesn't want to meet me.

I wondered how many people would miss her. Truly miss her.

"If you want, I'll wait for a cab with you downstairs," I offered.

Back home, back at school. Out in the world.

"Thanks. But I'm okay."

"Seriously. I mean, I can't sleep, anyway. It's no problem."

How many were there?

"Well, okay. All right."

How many are you?

I threw on my jeans and sneakers. She appeared a bit harried and rushed but shouldered her purse. "I'm ready," she said.

And are you scoring at home?

"Let's do it," I said.

"I appreciate it."

When I grabbed her in the hallway outside the room, she was much too startled to muster much resistance. As I dragged her across the hall to Room 211, she squirmed and whimpered, her fragrance strong in my nose. I felt like Peter Parker after being bitten by that radioactive arachnid. And since "with great power, comes great responsibility," I jammed my hand over her mouth so she couldn't properly scream.

I knocked hard on the door. She was already crying, eyes big and streaming wet in their sockets. She never knew what hit her. Which was pretty savvy of me, no? Guess I was capable of a little mystery, after all.

"Even diabetics know where to find the candy," I whispered to her. I've never seen anyone so terrified in her life. Well, until a few moments later.

WARFIELD

I was still stewing in my seat on the patio when I was alerted to voices inside the room. I glanced through the screen door and saw Special Ed and Early Man struggling with Doc Holiday's girl. Special Ed had her in the strangled grip of a full nelson.

Appalled, I charged inside. "What the hell's going on?!"

"She's looking for an audience," Early Man said.

"No, I'm not," she whimpered.

"Everyone is," Early Man said.

"Let's energize her fan base," Special Ed gushed.

"What the hell're you talking about?" Early Man said.

Special Ed just shrugged. "Um. Nothing. She's up for it," he said.

"She doesn't look up for it," I said.

Early Man shot me a taunting look. "And what's your excuse?"

"Where's Doc Holiday?" I asked Special Ed. "What is this?" But he just mooned about excitedly, uttering to himself: "Crazytown. Crazytown. Crazytown." Some kind of eerie incantation as invoked by a brain-dead shaman.

"Shut your hole," Early Man scolded him, and he instantly clammed up, pacing the room in a gathering frenzy.

"Guys, come on. Let her get outta here. Let her go," I pleaded. "This isn't funny."

"Do you see anyone laughing?" Early Man snapped at me. Special Ed snickered. Early Man gave him a nasty stare. Special Ed stopped snickering.

"It's my fuckin' room, okay?" I protested. "Get her out of here."

"It's our room," Early Man reminded me. "Let's share everything."

"What are we… what're you doing? I mean, we can't do this," I commanded. But they'd already wrestled her down onto my bed. She kicked and flailed, desperately thrashing at them with all four of her limbs.

"Settle down or we'll knock you out," Early Man warned her. She complied and momentarily ceased her resistance. I started to pace the room. I had to do something, had to stop this from happening. "Little help?" Early Man said to me, pointing to his bed.

"What?"

"Strip my bed. We need the sheets," he said. But I wouldn't budge.

"Crazytown," Special Ed said, swiping sweat from his round face.

"Hey, even the Wright brothers needed wings," Early Man said and then gagged her mouth with a dirty sock. He glanced at Special Ed. "Take off her clothes," he said.

"Me?" Special Ed asked.

"No. The *other* short, bald mongoloid in the room. Yes, you!"

Special Ed removed her shorts and Polo shirt, stripping her down to her bra and underwear.

"Noooo!" Jill whimpered behind the sock, a garbled protest that fell on deaf ears.

"Welcome to the Honeymoon Suite," Early Man said. "Now don't be a cunt." She continued to thrash at us. "What's the matter? Never been with older guys before?"

"You smell good," Special Ed told Jill, sniffing at her like a pesky dog.

"Dude, don't make it weird," Early Man said.

"'Don't make it weird?'" I said.

I wanted to kill these crazy maniacs. Jill's frightened eyes met mine – bulging and desperate with purpose – and I realized she was counting on me to call a halt to this madness. Early Man saw this covert exchange and appeared to sense the connection between us. And he needed to disconnect it. "Strip the other bed!" he repeated. "Two's company, three's a crowd, but four's a party!"

But I just backed off, never having been more scared in my life. There was no way I'd be a party to this. "No way, guys," I said. "No way!"

SPECIAL ED

Warfield stripped the other bed about six seconds later. When in Rome, no? Early Man goaded him. But first, Warfield needed reassurance.

"What about Doc Holiday?" he asked. "What're we going to do about him?"

"We'll blow up that bridge when we get to it," Early Man said.

I guess that was good enough, because Warfield stripped the sheets on the other bed and then helped us tie Jill down. She stared up at him, horrified and disbelieving but he wouldn't look at her. He couldn't do it. Know why? Because he'd just bought a time-share in Crazytown. LOL.

EARLY MAN

Warfield was married, so needed all his bases covered. I understood his concern. But Doc Holiday owed us, anyway. Needed to share the wealth. We'd saved his ass back at Barnacles when those college kids were about to annihilate him. The more the merrier. Safety in numbers.

I smiled down at our new girl and made the introductions. "We're the Boogeymen," I said. "And we're not for the squeamish."

WARFIELD

After she was fastened down to the bed in four-point restraints, the guys and I exchanged looks of dumbstruck awe, like novice fishermen who had inexplicably reeled in a one-hundred-pound tuna, but were clueless as to how next to proceed. What happened now?

SPECIAL ED

Early Man removed one of his celebrity magazines and held a photo up before Jill's face: a bikini shot of Jessica Alba from the movie *Into the Blue.* Awesomely hot girl, that one.

"Let's warm you up first," he said, freeing up one of her hands and planting it onto her beaver. "Foam your runway for us. Come as you are."

Warfield grimaced. "I thought we weren't making it

weird."

Early Man ignored him and slapped Jill's face with the magazine. "Masturbate for us," he repeated.

"Hey, if you don't, I will!" I said. The guys scowled at me. I shrugged. Tears streamed down her cheeks. One fat tear even rolled down to the base of her chin. I don't know why but I distinctly remember that one.

"Rub your 'baby dick.' Anchor properly with your thumb. Come on. It's Spring Break. No strings attached," Early Man instructed her. "Anchors away."

"'Baby dick?'" I asked. Sounded gross.

"Clit," Early Man explained. I shrugged. Sounded less gross. LOL. "Dance with the ones who brung ya," he admonished her. "Shop alone for the boys."

Jill stared at the shot of Jessica Alba. Not the one-night stand she had in mind. I wondered what she was gonna choose to do. I imagined her simultaneously weeping and pleasuring herself. Don't see that too often where I'm from.

"Come for us," Early Man commanded. "Then we'll let you go."

Jill's frightened eyes searched our faces, ticking to each of us: from Early Man, to me, to Warfield. Weighing her options, I guess. But she shook her head. She wasn't gonna do it because she couldn't trust us.

"Forget the magazine," Warfield said. "This is fucking ridiculous."

Undeterred, Early Man unzipped his jeans and removed his dick. "Is this better?" he asked. Here came trouble. "Masturbate for us. Or this goes inside you," he told her.

"Jesus," Warfield muttered. He stared at me, as if to say Are you kosher with this?

"Crazytown," I said, grinning. Special Ed likes kosher.

Jill had no choice but to go off to the races, choosing the lesser of two evils: she pleasured herself and wept. Not exactly walking and chewing gum at the same time but still pretty impressive.

"How cool is this?" I said but the guys totally ignored me. We watched Jill weep and maybe come, and afterward Early Man inquired about coffee and bagels. Crazytown, huh?

These guys sure knew how to party.

EARLY MAN

When you think about it, Viagra is the best date-rape drug of 'em all. But they don't mention *that* as a possible side effect, do they?

WARFIELD

Early Man handed each of us a hit of Ecstasy, but Special Ed declined. Early Man and I ingested those little white pills and chased them with beers. I'd never come even close to taking this drug, but tonight was a first time for everything.

"Our Fair Princess," Early Man said, a dark smile creeping across his face. But one person's fairy tale is another's horror tale, and one look at Jill was a reminder. No one said a word. The look on her face, man. Never forget it. Never. And though you weren't there, trust me: you'd never forget it, either. Her whole life was turned upside down in a matter of moments. Not to mention ours.

It happened so crazy fast, I'm telling you. Sound judgment? Forget about it. Common sense? Not a chance. What we did was brutal and inexcusable, but a snap decision or indecision can cost you for the rest of your life. I know that now.

But I didn't really know these guys and I certainly didn't know this girl. So I wasn't going to be civil or democratic about it. This runaway train had left the station. I wished it hadn't, but it had. All aboard. And that's why I decided to go first.

EARLY MAN

"Two's company, three's a crowd, but four's a party," I said, looming over her splayed form like a giant monster over a defenseless city. If I was Godzilla, she was Tokyo. But all of us were breathing fire.

"Please," our Fair Princess managed to mutter through her gag.

I told her she had to blow all of us, and after that we'd let her go. That was the deal. In the grand scheme of things, it wasn't such a high price to pay for her freedom. But she shook her head. It wasn't gonna happen.

"Come on. Add us to your oral history," I said. "Or maybe we'll kill you."

Warfield and Special Ed glanced at me, unsure if their fearless leader was bluffing or not. Our Fair Princess flailed and fought to remain defiant and "empowered" in the face of such chaos. That's when Warfield made his big proclamation.

He wanted to be the lone gunman on her grassy knoll.

SPECIAL ED

Early Man started scrolling down Warfield's iPhone. He sparked a joint and grinned my way. "We're takin' some dramatic liberties," he said, French-inhaling some smoke.

"Crazytown," I said.

"Go across the street and get us some coffees," he said. "Maybe a few bagels."

EARLY MAN

When Warfield was finished with our Fair Princess, he glomped past me and into the bathroom. He slammed the door shut and turned on the shower. I scrolled down the numbers programmed in his iPhone. Two were of especially pertinent interest: one listed as NIKKI-CELL and another one – HOME. You can never be too prepared when you vacation. I was nothing if not pragmatic, so I programmed these numbers into my BlackBerry.

Our quarry lay sprawled across the bed, trembling and crying and disheveled and brutalized. Flushed nearly orange from tears. Mother-naked and curvy, too. Doc Holiday certainly had good taste. I guess if you're bold enough to stand in the batter's box, you may as well swing for the fences. But now it was our turn at her plate.

"Look, we apologize if we're 'objectifying' you," I told her. "Not that, right? But you got one stand-up vagina." She pinched her eyes closed, even as she continued to blubber through her tears. "Guys like us don't like to be forgotten, ignored, or left behind. So we wanna ensure that you always remember us. Is that fair?"

She opened her eyes again. "Please stop. Please... let me go."

"Let's wait until the coffee comes. Caffeine's a good antioxidant, they say. In the meantime, baby, open big. Lemme show you my MTV."

I fucked her in the mouth. Her eyes were pinched close again, but she wept onto my cock. It wasn't the ideal lubrication, so I jammed it in harder, faster, nearly choking her. But she got it right. The good girls usually do.

I thought I heard Warfield crying in the shower. I hoped Special Ed remembered that I took cream, not milk. "Come on, honey. What're strangers, but friends waiting to happen?" I gently assuaged our Fair Princess. "Got room for cream?" I asked, before blasting my load in her face. "Nutsack goulash," we used to call it back in high school. "Cock-snot," too. Good times.

We dared a might thing, the boys and I. We'd turned some kind of monstrous corner, but a clear and present danger lurked at its edges. There was no going back. I knew that. I think we all did. I hoped we all did. I stared at our hard target, wondering what our next course of action would be. The consequences of whatever we chose to do needed to be carefully analyzed and examined. We'd have to dot our Is and cross our Ts as best we could.

Special Ed arrived with our coffees, saying they were out of bagels. Bummer. But he bought a few blueberry muffins. So we sipped our drinks and nibbled our muffins and ran our eyes over the girl. Drinking her in like she was some kind of pricey museum piece of which now was our personal possession: The Moaning Lisa.

Warfield emerged from the shower, wrapped in a big white towel. Florid and ornery, he cracked open a beer and didn't say a word. No coffee for him. When Special Ed offered him a muffin, Warfield angrily slapped it out of his hand.

SPECIAL ED
Apparently not a breakfast person.

EARLY MAN
Warfield slumped in a chair and nervously checked his iPhone for messages. Special Ed wasn't interested in joining our party. As if he was the gentleman of our peanut gallery. He didn't wanna touch the girl any more than he already had, seemingly content to be a voyeur happy enough to have done the shopping. Go figure, right? He was like the pedophile who decides to give up the life to go write children's books.

So we just hovered over our Fair Princess and stared at her. She was walleyed with twitchy delirium, like some kind of mental patient.

"Our little Maserati. Stuck in traffic," I said.

"Crazytown," he muttered, almost to himself. "Crazytown."

And this time, who could argue?

DOC HOLIDAY

When I finally rolled out of bed around 10:30, I realized that Special Ed was gone. More preoccupied with wondering if Jill and I had exchanged numbers the night before, I scrolled through my BlackBerry contacts. No luck, and no voice messages from the other guys.

After a long hot shower, I got dressed and tried calling them. My calls went straight to voicemail and I figured they were either on the beach or having breakfast somewhere. I knew Jill would be calling her phone as soon as she realized it was left behind, so I pocketed it and left the room.

A DO NOT DISTURB sign was hanging on the doorknob to Room 211, so I didn't bother knocking. I'd hook up with them later. The beach was over a mile away, but I was happy to walk, nursing a hot Starbucks coffee and basking in the 80-degree sunshine beneath an azure, cloudless sky.

At the beach, I found a good spot on the pier behind Barnacles. I kicked back on my towel and rubbed sunscreen onto my face and arms. A scattering of college kids were lounging and sunbathing. I may've appeared mysteriously incognito behind my dark shades and beneath the battered Red Sox cap, but didn't care much. I was feeling pretty good.

I lobbed in more calls to the other guys, but kept getting their voicemails. I left them messages: I was on the beach on the pier behind Barnacles. Where the Hell were they? It's a beautiful day. Come on down.

EARLY MAN

We sipped our drinks around a small table, squirming anxiously and brainstorming our next move, like a chess game played by amateur madmen. We bandied about ideas about how to possibly spin the story. But to whom?

Our Fair Princess was shuddering and sobbing beneath the blankets, her coloring now more waxen than orange. She appeared to have shrunken overnight. Bound, gagged, and flailing meekly against her restraints, she almost resembled a creature in a science fiction movie awaiting some kind of sinister experimentation.

And maybe she was.

WARFIELD

I broached the idea that maybe we could explain to Doc Holiday that things got crazy with Jill. They had been completely consensual at the outset, but she freaked out when it was over, and claimed she was raped. So now we were freaking out and unsure how to proceed. In other words: We Said, She Said. But could we take such a chance? Thoughts? The guys were against the idea. That was the vote. And I guess they weren't wrong.

SPECIAL ED

We stared at our cell phones, hoping none of them would ring again. Early Man said we shouldn't shut them off just yet.

WARFIELD

The rustle of Special Ed's bag of Fritos was driving me nuts.

EARLY MAN

Warfield looked almost possessed, capable of erupting in either tears or laughter at any moment. FYI: never vacation with a married guy. Special Ed fidgeted nervously, drinking his coffee too fast and too noisily and gorging on a giant bag of Fritos. He paused to study the fine print on the back, as if it foretold the secrets of his retarded universe. "Why does Frito-Lay need like, their own website?" he asked. I wanted to punch his teeth out. Warfield glowered at him. Special Ed merely shrugged, yet felt the need to finish his thought. "I mean, what else do we need to know?"

WARFIELD

Early Man beat me to the punch and told Special Ed to shut the hell up. Fritos weren't the problem here. What the hell were we going to do with this girl?! That was the problem. And this idiot had issues with fucking Frito-Lay?

EARLY MAN

Doc Holiday had left each of us voicemails, wanting to know where we were. I'd hung the DO NOT DISTURB sign around the doorknob outside our room, but it was only a matter of time before he came looking for us.

When the motel room phone rang, it jolted us. Special Ed flinched so violently, he nearly knocked over his coffee. The boys and I traded looks of creeping dread. We stared at the phone until the ringing stopped.

I grabbed up the phone, pressed VOICEMAIL, and listened to the message.

"It was him," I said. "Same message. He's on the beach behind Barnacles."

Warfield sputtered relief and checked his watch. "Thank God."

"Why's that?" I asked.

"So we can get the fuck out of here right now."

"Where are we going?" I asked. "Did you forget about her?"

WARFIELD

We gazed over at Jill, weighing decisions and indecisions. We had no plan. None. We needed an exit strategy. What the hell do we do with this girl? We couldn't just drop her off back at her hotel and then flee Canard Beach. She'd call the police or her friends would, and we'd be dead meat. Our lives would be over. I wished we could've forgotten about her. But we couldn't. And we never would.

SPECIAL ED

It didn't seem like we had a plan at all.

"What do we do with her?" Warfield asked, starting to panic now.

"Shoulda thought of that when you were putting it in her pail," Early Man said.

"Jesus, man. Think," Warfield said.

"Well, we can't just chew and screw," Early Man said.

"Maybe we can talk to her," Warfield said.

"And say what? 'I'm sorry?'" Early Man said.

"I am sorry," Warfield said.

"You think she's gonna negotiate with us?" Early Man said.

Warfield got to his feet, a man on a mission. "We gotta try something."

"Go for it," Early Man said. "Close the deal. You're the salesman."

WARFIELD

I grabbed a bottle of water and cautiously walked over to the bed. I carefully removed the gag from her mouth. She coughed, but her eyes remained focused on the ceiling.

"Drink some water," I said. She weakly shifted herself up and allowed me to pour some water into her mouth. "Look, um… We'd like to get out of here, too," I continued, attempting to give it my best shot. "It's just that we… in order for us to let you go… Maybe we can make a deal? Or, I dunno… an arrangement." But she refused to even dignify my words. "Look, things got crazy. Crazy. But we're sorry."

Her fierce red eyes finally met mine. "You will be," she said. "You fucking will be." The scary part was that I believed her.

"Gag her!" Early Man cried out from across the room. I grabbed the gag and gently stuffed it back inside her mouth. I returned back to the guys and slumped back down in my chair.

"No sale, huh?" Early Man said.

EARLY MAN

I wasn't surprised. I wouldn't have negotiated with us, either. We had the bait, not the switch. There were no sweetheart deals available in our kit bags. Negotiations were off the table. What act of good will could we possibly offer her, other than letting her go? Buy her a gift card? Any inaction of ours could be even more detrimental than any action, so we'd have to carefully weigh the pros and cons.

"So what now? What do we do with her?" Warfield asked.

"Something probably not very nice," I said.

DOC HOLIDAY

I didn't know where those guys were but didn't much care. To be honest, they were a trifle creepy and my game plan was to hook up with Jill and take it from there.

I called Beachfront Property. After learning they were booked solid, I followed up on their recommendation: The Cabana Inn. It was just a few blocks down from Jill's hotel and they had vacancies. I wouldn't be able to check in for another hour, but this was perfect. I booked a room for three nights.

I turned over onto my stomach. Sprawled out like a Bowery drunkard, I was perfectly content and comfortable. With the briny smell of sand in my nose, coffee in my belly, the battering heat on my back, and a glimmer of female promise probably still asleep back at her hotel, Day 2 in Canard Beach was off to a pretty good start.

EARLY MAN

"Should we blind her?" Special Ed suggested with alarming earnestness.

WARFIELD

When he said those words, I knew I'd stepped into some serious shit in Canard Beach.

SPECIAL ED

Warfield growled indignantly at me. "Are you on serious fucking meds, or what?"

"She's seen our faces, guys," I said, attempting to justify it. "So that way, she'd never be able to recognize us again."

"Keep your day job," Early Man said.

"You want to blind her?" Warfield asked me. "Why don't we just cut out her tongue while we're at it? So she can never testify against us?"

"Crazytown," I said.

"Jesus," Warfield said. "This isn't funny."

"Too soon?" Early Man said, smiling.

"You wanna disfigure her? You think that's the answer?" Warfield said.

"Raping her is okay but blinding her is a no-no?" I asked.

Early Man laughed. "The boy does make a point."

Warfield glared at me. "How do you suggest we blind her? Just to play this game?" he asked me.

"Ah, so now we're actually playing this game?" Early Man taunted him.

"I don't know," I said. "Maybe we can go buy some acid somewhere. You know, lye. Or whatever. Something like that."

Early Man snickered at me. "Clearly, you don't abduct chicks often, do you?"

"Do you?" Warfield asked him.

"Nope. But I've thought about it. And that's half the battle," he said.

"Crazytown," I said.

"Stop fuckin' sayin' that!" Warfield yelped at me.

"Sorry." "There's no such thing as a perfect crime, just a perfect alibi," Early Man said.

"But we don't have one," Warfield said.

"I do," Early Man said.

"What is it?" I asked.

"You guys," he said.

"What?" Warfield asked.

"You guys," Early Man repeated.

"What the hell are you talking about, Warfield asked, growing unhinged.

"And Doc Holiday," Early Man added, not answering the question.

"But Doc Holiday had nothin' to do with this," Warfield said.

"He didn't? He fucked her first, didn't he? Sounds like he had a lot to do with it. So let's use that to our advantage." We looked over at Jill, who was ashen and wide-eyed. "And what difference does it make? It's Spring Break semantics, really."

"Semantics?" Warfield asked.

"This wasn't rape, anyway," Early Man said.

"What was it, then?" I asked.

He grinned and lit a cigarette. "Forced enjoyment," he said.

Warfield kind of bit back a furious scowl, having heard enough of this. "Go pack your shit," he said to me. "Hurry!"

DOC HOLIDAY

I watched a beach volleyball game get underway. Pretty girls jumping and leaping beneath the unremitting sunshine. Good, clean fun. I removed my BlackBerry and clicked onto Facebook, thinking I should finally utilize the "check-in" feature: "Doc Holiday has checked-in at Canard Beach Paradise!"

Instead, I did another random Facebook Search for Camden. But of course, she was still nowhere to be found. I could only hope I'd have better luck finding Jill.

WARFIELD

When Special Ed returned to his room, Early Man remained eerily incautious and calm, casually smoking. This was a guy who'd been running Stop signs his entire life. He even cracked open a beer.

"Any thoughts?" I said. "Jesus. Come on, man. Vacation's over!"

He stared into his beer, ruminating. And as he did, I had to wonder if myself, Special Ed and Doc Holiday were his first online seductions. Or had earlier overtures to complete strangers failed before he finally hit pay dirt with his old camp friends? Was he some sort of online terrorist? Not that any of it mattered anymore.

Nothing did except for this girl in that bed. The hostage now keeping us hostage.

EARLY MAN

I started spitballing ideas and options. Killing her was off the table. That was just insane and incomprehensible to consider, and you don't cover your tracks by creating new ones. Yet a true Adventure Captain has to test the waters. And that's what I did.

"Are you happily married," I asked Warfield. "Or just regular married?"

"What? Yeah. I mean, sure. Happily married."

"Lemme guess: did you secretly register for wedding gifts at Smith & Wesson?"

"You're not funny. Jesus."

"Nikki, huh?"

"Yeah, Nikki. Let's leave her outta this, okay?"

"Maybe."

"Come on. We gotta make a decision here! We gotta do something."

"Are you sure you're happily married?"

"Yes, yes. Fuck, man. So what now? Thought you were the adventure captain. Thought you were the Man with the Plan."

I didn't appreciate the mocking nature of his challenge, his caustic tone implying that he doubted me. He thought I'd honeyed them down to Canard Beach with false promises, and now wasn't being accountable for my actions. Our actions.

"Did you know that 1 of out every 100 Florida citizens is on a waiting list to see an execution? I asked.

He scowled utter dismay at me. "What the hell're you talking about?"

I pointed to our girlfriend. Because maybe it was never really off the table.

"We have to kill her. Don't we?"

WARFIELD

That's when I knew I had stepped into even more serious shit in Canard Beach.

EARLY MAN

"You're not in Kansas anymore," I informed our quivering captive. Warfield muttered how "none of us were." I saw tears in his eyes. It was time to separate the men from the boys. I called over to the girl: "We just might have to remove you as a friend."

DOC HOLIDAY

It was probably a good thing Facebook didn't exist when I was in high school because I would've probably grown jealous every time Camden added a new "Friend." I might have tried to invent a feature that could remotely "remove," "hide," or "block" any "Friends" of hers I didn't care for. Kill her darlings, as it were.

When she started dating boys in tenth grade. I grew embittered and embattled and and crumbled into a reckless tailspin. I'd wander the high school hallways, brooding and miserable, reeking of cigarettes or weed. I was Black Bile Guy –

often grumpy, rude, and moody. Always high, even at my lowest. I hated seeing Camden every day but loved seeing her, too. I never missed a day of school. Never. I couldn't miss a day.

Erratic and irresponsible, my grades plummeted nearly as low as my self-esteem. I was failing math and my parents wanted me to see a tutor. I loathed math and didn't understand why it was a core requirement. I promised my parents I would study harder, and I did. But I studied Camden with much more scrutiny and attention to detail. The results were mixed on both accounts. Between math and Camden, I was never sure which subject was trickier to comprehend.

Reese and Lansky often teased me about her, theorizing that her vagina must be made of either gold or chocolate. I wasn't a fan of these taunts, but when too lazy not to play along, I trumped them with my own theory: it was cashmere.

Once she got busy with boyfriends, it was difficult to cultivate or maintain a friendship with her. She was always occupied and constantly on the go. So I proceeded to commit to memory the makes and models of all her boyfriends' cars, all in the hopes that maybe it was true: practice really did make perfect. That it wasn't just some tired old cliché, or urban myth. And wasn't perseverance, persistence, and attrition supposed to pay off for the good guys? Hadn't such peachy wisdom been drummed into our brains since we were children, that if we worked hard enough at something, anything was possible? Okay, so maybe that was all bullshit.

It caused me considerable mental anguish, but I tried keeping a respectful distance from this runaway bandwagon. I chose to be a "Spare Tire" rather than a Third Wheel because the spare has an outside chance to get in the game, whereas The Third Wheel is content to watch from the sidelines.

It was akin to investing a wealth of emotional capital in a favorite sports team: you live and breathe for that team. They may break your heart to pieces, but there's always next year - always that kernel of promise you could hold out for.

Camden was a lot more draining, a year-round emotional siphon, not merely a seasonal depression. If I suffered from "Seasonal Affective Disorder," it knew no deadline. The seasons would change, but I never changed with them. Fall, winter, spring, or summer, it didn't matter. She always messed me up.

"Goodbye to you my trusted friend/We've known each other since we were nine or ten... "

EARLY MAN

"We could suffocate her and then leave her in the other room. So they'd find her in there," I suggested. A series of frightened tics danced across Jill's face, her darting eyes glassy with growing terror. She was living out a nightmare in real time. The sock gag muffled her whimpers and tears ran down her face. We had no choice but to sort of ignore her, Warfield finding it more difficult than I.

"But then Doc Holiday would be implicated in her... in all this," Warfield said.

"Exactly."

"No way. No way."

"You really care if some old camp friend asshole takes the rap? You don't even know him anymore. Practically met him on Facebook this time. It means nothing."

"Hey, that was your idea, this whole thing was your idea."

I pointed at our Fair Princess. "She wasn't my idea."

"Mine, either."

"So after raping her, now you have a moral conscience?" It was a rhetorical question to which he had no answer. "The cops will theorize that Doc Holiday killed her," I reasoned. "Then he split and checked out of the motel."

SPECIAL ED

As I packed my bags in my room, I was unsure what our plan was. Could we write a ransom note? A fake ransom note? We needed to be creative.

EARLY MAN

"Or both he and Special Ed will be implicated. They killed her together. Is that better for you?" I asked.

Warfield stared at me, unblinking and aghast. "You've put a lot of thought into this."

"It helps, doesn't it?"

"You're fucking really...You're totally insane, aren't you?"

I shrugged. "Pretty much."

He sneered at me. I just smiled and exhaled smoke in a nifty spiral. Warfield needed to know that the truth is always overrated. Just ask any good liar.

WARFIELD

Jill watched our entire exchange, and God knows what she was thinking. *This wasn't happening to me.* And to be honest, I was thinking the same thing: this wasn't happening to me. If we had a series of options, every one was as repugnant as the next. We were fucked and she knew it. We were frenetically indecisive and growing more frightened and desperate by the minute. We didn't know what to do next and time was of the essence. We had to get out of Canard Beach right away. I had to, anyway.

"No, man. No way. I can't kill anyone," I said.

"Can't you, though?"

"No. Never."

"But I thought we were playing this game."

"Can you do it?" Just asking the question made me want to die, and it backfired.

"How about this: you do it? Or I call your wife and tell her we're even having this conversation." He waved his BlackBerry at me. "I have her number."

"Jesus. No. No way. Please… We'll figure something out," I said.

"Good argument for remaining single, isn't it?"

"Fuck you."

He stabbed his cigarette at me. "This is how I see it: the guy who's got the most to lose will do the most to protect and preserve that. And that's you. Isn't it?"

"What are the other options? What about a suicide note?"

It was horrifying to think that, yes I was playing this game. He looked impressed. "Not bad. I have sleeping pills. We could give her a bunch and booze her up. Make it look like an overdose."

Given the hideous circumstances, I was nearly excited to have hatched such a clever idea. In six years in sales I don't think I'd ever harnessed such creative energy.

"It's the safest play," he said. "We'll clean her up as best we can. We'll throw her in the shower. But it's our only chance."

DOC HOLIDAY

In the fall of 11th grade, Camden started dating a senior named Dicky Marrota. He was a Motorhead and her first serious boyfriend. He was a bit of a "bad boy," but not too bad. Any "edge" he may've possessed was blunted by weaknesses for country music and Wine Coolers. Carefree, cocksure, and only occasionally menacing, Dicky seemed not to have a worry in the world, unless deciding on whether to go with mayonnaise or mustard on a sandwich qualified as such. He wasn't the brightest bulb in the chandelier, but it didn't matter because he was banging the blood out of Camden. And that did.

Underachieving bad boys like Dicky often landed the pretty girls, and maybe that was the subconscious rationale for never giving math my best efforts. Camden always liked the bad boys, too. And who knows, maybe that was the subconscious rationale for me drunkenly decapitating her snowman on Christmas Eve.

It was just after midnight. There was booze in my bloodstream and black bile in my heart, as I wavered unsteadily before the snowman occupying her lawn. If you were that little silly Drummer Boy, you wouldn't have wanted to run into me. Winds battered against colorful festive lights adorning the house. The snowman was rooted there like a sentinel, with its long orange scarf, Derby hat, carrot nose, black-pebbled eyes, and swishy I-Know-Where-The-Bodies-Are-Buried smile.

What the Hell was *he* so happy about? I thought it was a reasonable question, so I charged that giddy asshole and tackled him. His head came apart from his body, and I stomped it into mush with my boots. Like a hate crime perpetrated by Scrooge. But when you're 17, stoned all day long, and madly in love with your neighbor, you didn't worry much about the repercussions. After lurching back to my feet, I dashed clumsily through the snow and scrambled back home.

Charlie Brown's Revenge!

WARFIELD

It was still going to look very suspicious once she was discovered: a girl overdosing in the motel room of complete strangers after writing a suicide note. Didn't seem logical. Every possible "solution" presented a problem. There was no playbook or manual.

     Jill started to weep, and this particular round of tears was a harrowing reminder of what we were attempting to do. I took Early Man aside because she didn't need to hear any more of this discussion.

     "If these rooms are in your name, we'll have to drop her somewhere else."

EARLY MAN

He was right. The better plan was to leave her off-campus, but removing her from the motel could present a challenge. Someone was bound to see us, since there were a million college kids running around. Warfield suggested we write the suicide note first before figuring out the rest of our plan. Baby steps. Forward thinking. I agreed to that much.

WARFIELD

As we carefully unfastened one of her arm restraints, she used her hand to tear out her gag and throw a solid punch in Early Man's face. It walloped him square in the hollow beneath one eye, and knocked the snot out of him. Seething, he throttled her by the neck, and for a frightening moment I thought he was really going to kill her. (Then again, isn't that what we were planning on doing?)

     "Jesus, stop it!" I said, restraining him like I was breaking up a playground fight. I was surprised he relented so easily, but I think he was genuinely hurt. He needed a time-out, and spent it pawing at the raw shiner building beneath his eye.

     Jill had the opposite of Stockholm syndrome, and it was contagious because I wanted out of there almost as bad as she did. And to be honest, it was kind of nice to see Early Man get a taste of his own medicine. I had to remind myself whose side I was on.

EARLY MAN

"Please, please. Just let me go," she begged. "I'll give you money, I have some. I have… you know… I'll give you anything you want. "

     I gagged her mouth again. "You already have. And that's the problem."

SPECIAL ED

The moment that changed everything was a text I got from Doc Holiday.

WARFIELD

Early Man emptied about 10 sleeping pills onto the table, then opened a bottle of vodka. It was insane to believe we were actually doing this. I almost hoped we were bluffing.

"So this is it?" I asked him, needing reassurance. "I mean, this is it?"

"This is it," he said and fired up a cigarette.

"And then what? Fuck. No, I can't do this, man. We can't do it."

A rapping on the door startled us. "It's me!" Special Ed yelled out from beyond it. I scrambled over to the door and carefully opened it. Special Ed bounded in.

"Good news!" he said. "Great news."

"What is it?" I asked.

"Doc Holiday's checking outta here," he said.

"Are you sure?" Early Man said.

"Crazytown," he uttered, nodding.

Special Ed had just received a message from Doc Holiday, saying he was checking out of the motel because he wanted to be closer to the strip.

Early Man winked at Jill. "The plot thickens."

"Now what?" I asked, unsure how or why this news changed our predicament.

EARLY MAN

"What doesn't kill you doesn't make you stronger," I said to the Fair Princess. "It makes you lucky. And don't let anyone ever tell you different." But the problem still remained: did she live or did she die? Yet first and foremost, we needed Doc Holiday completely off our scent. We'd formulate a better plan once he checked out of the motel.

WARFIELD

If nothing else, we'd bought ourselves a little more time. Jill had, too. For us, we'd use the time to design an exit strategy and I'm sure she'd privately do the same. None of us were going anywhere right now. It was the only thing we'd ever have in common with her. Of course, I was tremendously relieved that she wasn't going to die now. Maybe I'd even aided in saving her life. Or at least extended it. But what happened later?

DOC HOLIDAY

I walked back towards The Island Oasis to pack my bags and check out. I decided I'd use Jill's phone to either call or text her friend Ashley and make some kind of plan. There was no crime in that. Not that I needed one, but returning Jill's phone was a good excuse to see her again.

I wondered why she hadn't tried calling her phone yet; it was past noon now. She must have still been sleeping it off, and unaware she'd even left her phone in my room. But when I removed it from my pocket, I discovered that its battery was totally dead. Which was frustrating. Shit, so maybe she had tried to call it. This was no good, because now I was unsure how to even get in touch with her.

As I crossed towards The Island Oasis, I noticed Special Ed reading the newspaper on the bench beside the reception office.

"Hey. Where've you guys been?" I asked. "No one's answering their phone."

"Warfield's at the gym. We're gonna get food and go to the beach when he comes back. And I got lousy service. It's in and out like crazy. T-Mobile stinks." He said Early Man got sick in the middle of the night and was still in bed.

"Well, you got my message?" I asked. "Hate to be a party-pooper, but I'm checking out. Hope you guys don't mind."

"Where are you gonna go?"

"Place called The Cabana Inn. Right on the beach. But we'll hook up somewhere tonight," I said, although to be honest, my old camp friends hadn't turned out as I'd hoped. In fact, they'd gone creepy. Maybe I was delusional to have expected otherwise. "Or tomorrow, for sure," I added. "But first I'd like to find Jill."

"Right, right. Yeah, she was crazy-hot. She was super pretty."

"She sure was. Cool, too. So we'll see." I headed into the

motel. "I'll be in touch. Tell the guys. Or whatever."

"Sounds good. Good luck finding Jill," he said.

"Thanks," I said. "Got a feeling I'll need it."

SPECIAL ED

When Doc Holiday said, "Got a feeling I'll need it," I cracked a smile he never saw. Role-playing in person can be fun. LOL.

WARFIELD

I parted the curtain just slightly enough to be able to watch the exchange between Special Ed and Doc Holiday. I wasn't sure if this hammerhead could pull off such wily subterfuge, but he insisted he could and Early Man inexplicably vouched for him.

It was going to be a close call, but chances were Doc Holiday wouldn't be popping in for a visit right now. Just to be safe, Early Man had locked himself in the bathroom with Jill, after we'd issued Special Ed stern warnings and careful instruction.

But what would happen if Doc Holiday discovered Jill in our room three minutes from now? I didn't know. What we'd done to her couldn't be undone, but at least all discussions of how to kill her would be over. But what if he threatened to call the police on us? What would we do then? Try and stop him? Or worse?

At least for the time being, the lesser of two evils was to utilize Special Ed as a decoy or diverson. We'd have to see where that would take us. I had to keep playing this game a little while longer. We all did.

EARLY MAN

She was unbound but still gagged, and seated against the wall. Dead-eyed and staring at the floor.

"You shouldn't take this personally, cuz we don't really know you," I said. "So we got nothing against you. But that's also why we don't care for you. We don't give a shit, either way. See the similarities?" Her eyes rose from the floor, fixing on me. "We're both just creatures of opportunity," I continued. "Only difference between you and me? You have tits and a college education."

The closest I ever got to college was watching the football games at a local junior college. I hated sports but liked cheerleaders, so I'd squirrel myself high up in the bleachers behind my black shades, and soak them in: those short skirts over long, lean legs, those pretty, cheering faces lockstep in the name of dopey school spirit. But they were inaccessible. Siamese twins at a singles dance had a better chance of scoring.

My favorite was a cheerleader named Taylor, a six-foot blonde with a sublime rack and strong, muscular legs. We chatted once after a game, but one of her co-cheerleaders cunt-punted me: a female cock-block. She called me a "weirdo goober" and that was the end of my courtship. John Hinckley had better luck communicating with chicks way out of his league.

The moral of the story: she was allowed to fuck the captain of the football team. But I'm not allowed to fuck the captain of the cheerleaders. I didn't handle rejection well, so stopped attending the games. Instead, I dreamed about the cheerleaders decomposing before my eyes, hunks of skin sloughing off their faces and bones and muscle and cartilage. Eyeballs noodled forth from sockets, dangling and dripping. Undeterred, the girls would keep cheering, whitening skulls beaming wide, puddles of watery gore settled upon what once were impossibly white sneakers. Their booming voices grew weaker, throatier, and more guttural. Until, like human dominoes, they toppled over from their formation. I hated sports, so that's how I best liked to remember them.

I asked the Fair Princess if she had ever been a cheerleader, but she didn't respond. If Dorothy had been a cheerleader, her secret, faithful bleacher admirers most definitely woulda been The Scarecrow, The Tin Man, and The Cowardly Lion.

But The Wizard... he's another story.

DOC HOLIDAY

I checked into The Cabana Inn, feeling pretty good about the move. My room on the fourth floor was real nice, bright and clean with sandstone walls and a pretty cool view of the beach. Even the air conditioner worked properly.

I walked out onto the deck and glanced down at the festivities at the hotel swimming pool. A swarm of college kids were frolicking about, swimming, sunning, and cocktailing. Some were lording over long plastic beer funnels. Girls were riding astride boys in the pool, and a few chicken fights were unfolding. Pretty cocktail waitresses were ferrying about drinks and snacks, dutiful behind their dark shades, snug shorts, baby blue T-shirts, and short white socks and sneakers.

After returning inside and unpacking, I went down to the gift shop and bought stamps and two postcards. These were earmarked for Reese and Lansky. I'd "check in" from Spring Break. They wouldn't believe it.

I wrote a brief, uniform message on my postcards: "GREETINGS FROM SPRING BREAK IN CANARD BEACH! DON'T ASK. Later, Billy the Kid."

After mailing them, I headed over to Beachfront Property to go looking for Jill.

SPECIAL ED

After we watched Doc Holiday get into a cab with his bags and drive away from the motel, Early Man hung the DO NOT DISTURB sign on the doorknob outside the room. It would have to remain there as long as we did. Warfield paced like a general in a War Room, working through the strategics.

Early Man started rooting through Jill's purse and removing its contents: chewing gum, make-up, a bottle of perfume, loose change, cigarettes, and credit cards.

"We need to be smart about this," he said, attempting to temper any growing fears we may've had. "Your average college jackass wouldn't be. But we're older and wiser. And we know better."

"Do we, though?" Warfield asked.

WARFIELD

It was a disorganized crime. How much longer could we try and sort this out? A few more hours? A day, at most? And maybe that was even being generous. The longer we stuck around, Doc Holiday was more apt to make the connection we had Jill. This wasn't rocket science. He'd find the solution to this riddle. I had to get the hell out of there.

I was fucking married.

DOC HOLIDAY

At Beachfront Property, the desk clerk told me that there weren't any rooms booked under a "Jill Cassady." Thinking on my feet, I inquired about her friend Ashley. But I didn't know her last name, and the desk clerk wasn't at liberty to provide me with those details. "Sorry, sir," said. "It's just our policy."

From her nametag, I saw that her name was Megan. "Megan, I understand you're just doing your job. But isn't customer service the idea here? I mean, I know for a fact she's staying here. Jill, I mean. And I have her cell phone." I removed Jill's phone from my pocket. "I just want to leave her a note and return it, that's all."

"Sorry, sir," Megan said. "I can't help you."

"Really?" I was pretty irritated with this snag because Jill and I had no way to get in touch. We hadn't exchanged numbers and her cell phone was dead. It was a wash.

"Sorry, sir," Megan repeated.

"Thanks, anyway," I said, beyond annoyed at this "policy."

I walked off, and headed out of the lobby. Maybe I'd try again later.

WARFIELD

After Early Man left the room to grab sandwiches from across the street, I secured a private moment with Special Ed.

"I think we should get outta here," I said. "Me and you, right now."

"Why?"

"What do you mean why?"

He glanced over at Jill. "And do what with her?"

I couldn't answer that. I could never really answer that. But I gave it a shot. "Leave her here."

He shook his head. "I don't love it."

"I don't love it, either. I don't love any of this. But you got any better ideas? Jesus, man. You snatched a girl, you didn't find the cure for cancer."

"But we're in this together. You know?"

"Hey, Early Man was willing to frame you for the whole thing. Just so you know. What do you say about that?"

"No way."

"I'm telling you. He doesn't give a shit about us. The rooms are in his name. We can do this, man."

He nodded, processing my message: that we should leave, that we had to leave, and that Early Man couldn't be trusted. I had broken through to him, finally allowing this insanity to finally cohere into a clear picture: we had to get the hell out of Canard Beach right now.

He looked at me quizzically. "You're still not into blinding her?"

Clearly, I hadn't broken through to him at all. He was useless ally material. I had lost this battle. I'd play along a little more in the hopes I'd win the next one.

"Jesus. No, man. I'm still not into blinding her."

DOC HOLIDAY

Back in my hotel room, I crashed out on the big bed and decided to order some Room Service. An NCAA hoop game was on TV. March Madness was winding down to the Final 8. And so far, my brackets still looked strong.

I planned on returning to Barnacles that night, hoping to maybe find Jill there again with her friends. I felt like I was somewhat on a comeback trail. Sometimes that happens in the most unlikely of places.

In October of our Senior year in high school, Camden's best friend, Tracey Finn, committed suicide by driving her Toyota Camry into a birch tree at 70 MPH. Tracey was a sweet, troubled girl who had battled an eating disorder since eighth grade. And who really knows what's inside someone else's head? We certainly didn't know what was inside Tracey's until it was too late.

I summoned up the courage to call Camden, who was understandably disconsolate. I expressed my condolences for her loss. "If there's anything I can do. . . "

After she provided me with the funeral details, I surprised both of us by asking if she'd need a ride to the church. We were neighbors, so we could carpool - for lack of a better word - if that would make things easier. I assumed she'd be attending either with her parents, her friends, or Dicky Marrota. She told me that she and Dicky were "fighting." (Apparently, Motorheads got real annoyed when your friends committed suicide).

And it was a shock when she agreed to go with me. It was a date. I panicked. I needed a suit. Maybe a haircut. I was in desperate need of both. Did I have a decent pair of shoes? Could probably use a new shirt, too. A new necktie wouldn't have killed me, either. Boy, this bereavement business could cost you an arm and a leg. Not bad enough someone has perished before his time, now they practically want a down payment on mourning gear.

The prospect of this funeral date was seriously stressing me out. I was unsure why I even bothered to ask Camden to go. It felt like a daunting task and I started having cold feet. Should I just meet her there?

At least I wasn't going to attend Tracey's wake. It was slated to be an open-casket affair and those are good for nobody. It's post-mortem pomp and circumstance, a trifle ghoulish and passive-aggressive for my tastes. There's no happy face for such an occasion. I remember standing over my father in his casket prior to his funeral. He looked maybe even too good because they'd gussied him up quite well. I almost asked, "So how about them Red Sox?" But of course, he'd missed the last few games.

Camden and I sat together in the church during the funeral service. Lansky and Reese were seated behind us along with Tracey's other friends. Camden wept uncontrollably throughout, choking back throaty sobs; she was really upset. At first it unsettled me and I didn't know what to do or say. Of course I expected her to be upset, but just not so audibly. It was like she was *over*-mourning. There's often that funeral or wedding guest who's crying tears of tremendous pain or joy much too loudly. And everyone's trading covert looks and shooting the offender furtive, annoyed glances, wanting to say *Simmer down, fruitcake.* But no one says anything.

I was dying for a cigarette, deeming it ironic that such a stress-inducing place — which warrants a smoking reprieve more than any other — is the same one that prohibits and enforces it the most. It's like banning laughter at a comedy show.

I sneaked a troubled look at Reese and Lansky as if to inquire if they had read Consoling Hot Grieving Chicks For Dummies. Camden was really falling apart. They sensed my clueless concern, but merely shrugged. They were out of bullets, too, and Lansky was more preoccupied with a pimple on his chin. It was the size of New Delhi.

So I held Camden's hand and squeezed it. I didn't know what else to do. She gave me a sad smile and rested her head against my shoulder. She managed to simmer down a little. Squeezed my hand a little harder. I was her rock. I guess. We were a team united in grief. I was quietly thrown: was I on the comeback trail... at a funeral?

I glanced back at Reese and Lansky again, seeking their approbation. Apparently they'd been watching, because Lansky signaled me a discreet thumbs-up sign. I forced an uneasy smile. Reese just rolled his eyes, probably unsure whose funeral theatrics were creepier, Lansky's or mine.

I felt slightly dizzy sitting there beside Camden's warm body and soft whimpers, her musky fragrance filling my nostrils, her hair falling against my cheek. But it wasn't bad. It wasn't bad at all.

And as awful as it sounds, I thought, *Too bad her friends can't die more often.*

WARFIELD

Jill was asleep and probably killing us in her dreams. We ate our sandwiches and continued to monitor the TV and Internet for any news about a North Carolina State college girl missing in Canard Beach. So far, there was nothing to report. I had to get out of there before there was. That much I knew.

My iPhone rang. Nikki was calling, so I let it go to voicemail. Shit, shit, shit. I insisted to the guys that I needed privacy to check in with her. I wanted to use Special Ed's room. "Just don't be long," Early Man said. "You have a missing girl to attend to here."

After Special Ed handed me his key card, I darted across the hallway and ducked into Room 209. The scene of the crime. At least one of them. I tried to envision the moment of Jill's abduction, this horrible crime of passion. What the hell was Special Ed thinking? We were all responsible for that girl across the hall, but he had pulled the trigger and now there was plenty of collateral damage.

None of these speculations or conjectures mattered, but what suddenly did was not calling Nikki. What mattered was leaving right now. I thought about it. How could I not think about it? The rental car keys were in my pocket. I could do this.

In a weekend of few proud moments, this wasn't my proudest, either: the idea of leaving Jill behind with those savages. But I had to do what was best for me. Sure, Early Man could still call Nikki and attempt to destroy my life, but maybe I could proclaim my innocence. Other than lying to her so brazenly, maybe I could swear the only thing I was guilty of was horrendous, irresponsible judgment: the decision to meet old camp friends in Canard Beach. Maybe I could say that I had been kept hostage as well. I could sell that, couldn't I?

But the problem was that, at the end of the day, Jill would never testify to that. The Nikki fallout notwithstanding, another option was to turn myself in to the police. It was a worst-case scenario, but at least I'd be able to plead down to a lesser offense. That's what people always did. It was the lesser of two evils.

A knock on the door jolted me, whirling me around, rigid to the spot. I was unsure how to respond, yet just knew it was Doc Holiday on the other side of that door. He must've left something behind before checking out. I treaded slowly towards the door, fixing on the peephole, when a woman's voice cried out beyond it: "Housekeeping!"

I halted, nearly dizzy with relief. Special Ed hadn't bothered to hang a DO NOT DISTURB sign around his doorknob. "Not now, please!" I called out. "Thank-you!"

I walked out onto the patio overlooking the parking lot. It was about a 10 to 15 foot drop to the pavement from the second floor, but it was worth a sprained ankle. As I began to straddle the railing, I glanced over at my rental car. Special Ed was leaning up against it. He grinned at me and waved.

SPECIAL ED
LOL!

WARFIELD
Seething, I climbed off the railing and returned to the patio, angrily kicking a plastic chair against the wall. Early Man had obviously sent him out there to test me or reaffirm his belief that I was not a loyal soldier. Maybe he figured the only way to avoid a mutiny was to play Special Ed and me against each other. He was wasting his energy, both of them were. We were trapped there, so

what those lunatics should've been doing was trying to devise a successful exit strategy for us. Whatever that even meant.

I slipped back inside the room. In no mood for conversation, I texted Nikki a message, promising I'd call her later. I considered just leaving the motel through the proper channels, go find Doc Holiday, and attempt to spin the situation in a more favorable manner. Or maybe that was as lousy an idea as it was three hours ago, or might be three more from now.

I went to the door and peered through the peephole. Early Man was leaning against the doorway of our room with his arms sternly crossed, like a middle school teacher waiting to reprimand a student caught cheating on a test. When he slowly turned his head and met my gaze with a smarmy smile, I flinched. It scared the Christ out of me.

It's when I knew I had stepped in the most serious Canard Beach shit of all.

EARLY MAN

When Warfield returned to our room, he looked like a gloomy, oversized child who was just informed that Santa Claus was a child molester. And that those weren't elves. We didn't even talk about it. We didn't have to. He knew his Adventure Captain was in charge and calling the shots. We had to trust each other. Who the fuck was he kidding?

"You can't go crying wolf when you're a member of the pack," I said.

"Watch me!" he said.

"Give me those car keys, or I call Nikki right now."

"Fuck you."

"We're in this together. A democracy. Safety in numbers."

"Then why don't I feel safe?"

I removed a computer printout from my backpack. "Spring Break risk factors," I read aloud. "'There is always safety in numbers. Don't travel alone and try to travel in threes. The idea of three is the hope that no matter how crazy you and the situation get, out of three friends one can be counted on to be the voice of reason.'"

"And you're the voice of reason?" he said.

"I'm trying to be."

"Well, you're failing."

"Got any better ideas?"

"I thought I just had one."

"Give me those fucking car keys," I said. "Or Nikki gets a call."

He chucked the car keys at my head, barely missing me, as they clattered against a wall. I gathered them off the floor and shoved them inside my pocket. He grabbed a beer and planted himself down against the wall. When Special Ed returned, Warfield wouldn't even look at him. Special Ed got a beer for himself and tossed me one. We were back to the drawing board.

WARFIELD

Jill stirred awake to discover us sitting quiet vigil before her, with cold beers and long faces. Early Man was gently pawing at the abraded skin beneath his eye. She must've discerned some kind of new weakness in our rank because something possessed her to softly speak.

"My friends will be looking for me," she said.

"They'll make new ones," Early Man said. "At your funeral!"

DOC HOLIDAY

After Tracey's funeral service, Camden and I repaired to the Finn residence for the "after-party." A dreary chorus of warm condolences and warmer casseroles. Mourners mingled about, eating and drinking, gamely trying to stay fat and, well, unhappy.

I sat with Camden the entire time, providing her with orange juice and extra napkins so she could swipe at her tears. Reese and Lansky rolled in a bit later. I watched them graciously extend their condolences to Tracey's parents and older brother. Right after imparting their sympathies, they attacked the buffet table. Because as sorry as they were for the Finns' loss, they were as equally hungry for their sandwich meats.

It was dusk when I pulled up beside Camden's house. There was a sharp chill in the air; the days had already grown shorter, of course, but tonight even the air smelled like winter. Soon the foliage would be gone, nature's decomposition, revealing cruel, skeletal branches in its wake. Another season expired. Another one beginning again. And Camden's best friend in the world, no longer around to see this next one unfold.

"Goodbye friend, it's hard to die... "

"Thanks for coming with me," she said, punch-drunk with grief, her face flushed and weary. All of that crying had taken its toll. "And staying with me."

"You don't have to thank me."

"Yes, I do."

"Well, you're welcome."

She slouched in her seat and tried to murder a building yawn. I racked my brain to come up with something that would make her feel better or help take her mind off such a grim day. ("That Bundt cake was pretty good, huh?") It was no mean feat, and I was out of bullets. I removed a pack of cigarettes from my pocket.

"You really shouldn't smoke," she said.

"I know it," I said, tossing the cigarettes into the back seat. She smiled. But it was the easier habit to quit.

She looked straight at me. "Can I ask you something?"

"Sure."

She pointed to her front yard. "If my sister decides to build a snowman this winter, can I assure her of his safety?"

I tensed. "What do you mean?"

"Come on, Billy. I knew it was you."

All of a sudden she was Nancy Drew? I attempted to see if my deceit had legs.

"I don't understand. What happened to your snowman?"

"You killed it."

"What? That's crazy, Camden. Why would I kill a snowman?"

She rolled her eyes. "I asked myself the same question."

She then informed me that I'd left my scarf behind at the scene of the snowman hate crime. I was busted. She nailed me. My deceit had proved to be as legless as that goofy snowman. (I never did know what happened to that damn scarf.) I fidgeted beside her, trying to quell my humiliation. That was no mean feat, either. Not sure whether you've ever been accused of decapitating the object of your unrequited love's snowman, but trust me: not recommended.

"Sorry," I said. "It wasn't my finest hour."

"No. No, it wasn't."

"But it was going to die eventually, so think of it as an act of euthanasia."

It was a lousy attempt at levity, and she obviously had more grinding troubles on her mind than the vagaries of my silly personal history with her snowman. She started to scroll down the numbers in her phone, stopping at a certain one. She swiped at fugitive tears and when she did, I knew she was staring at Tracey's number. She would have to delete the name from her phone and e-mail address book. Essentially delete Tracey from her life. It wouldn't be easy to do.

Tracey had been a friend who was a stranger waiting to happen. She wouldn't be in school anymore and they would no longer gossip at their lockers in between classes. No more impish chatter about cute boys and catty girls. No more study sessions together. No more sneaking cigarettes on tipsy Saturday nights in the baseball bleachers at Franklin Field. (Tracey preferred the Clove ones. "They burn slower, so you live longer," she'd joke, unaware of the irony as it pertained to whatever briefly remained of her own life.) No more late-night telephone bull sessions or shopping expeditions at the mall. No high school prom. No college, no husband, no children. No future at all.

Camden glanced at me uncertainly. "Do you miss your father?"

The inquiry threw me. "Yeah. You know. Sure."

She cracked a rueful smile. "I miss him for you, too."

"Thanks," I said, realizing she was moving closer to me. It seemed to take forever to negotiate that short distance, but she was indeed coming over to my side of the ball.

And then we were kissing. A few legitimate, serviceable thrusts. Tonsil hockey with Camden Miller. *Fuck,* yeah! And me hoping it would go into overtime, and wondering if napkins and orange juice were top-secret aphrodisiacs. It didn't last very long, but seemed long enough.

"Goodnight, Billy. See ya in school."

"Goodnight. Okay. Totally," I said. It came out so wildly discombobulated that she frowned. I shrugged. I was never too cool around her. She put a hand on my shoulder.

"Thanks for the ride."

"Of course. No problem."

As she climbed out of my car and I waited until she slipped safely inside her house, I wanted to say more. I wanted to call out something like, *How about we go for coffee and Quaaludes sometime?* Anything that would forestall her departure, because I desperately wanted to keep the conversation going. I wanted to extend the moment. You always do. Because she really messed you up.

God knows I had put in the work, ever since we were in grade school, when we were bite-sized innocents, the infatuation building each year. The older we got, the prettier she got, the friendlier we became. Like some damaged, punch-drunk boxer on his last legs, I never let her out of my crosshairs.

And tonight I had finally hit the bulls-eye. This was crazy! Camden and I had spent the entire day together. Obviously the circumstances were not ideal – in fact, they were tragic and terrible – but the day had resulted in a nice kiss. And in high school, you drink up happiness wherever you can find a spigot.

I imagined the headline in school the following week after the rumor inevitably took flight: *Boy Finally Scores with Carpool Crush. Snowman Not Reached for Comment.*

WARFIELD

Jill sat propped up in bed and nibbled pensively on her sandwich with her only free hand. We sipped beers and watched her closely, trusting that she wouldn't scream. If she did, well, I don't know what would've happened next. She wasn't taking any chances, though, and didn't utter a peep. I couldn't believe she was still here. I couldn't believe we were.

I needed to expedite whatever it was we were going to do to solve our problem, because had her friends known she was coming back to this motel with Doc Holiday, we were doomed. It'd only be a matter of time before they showed up looking for her.

"Do your friends know you're at this motel?" I asked her. But she wouldn't answer the question or play this game. Maybe she figured the worst was over and she had nothing to lose anymore. Only we did. Maybe she was right. The room was getting smaller. None of this was going to resolve itself well.

SPECIAL ED

Some movie with Bernie Mac was on TV. Early Man wasn't impressed. "Think anyone will really miss his contributions to cinema?" he asked. Not a chance, I said. LOL.

DOC HOLIDAY

After the college basketball game ended, I decided to head over to Barnacles to watch the sunset and look for Jill. After snooping around and failing to find her, I grabbed a seat at the bar and ordered a drink. I texted Special Ed and asked if they wanted to meet me for dinner. A little down time with the other Boogeymen wasn't going to kill me.

WARFIELD

Special Ed said he'd just received a text from Doc Holiday at Barnacles. All of us agreed that we needed to properly respond to him, so Special Ed texted him that we'd catch up with him later.

SPECIAL ED

"Hey, do you have T-Mobile, too?" I asked Jill. She hesitated to answer, which I thought was strange. But then she nodded. I smiled. "I knew we had something in common."

WARFIELD

"Guys, we gotta get the hell outta here!" I said. Doc Holiday was closing in on us, I could feel it. I think we all could.

"And go where?" Early Man asked.

Home would've been nice.

EARLY MAN

This native was getting restless, too. I removed my package of blow and started dicing up some fluffy lines onto a picture frame. I considered forcing our Fair Princess to provide us with her ATM PIN and password, just in case we needed to withdraw funds from her account. Otherwise, the authorities would grow suspicious. It's what they did: monitor bank transactions. When someone goes missing for a period of time and no money has been withdrawn, it's often a dead giveaway that he/she is probably dead.

But it was far too early for such hysterics. A missing college chick on Spring Break for only 24 hours wasn't news. It might even be love.

WARFIELD

Early Man starting snorting cocaine. Special Ed stood by the patio door, gazing up at the dark sky. I sat brooding in a chair, nursing a beer. We were quiet for too long, having grown restless and antsy with a rabid strain of cabin fever. The room was rank from the stenches of body odor, farts, and beer. The guys had grown bored and irritable and that notion scared me more than anything. I didn't know what was going to happen next, just that the clock was ticking.

"Wow. Guys, look at the stars," Special Ed said.

"Fuck the stars!" Early Man thundered.

Special Ed flinched. "Okay."

DOC HOLIDAY

After downing another drink and hoovering some cheeseburger sliders at Barnacles, I started walking over to Jill's hotel again. Round two. The strip was teeming with bawdy, boisterous college kids. I passed a photo booth kiosk similar to the one the Boogeymen had posed in at the PlayTown amusement park all those summers ago. Two girls were flanked beside the red curtain, giggling at a photo printout that had captured them.

I texted Special Ed again: "Change of plans. Going to the bar at Beachfront Property. That's where I'll be, you lazy assholes."

SPECIAL ED

"He's going to the bar at Beachfront Property now," I reported to the others.

"That's my hotel," Jill softly said.

WARFIELD

I wasn't sure if she was gathering confidence or courage, only that the rest of us were lacking in both departments.

"What if I go meet him there?" I offered. Early Man shot me a frosty stare, obviously not trusting me at the moment. But I still attempted to qualify my idea. "Look, if he sees one of us beyond this motel, it'll distract him. We can create a diversion because he's obviously looking for her."

"And then what?" Early Man asked. "What does that solve for us?"

"Maybe it buys us some more time."

EARLY MAN

I looked at Special Ed, who had a finger drilled up one nostril. "What do you think?" But Warfield interjected: "Who cares what he thinks? This is the guy who wanted to blind her." Special Ed fired back: "And you're the guy who wanted to split without us!"

"Settle down, boys," I said. "We'll figure something out."

WARFIELD

I was just plain scared. How do I get the hell out of Canard Beach?

DOC HOLIDAY

I couldn't find Jill in the Beachfront Property lounge, so I grabbed a seat at the bar and ordered a drink. I made some small talk with a few college kids. They told me there was a party outside by the pool, which is where they were headed.

I decided to check it out, but not before hatching an idea. It was probably a Hail Mary attempt and something I should've thought of earlier, but it was still worth a shot. I texted Special Ed again.

SPECIAL ED

It was another text message from Doc Holiday that changed everything. Everything.

EARLY MAN

Special Ed read us Doc Holiday's text: "Hey, if Jill shows up there looking for her cell phone, tell her I have it. Maybe I'll call the front desk, too. Remember, I'm stayin' at The Cabana Inn. Still can't find her. Thanks."

The three of us went wide-eyed and mystified. Special Ed looked personally affronted, like it was now only raining on his personal parade.

"You had a cell phone?!" he asked the Fair Princess.

A nearly Satanic smile swept over her face. "Does T-Mobile ring a bell?"

WARFIELD

That's when we all became completely unglued, when it all unraveled. In his abduction haste, Special Ed had forgotten to retrieve Jill's phone. And now both he and Early Man finally appeared to understand the enormity of our crisis. How could they not?

Our window of opportunity had quickly narrowed. We had to make a move, had to get off our asses and really improvise now. At least I needed to. Early Man was now pretty goosed from that cocaine and furiously hurled his sandwich against the wall. It landed with a splat above the TV, a Rorshach blob of roast beef, lettuce, and tomato. Special Ed started to pace and repeatedly utter, "We need to be heroes." Jill broke down in fresh tears. The walls were closing in on us.

I knew it was over then. Time was on Jill's side, not ours. We had to think fast and act faster. Her friends were bound to call or text her phone, and once Doc Holiday learned she was missing the trail of breadcrumbs could lead back to us. As I had feared.

Enough was enough. I started to throw my clothes into my bag. "Here's the deal: I'm going home, party's over for me. You guys do what you want after that."

Early Man merely laughed. "You think we're just gonna let you leave? Let you go home and fuck your wife and live your life? Really?"

SPECIAL ED

Early Man removed his BlackBerry and pressed it to Jill's ear. "What if we call your wife right now?" he threatened. "And let the Fair Princess here say a few words to her? How 'bout that? I bet she'd just love to." He gazed at Jill. "Wouldn't you?"

WARFIELD

Jill put down her sandwich and glared at me. When I saw her crack a smile, I had to remind myself whose side she was on. "I bet you were once a good father," she said. The guys kind of snickered at me. And suddenly, I was as terrified as she was.

SPECIAL ED

Warfield was the most scared I had seen him yet. He paced like a caged animal about to be euthanized. So we were super surprised at what he said next.

WARFIELD

Despite Early Man's efforts to blackmail me, I'd made my decision: I was going home.

"Give me my car keys," I said to Early Man. "I'm out."

"If I give you the keys, I call your wife."

I shoved him against the wall, about to pummel the snot out of him. But Special Ed interceded by jumping on my back, pleading for me to stop. That fat bastard was heavy, and we ending up colliding into a table. We managed to knock over some empty beer bottles and two chairs before before landing on the floor in a clumsy heap. I think Jill even giggled at the sight of us.

As I got back to my feet, Early Man just smiled at me. "For a happily married guy, you managed to do some pretty good damage down here: ya lied to your wife. And prob'ly your boss. And who knows who else… Then ya dabbled with a college girl. So naturally, it begs the question: can I book you for next year's Spring Break?"

"You know where to find me," I said.

And then I took off without those car keys. It was time for Plan B.

SPECIAL ED

When Warfield split, I got really freaked-out, because no longer did it seem like there was "safety" in our numbers. But Early Man calmed me down. He said that Warfield wasn't dotting his Is and crossing his Ts, because he'd have to return his rental car in Miami or be in a world of trouble. Paper trails needed to be avoided at all costs.

Early Man tried calling Warfield. He got no answer. "You wait here," he said. "I"ll find him. Don't answer the phone unless it's me, okay? Just wait fucking here."

When he left to chase after Warfield, Jill and I were alone together for the very first time. I sat down beside her, and she flinched and wriggled as best as her restraints would yield. Tears streamed from her eyes. But I had no interest in hurting her.

"What do you want?" she asked me. "What do you want?"

I shrugged. But as long as she was taking orders, I decided to answer. "I wanna tell you about drought and famine and Natural Selection."

EARLY MAN

It was time to bring out the heavy artillery. The best defense is a good offense. Warfield needed to be stopped. He couldn't be trusted. Married dudes never can be.

WARFIELD

I raced towards the strip, adrenalized and invigorated by the fresh air. This had to end now. I had ignored Early Man's calls, because I'd made the decision to find Doc Holiday at Beachfront Property. I needed him on my team. I considered texting him first, but providing too many details would be dangerous. It always is.

When I saw Beachfront Property in the distance and started picking up the pace, my cell buzzed with a text. The sender was Early Man: "Do you know that if you decapitate a rattlesnake and attempt to pick up its severed head, it's still capable of biting you?"

I texted him back: "And your point, asshole?"

He texted me a photo: me having my turn with Jill on Friday night. I shuddered, halted to a stop. Jesus Christ, he had pictures, too. He had fucking pictures.

"And there's four or five more of those snaps," he added. So how you gonna explain those to Nikki? PhotoShop? ☺."

I planted myself down onto a park bench across the street from Beachfront Property. There was now no way I was going inside to look for Doc Holiday. I stared down at those horrible photos in my cell. There was no way of getting around those.

Diversion is one thing, perversion quite another.

DOC HOLIDAY

A huge party was raging around the hotel pool. Masses of gyrating girls were bumping and grinding, wild-eyed and disordered with booze and drugs. EDM pulsing through their undulations like lifeblood. Two mindless girls were making out, tousled hair dangling in their faces. I saw an exposed tit and a girl dragging her tongue across it. Girls were drinking long bottles of water and knocking their asses together to the music in Ecstasy-fueled nirvana.

I had no luck finding Jill after walking a few laps around the pool in search of her. She was probably out somewhere with her friends again, having fun. There was no crime in that. But most people completely panic when they lose their cell phones, and it seemed pretty strange that she hadn't yet made an effort to find me. All I knew was that I felt pretty old and alone. If anyone cared to notice at all, I must've looked like a bartender's older brother cadging free drinks, and hungering for eye candy on a Saturday night.

But what else was there to do? So I ordered two shots of whiskey, and after killing them, lazily reposed on a poolside lounge chair. Now pretty hammered and resigned to the idea of not seeing Jill again. It had been a Spring Break one-night stand, that's all. Over before it really even started. I'd thought I was on some kind of comeback trail, only to step in a landmine. I was pretty sure I'd never see Jill again.

It had been the same way with Camden. We actually spent Senior Prom Night together, despite the fact that neither of us was attending. She had since broken up with Dicky Marrota, who was going into the Army in the fall to Be All That He Could Be. (Which wasn't likely to amount to much). Since Tracey Finn had died, Camden had been pretty morose and withdrawn in school. She'd chosen to be boyfriend-free, intent on playing out the string until graduation. If misery is cyclical, this was her time.

It was a balmy, spring night, the days having stretched longer. Spring in New England is pretty great. A jaunty time and frivolous engagement. The warm weather and extended daylight were Mother Nature's therapy, either fueling or renewing your optimism. Hope and vigor were rekindled. The smile on your face stuck around longer.

The day of high school graduation was less than a month away. Looming there like a blind date with a hangman. A foreboding development and day I was dreading; I wished I could blow it off rather than honor with my presence. It was an achingly bittersweet time, mainly because I felt I was running out of it. And Camden was still keeping me up nights.

I decided to cruise over to the 7-Eleven and buy a jumbo bag of Camden's favorite candy: Peanut M&Ms. I drove over to her house and parked across the street. Even though I knew it was the grief that had been navigating her tongue on the night of Tracey's funeral, she and I had bonded since, and high school life was ending in less than a month, so...

Bracing myself, trying to muscle through a bout of sudden disorientation, I rang the doorbell. And instantly second-guessed myself to the point where I almost pooped my trousers. Maybe more hopeless than hopeless romantic. Let's face it – there's a fine line between being romantic and pathetic. One person's "he was really sweet," is another's "he was really creepy." I guess you have to know your audience.

She answered the door. Barefoot and a little beleaguered. Wearing sweatpants and a short T-shirt. Never hotter. "Hey. What are you doing?" she asked.

"Hey. Is this a bad time?" Which, by the way, is a question that should be surgically removed from our lexicon. You might as well ask, "Am I freaking you out?"

She eked out a little smile. "Not at all," she said. "Just watching TV."

"I brought candy," I said, maybe a bit too proudly, raising the bag in the air.

"Why?"

I frowned. Not the answer I was looking for. I shrugged. "No idea."

Thank God she laughed. She was so pretty, so sweet, and so willing to generously engage with the clingy, obsessed boy who lived up the street. We sat together on her front steps, bathed in the glow of floodlights and swatting away pesky mosquitoes. "Don't take this wrong way or anything, but... " I started.

"But what?"

"You look kinda great," I finished. And she did, she always did.

"Thanks for the candy. It was sweet," she said, not bothering to acknowledge my compliment. Which was annoying as fuck, but whatever. She knew I still lusted for her friendship. I wasn't subtle about that. This was a consolation prize she was offering, because I was never going to succeed in lusting after the rest of her. She wasn't subtle about that, either. You might say we both knew our audience.

When she plopped a few Peanut M&Ms into her mouth, she had no idea that I was terribly allergic to peanuts. And when she offered me the bag I didn't betray this intelligence, choosing instead to lodge a bunch of them into my mouth with such velocity, you would've thought someone had a gun to my head. I was just happy to be there.

I knew I'd break out in a heinous rash, but I'd worry about that later. I assumed my mother had a good, reliable ointment back home. And life is short.

Except I almost died, that's how bad my allergic reaction was. My throat tightened, and a spasm of wheezes and coughes ensued. It was a struggle to breathe. Camden grew alarmed. Was I okay? I insisted that I was fine, not because I was, but because the indignity of dying on her front steps from a goofy candy overdose was enough to entrench me in such stubborn denial. (To be honest, her father never liked me to begin with). But as diarrhea reared its head and I nearly threw up in my mouth, it was obvious her candy Casanova was falling apart like a crumbcake. At some point, I lost consciousness.

When I woke up in the hospital sometime later, Camden was sitting in the room, mindlessly thumbing through a magazine beneath those unremitting fluorescent lights. After conferring with my mother and a doctor, Camden and I were alone again. In the canon of inglorious "Prom Night Stories," this was up there with one of the worst.

I apologized for scaring her and not mentioning my peanut allergy. She asked why I hadn't told her. It was a rhetorical question, and I stifled the urge to blurt, "Because I love you!" She was already aware of that, of course. There was no more mystery. Never had been much of any. And that sucks. I had revealed my cards way too early: around first grade. Hopelessly smitten at six years old. Early puberty. Not recommended.

And the toxic fallout? An allergic idiot eating Peanut M&Ms in her presence, several painstaking years later. So yeah, the damage had been done. One of us had fallen down.

Camden smiled and rolled her eyes, not expecting an answer to her question, because she already knew what it was. To wit: a boy who jealously decapitates his neighbor's snowman and eats candy he's deathly allergic to, only because it's her favorite, isn't exactly playing his emotions close to the vest.

"Billy, you're crazy," she said, casually defining and maybe dismissing my entire existence in three words.

"Guilty," I said, confirming it in one.

We shared a bout of uneasy laughter. We really needed to stop meeting at funerals and hospitals. A month from now we'd be graduating and then going off to college in the fall. We were cutting the cord and just when we were finally getting along, too, our parallel universes perhaps growing closer in proximity. Things between us were becoming less unrequited and more unpredictable. This was progress for me.

But our universes would never truly merge because now it was over. The notion of not seeing her in school every day was devastating. She was finally leaving my crosshairs, and it wasn't likely we'd be staying in touch. I wouldn't bother to try. I'd grant her the space she deserved. I guess you're always either leaving someone behind or someone's leaving you behind.

Camden said she rode in the ambulance with me, her maiden voyage in such a vehicle. It had freaked her out and her ears were still ringing from the blaring siren.

"Sorry about all that," I said.

"As long as you're okay."

"Well, thanks for the ride." She smiled just a little. But it was enough.

I wasn't a big Fate guy. I'd seen too many shitty John Cusack movies to know better. But this was nice. We were graduating and moving on and starting over. It made me feel good. It really made me feel good. But it also really made me feel sad.

But like the haunting funhouse ride that was high school itself, I suppose it was the best of times. And it was the worst of times.

Think, say, the Stones playing Auschwitz.

SPECIAL ED

I was getting super impatient. Where were those guys, already? I began to worry they might leave Canard Beach without me. What would I do then?

"I'm leaving to go back to school tomorrow morning," Jill said. She appeared to have some swagger to her now.

"You are?"

"The buses to the airport leave my hotel at 9."

Crazytown!

DOC HOLIDAY

I sneaked two fresh beers off the hotel grounds and walked down to the beach. Dark and quiet and steeped in tenebrous shadows, there wasn't a college soul in sight. It was placid and peaceful. Perfect.

I found a stray lawn chair and splayed myself onto it. I sipped a beer and watched the waves crashing. I figured the guys and I would have breakfast in the morning and sort of start over.

EARLY MAN

Warfield was waiting for me on a bench across from Beachfront Property. That same gloomy oversized child again. Without saying a word, I sat down beside him. I lit a cigarette. Safety in numbers, I reminded him. Safety in numbers.

Some filthy panhandler shambled by us, bumming change and strumming an acoustic guitar to the song "I'm Your Boogie Man." I dropped three bucks into his change cup, and asked if I could sing along. "Bless your heart," the panhandler said. I vaguely heard Warfield mutter to himself: "I can't believe this is happening."

SPECIAL ED

"You'll never survive this, anyway," Jill said.

"Why not?"

"My father used to work for the CIA. Black ops."

"Cool job. But so what?"

"My sister swore me to secrecy about something he was involved with a long time ago. They were interrogating someone who wasn't cooperating, so they injected him with some steroid. His body temperature rose to 110 degrees. He melted to death."

Crazytown!

"I hope they fucking melt you to death," she continued.

Yikes! That was scary to consider. Melting? That's not for me. I panicked. This was bad on at least three accounts: Doc Holiday had her cell phone. She was scheduled to leave town in the morning. And her father melted people for a living?! We were running out of time and those guys needed to get back here soon if we wanted to be heroes.

"Let me go!" she suddenly yelped, and it was the first time she'd raised her voice since Friday night. I jumped atop of her and jammed the sock gag back inside her mouth. She fought to muscle free from her binds, her veins popping out from the strain of her effort. Hair hung in her eyes and more tears rolled down her face. I still had no interest in hurting this girl.

But I did have a question for her: "Wanna hear an old camp ghost story?"

EARLY MAN

"I'm your boogie man, that's what I am
I'm here to do whatever I can
Be it early morning, late afternoon
Or at midnight, it's never too soon."

SPECIAL ED

All I wanted was one super nice kiss from her before "Plan 9 from Cyberspace" was gonna launch out of Canard Beach. I didn't think it was so much to ask.

EARLY MAN

"I'm your boogie man, I'm your boogie man
Turn me on
I'm your boogie man, I'm your boogie man
Do what you want."

DOC HOLIDAY

After knocking some sand off my BlackBerry, I clicked onto
Facebook. An idea had taken root in me: was it possible Jill had
"checked-in" somewhere in Canard Beach?

Maybe that was a way I could find her. It was worth a
shot, so I went to her Facebook page. But even if she had been
"checked-in" somewhere, there was no way I could locate her
whereabouts, because we weren't yet Facebook friends. Oh, boy.

Where the Hell was she?

EARLY MAN

"To wanna please you, to wanna hold you
To wanna to do it all, for you
I wanna be your rubber ball
I wanna be the boy you love most of all."

SPECIAL ED

I removed her gag and pressed my mouth towards hers. But she
slammed her head against mine. So I guess I kind of strangled
her.

DOC HOLIDAY

No Camden Miller on Facebook. No Jill Cassady in Canard
Beach.

SPECIAL ED

I think I've already told you that I never ate anything that has a
face.

DOC HOLIDAY

Sometimes The Girl Next Door goes away.
"But the stars we could reach/Were just starfish on the beach... "

SPECIAL ED

But hers was real pretty.

PART SIX

CREATURE VIOLENCE

"Sick as a dog. What's your story?"

-- Aerosmith

WARFIELD

Early Man and I quietly discussed our plan as we walked back to the motel: we would wait until around three in the morning to make our move. Since the motel seemed mostly deserted, we agreed these elements could work to our advantage. There was a slim chance anyone would see us escorting Jill into my rental car. What happened after that was anyone's guess, and something I didn't want to think about. We were essentially taking our indecision elsewhere. But we definitely had to disappear from Canard Beach. It was important we agreed to that much.

EARLY MAN

We could drive her fifty miles out of Canard Beach, find some small shit town in the sticks, and maybe chain her to a tree in the woods. By the time someone found her later, we'd be in the fucking wind. (With any luck, her vagina would never be able to keep its story straight.) Was it crime scene Camelot? Of course not, but it seemed like our best viable option.

Warfield agreed. We were on the same page. It was settled. Cease-fire. We even shook on it. There was safety in numbers. We were quiet for a few minutes, before he offered me a nervous smile.

"You couldn't even find a decent motel for us, but think we're really going to get away with this?" he said. We actually laughed, which eased the tension for a minute.

WARFIELD

We were crossing through The Dove's Nest parking lot when he joked that he couldn't believe Special Ed snatched a girl, but left her cell phone behind. Hello? Where was his sense of responsibility? I cringed, but we managed to share another dark chuckle. I just wanted all of this to be over. Please. Just let this be over.

But that's when we saw him.

EARLY MAN

He was sitting alone at a corner booth of The Dove's Nest, and staring out a window. He looked like some kind of spooky bald ghost beneath those bright lights. What the fuck?

SPECIAL ED
When I saw the guys approach, I knew I was in big trouble. I sipped my Ginger Ale and hoped for the best. They sat down hard across from me and leaned forward.

"What the hell're you doing here?" Warfield asked.

EARLY MAN
Special Ed looked painfully reticent, like a small retarded child who pooped on his birthday cake and was now trying to distance himself from the transgression. But before he could respond, a chirpy waitress danced over to us.

"Hi, guys. I'm Emma and I'll be your server. Ready to order?" she asked.

"We'll need a minute, please," I said. When she walked off, I glared at Special Ed again. "What's going on? Why aren't you in the room?"

WARFIELD
"She was supposed to fly back to school tomorrow morning," he said. Early Man and I traded a look.

"Supposed to?" I asked.

He nodded. "Was supposed to."

Oh, God.

EARLY MAN
"What do you mean?" I asked, but he looked about to get sick, red splotches surfacing all over his face. He gulped his soda. "Sour stomach," he said, changing the subject.

"What the fuck is going on?" Warfield said, trying not to raise his voice.

WARFIELD
He grew really pale, trickles of sweat spidering down his face. He retched and we recoiled, fearing the worst. Not just the idea of his vomit, but the notion of calling any attention to ourselves at all. Our margin of error was slim. We were 34 year-olds on Spring Break with a missing girl inside our motel room.

But he retched once more and we flinched again. And then he puked onto the table, a throaty purge; it was mostly a liquid, puddled splatter, which fortunately didn't reach us. But there was something else, too.

And it was much worse than we feared.

EARLY MAN

An eyeball. Slowly spreading apart, shiny and unblinking, the raw nerve endings floating in its gooey wake; the wispy tendrils interlaced. It almost resembled a runny, sunnyside up egg. Warfield gasped at this most unspeakable of regurgitations. I cringed all over.

Special Ed no longer appeared like the gentleman of our peanut gallery.

"No. No," Warfield uttered.

"Grab it," I said to him. "Hurry."

"Grab it?"

There was no time to argue, so I scooped up the eyeball in a quick deposit, the way you clear crumbs from a table: one deft, sliding hand stroke feeding them into your other one. Special Ed mopped up his gastric goozlum with some napkins. He wiped his chin.

"Meet me outside. Go," I charged them. They scrambled out of the booth and fled the diner. I jumped out of the booth and headed for the Men's Room, a glutinous piece of the Fair Princess held carefully in my fist.

WARFIELD

Special Ed and I regrouped in the parking lot. He was shaking like a shitting dog. This was his idea of blinding her?! I couldn't believe we allowed this to happen. Not this. Not fucking *this*.

"Is she… is she dead?" I asked him.

"I think so."

"What? You're not sure?"

"Do you know CPR?" I shoved him hard, nearly toppling him on his ass. Early Man charged out of the diner, wiping his hand on the back of his jeans.

"I flushed it down the toilet," he said. "Let's go."

"Jesus," I said, fearing whatever atrocity awaited us inside our room.

"Come on, dude. Safety in numbers," Early Man said.

EARLY MAN

Special Ed had deposited her lifeless form inside the bathtub, beneath a blue blanket. The three of us stared at it, big-eyed and speechless.

"We've gotta get rid of her," I said. "Right now."

"Where do we bring her?" Warfield said.

WARFIELD

We returned back into the room, and Early Man opened his laptop. A Google search was in order, he said, because I was right: we needed to find a place to bury our dead body. I almost thought he was kidding.

"You're gonna leave our fate up to Google?" I asked.

"Don't we always?" he said.

He Googled "best place to bury a human body." Almost 377,000 links came up, but most of them concerned pet burials. One link was even called "A Place To Bury Strangers."

EARLY MAN

But there was one nasty surprise still in store for us. We heard noises from inside the bathroom. Movement. A struggle. The three of us, we froze. Warfield's jaw hit the floor. Special Ed whimpered something moist and unintelligible. We traded mortified glances and bounded back inside the bathroom.

Our Fair Princess was still alive. She had stirred awake in the tub and partially removed herself from beneath the blanket. Twitching, moaning and disoriented, she flopped around like a worm on a waffle iron. I sneered at Special Ed. He couldn't even kill her right.

And now she was running her fingers over her chunk of missing face, gore lacing around them. She seemed as shocked as we were that she was still alive. We backed away from her, retreating like she was a movie monster stubbornly refusing to be vanquished.

We watched her groping around, this installation of grotesquerie on display. A ribbon of retinal gunk streaked down her face like some kind of hideous war paint.

But her one shiny eyeball was fixed in our direction, washing over us, a life unto itself. And with her every small movement, we recoiled and edged further away, like maybe she was growing stronger or more resilient and summoning forth her second wind. Like she was re-animating herself. Like she was winning.

SPECIAL ED

And suddenly, what she did next... that's the thing I'll never forget. I'll never forget what she did next. She eyeballed us. And smiled.

EARLY MAN

Warfield couldn't take it any more. He snapped her neck. It made a noise.

WARFIELD

At that point, I honestly felt we had no choice but to put her out of her misery. Not to mention ours. It was a necessary evil that had to be done to hasten both her departure and our own. I'm sorry, but it did.

SPECIAL ED

When it was over, I felt palpitations boomering inside my chest. Early Man perched an unlit cigarette between his lips. It quivered there a moment, bent and trembling. I knew he was super scared, too. Warfield's face was full of crazy, bubbles of perspiration forming on his forehead.

"Now what?" I asked.

"We have to go shopping," Early Man said.

"Huh?" Warfield said.

"Shopping?" I said. Early Man didn't look pleased with either of us.

EARLY MAN

FYI: never kill a new girl with old camp friends.

WARFIELD

Back inside the room moments later, Early Man started compiling a shopping list: power tools, bandsaws, hacksaws, plastic buckets, rubber gloves, and various cleaning products. It was fucking beyond incomprehensible to fathom the mess we were in. Early Man said we needed to make the body "portable and aerodynamic. Travel-friendly." And then figure out where to travel with it.

We were having this conversation.

SPECIAL ED

Warfield drove us to an Ace Hardware store a couple of miles away. We tried to play it cool as we entered the building. The sign in Aisle One read *Air Fresheners Laundry Detergent Household Gloves Mops & Brooms Squeegees.* Early Man tasked Warfield to retrieve the cleaning products on his list, while we went looking for the power tools.

EARLY MAN

When Special Ed saw a shelf lined with cans of lighter fluid, he brightened with an idea. He said he'd once seen a corpse burned beyond recognition during his security work at the morgue in Seattle. So he suggested an alternative plan: toss our dead body into a garbage Dumpster, and then it light it ablaze. He was annoying. Maybe next time, I said, and kept walking.

WARFIELD

When we returned back to the motel, I watched the guys remove the tools from the bags, and as casual and workmanlike as if they were assembling something from IKEA. The inmates had truly taken over the asylum.

My life was over. I tried not to look at them, tried to ignore them. To ignore every part of it. But this was really happening.

SPECIAL ED

The guys forced me to start in the bathroom first because I had created this problem. I protested. What happened to teamwork and safety in numbers? But there was no time to argue, so I removed most of my clothes. I pulled on a pair of rubber gloves, grabbed some tools, and then entered the bathroom. Warfield closed the door behind me. I could only hope Jill was really dead this time.

I didn't know where to start. I wondered how I'd gotten here, and how we were gonna get out of there. I wondered about how you dismember someone. I needed to think of something else, had to somehow try and keep my mind off what I was doing.

So I began thinking about Rita the Eater, as I began sawing through the gristle beneath Jill's left shoulder. Maybe if Rita had loved me back none of this would've happened. I wouldn't be in Canard Beach holding a bandsaw. Yeah, maybe the "mightiest thing" I would've ever dared was proposed to her. I could've hosted her party. A little happiness wouldn't have killed old Special Ed, you know. But no… she had to eat and run. And now I was doing the same.

It might be nice to see Rita again someday, I thought. I'd sure have a ghost story to tell her. Safe travels, Rita, wherever you are. Maybe in the next life, right?

I'll be looking out.

WARFIELD

I'm not sure how much time passed, but Early Man got impatient with Special Ed's progress in the bathroom. I reluctantly trailed him when he went inside to check on him. Standing just inside the doorway, I glimpsed Special Ed clutching a bloody cutting tool.

"Crazytown," he said.

"What have we done?" I said, barely above a whisper.

"We fell in love," Special Ed said.

EARLY MAN

My old camp friends hadn't changed a bit.

DOC HOLIDAY

I stirred awake on the beach with a ghoulish, handicapping hangover, thanks to a sliver of blistering sunshine. Cramped, achy, and shivering, my throat a parched tunnel of phlegm, I shoved up to my feet and knocked sand off myself. I was stretching my limbs and fighting a sudden urge to vomit when, like some kind of hectoring wake-up call, I heard a burble of sirens just beyond Beachfront Property.

Wincing through the rancor of sirens, and in desperate need of coffee, aspirin, and a shower, I dragged my ass through the rear entrance of the hotel. I was going to grab a coffee from the restaurant, then go back to my hotel and sleep the rest of it off.

A scattering of college kids were massing in the front lobby, staring out the windows, blue flashing police lights playing off their faces. Some of them held travel bags, and chirped into their phones. Others were using theirs to shoot pictures and video. An eerie buzz hung in the air, palpable and contagious. Dark gossips were exchanged. Rumors were fueled from troubled faces.

Something was definitely wrong, so I shuffled over to see what was going on. Four of five airport shuttle buses were parked like sentries alongside the hotel.

"What's this all about?" I asked a college boy.

"Some chick went missing from Barnacles Friday night," he said. "Her friends are freaking out, cuz she was supposed to leave town today." He pointed to a few harried college girls being questioned by the police. One was crying and trembling. Two of her friends held her steady, attempting to calm her. I thought she looked vaguely familiar.

"I guess they're looking for the dude she left the bar with," the boy added.

When I noticed the black rubber bracelets circled around the trembling girl's wrists, I blinked. Oh, boy. No way. No fucking way. Yes, way.

It was Ashley, Jill's friend. A noxious dread bloomed inside me. Swooning with alarm, I was suddenly wide-awake with bowels hot, wet, and straining against the gate.

It was obvious: *Jill* was the missing girl.

Now it was me who was freaking out. I slowly backed off, rubbing hands over my face, attempting to compose myself. Fighting to get my faculties in working order. I continued to creep back into the lobby, not wanting to run, lest I arouse suspicion. More suspicion. Jesus. They were looking for me?!

More important: where was Jill?! I was in the worst possible place at the worst possible time. That's all I knew. So I panicked and ran like Hell.

EARLY MAN

We packed Warfield's rental car quickly and discreetly. We'd used the cleaning products to scrub the bathroom clean as best we could manage. It took hours. You can never be too prepared when you vacation. But was it good enough? Probably not, but any physical evidence left behind would surely be contaminated by whoever checked into that room next. Hopefully sooner than later. So maybe we had that going for us.

We heard sirens in the distance, which could've meant 100 different things in a town like Canard Beach, but I knew there was a good chance the police were now looking for the girl's whereabouts. We moved even faster to effectuate our escape.

"You made a mistake," I said to Special Ed after we finally climbed into the car. I thought a little humor might be nice to grease the skids.

"What do you mean?" he asked.

"You shoulda snatched a black chick, instead."

"But I don't like black girls."

"That's not the point."

"So what do you mean?"

I grinned. "You snatch a black chick, no comes looking for her so fast."

DOC HOLIDAY

I emerged back onto the beach, harried and trembling in the shadows and unsure as to my next course of action. They were looking for me?! The shrill squawk of seagulls soared overhead, an ear-piercing cacophony that bit into my nerves. If I'd had a shotgun, I would've blasted them out of the sky.

It dawned on me that I was on the fucking beach editorializing about seagulls. Not the move. Thinking on unsteady feet, I reached into my pocket for my phone. Maybe someone had called looking for me, too. But I removed Jill's phone by mistake. I stared at it. Oh, boy. This was no good, either.

I actually did a quick Google search on my BlackBerry, and learned that as long as a battery remains inside a cell phone, even if the device is turned off, a GPS signal is sent out that police can track. It's essentially a map for them to follow after they bring it up on their computers.

That's when I completely snapped, and tossed Jill's phone about thirty feet into the ocean. I watched it disappear into the drink, the seagulls continuing to shriek, as if either surveilling or mocking me. I finally started to race down the beach, slicing through the eerie gloom in a desperately uneven scramble, the swift of foot being the province of others.

I hoped to arrive at my hotel before the police did. If not, I'd have a lot of explaining to do. They'd have questions I had no answers to, questions I needed answers to myself.

WARFIELD

We discussed the need to dispose of Jill's personal effects, as well – her purse and its contents. I wondered if it was too risky to purchase something online, using Jill's credit card. It might give the police the illusion she was still alive, and buy us some more time.

But Early Man informed us why buying something online with her credit card was a dangerous and incriminating idea. He read something to us from his phone.

"When you send emails, post on web forums, use instant messengers or access any online accounts, your computer's IP is logged by the network receiving communication requests. This is an essential step that cannot be avoided and contributes to various technical, security and privacy aspects."

"Everything leaves a cyber footprint," he said. "Every search, posting, text or Tweet. It's true what they say: privacy is dead. They really got you by the balls."

DOC HOLIDAY

Back inside my room at The Cabana Inn, I quickly packed my travel bag, and decided to call the other Boogeymen. I knew of nowhere or no one else to turn. At least they could vouch for me. They knew I'd checked out of The Island Oasis to be closer to Jill's hotel. Maybe I'd go to the police with them and explain myself.

EARLY MAN

Carpool from Hell: Warfield driving us out of Canard Beach. No one said a word. It was another gloriously beautiful day, belying the grisly contents in the trunk of the rental car. Our bags were packed and our cell phones were off. The show was over and the Boogeymen were going home to clear our histories.

SPECIAL ED

The troops were withdrawing again. The Boogeymen would be saying farewell very soon. "I always felt sad at the end of camp," I said. "Especially that last summer." The guys just looked at me. But I think they might've even smiled.

WARFIELD

I wasn't sure if we weren't making a tactical mistake in turning off our phones, but Early Man convinced me otherwise. He reasoned that Doc Holiday would assume his calls went straight to voicemail because we were sleeping and our phones were off. We would appear either guilty or wildly suspicious if we answered them so early. It made sense. And besides, any conversation with Doc Holiday would be far too dangerous. Less was more.

DOC HOLIDAY

I took the elevator down to the lobby and checked out of my room, careful to keep small talk to the barest of minimums.

I hurtled myself into a taxi outside the hotel. "The Island Oasis, please," I said to the cabbie, fighting to remain calm. As we merged onto the main strip, we passed a familiar scrawl of graffiti: "I'M CREEPIN' WHILE YOU'RE SLEEPIN."

I tried to wrap my head around the events of the past 24 hours or so. It remained unclear why Jill was gone from my room yesterday morning, but I suppose I'd chalked it up to the impulsive, capricious nature of a young girl on Spring Break. To be honest, I hadn't dwelled much on the "why" of it. I suppose you could chalk that up to the impulsive, capricious nature of a 34-year-old guy on Spring Break.

It was true that Jill could very well be perfectly safe somewhere, maybe even shacked-up with another boy. It was entirely possible she'd been a little careless or irresponsible, causing her to be late for her bus. Wouldn't be the first time that's ever happened to someone on Spring Break. In fact, it was probably an occupational hazard. I could only hope.

EARLY MAN

I underscored what our imperatives were once we returned back home. For starters, we'd need to go dark and completely vanish from the online grid. And get Doc Holiday off our scent.

SPECIAL ED

We had to "clear our histories," he said. We were undertaking a covert mission. We'd have to change all our contact information except for the dummy Facebook accounts we'd set up. We'd communicate with each other that way but only when absolutely necessary. Emergencies only. No Video Chat or Skyping. No profile pictures, either. Early Man warned that we needed to disappear faster than our Fair Princess did.

WARFIELD

Doc Holiday would obviously remain the problem. It's not like he didn't know our names and know where to find us. He'd call the police and tell them what went down in Canard Beach. I voiced this concern to Early Man.

EARLY MAN

Or we could call the police and tell them what happened in Canard Beach: the last time we saw Doc Holiday he was waltzing off with the girl who was now missing. Stored in my BlackBerry was the photo of them I had shot in the Barnacles parking lot. Was it Camelot? No. But at least it would be our word against his, if it came to that. Three against one. Safety in numbers.

DOC HOLIDAY

At The Island Oasis, I hopped out of the cab and rumbled up two flights of blue metal stairs. I went straight to Room 211, struggling to modulate my panic. The shades were drawn and a DO NOT DISTURB sign hung off the doorknob. I throttled it, but it was locked, so I rapped a fist against the door.

"Early Man! Warfield!" I called out. "Open the door, guys. It's Doc Holiday. Wake up!" No one answered, so I descended the stairs and crossed the parking lot. I slipped inside the reception building, where a young desk clerk was drinking coffee and reading USA Today. He was a different guy from the one who'd checked me out the day before.

"Can I help you, sir?" he asked.

"Well, um… I'm here to see some friends," I said. "In Room 211. But they aren't answering the door or their phones, so… I'm sure they're still sleeping. And it's kind of important."

He slid the black house phone across the desk to me, and told me to give that a shot. I dialed the room number: 211. It rang four times before going to voicemail. I hung up. No luck, I said. He killed the dregs of his coffee and punched something up on his computer. "Actually, they checked out at eight this morning," he said.

"They what?" It had to be a mistake. "Are you sure?"

"I'm sure," he said. "Eight a.m. They checked out."

A horrid foreboding crept through me. And as I turned around to glance back up at room 211, the cobwebs were starting to clear. I started to squirm with apprehension and flowering dread. Cold sweat drizzled at my temples.

Because I didn't like what I saw coming into focus.

The strangers who were friends waiting to happen… they checked out.

Why?

SPECIAL ED

Of course, I can't tell you where we planned to deposit Jill's body. I'm not that crazy, you know. Magicians don't tell audiences the secrets to their tricks, right? Then it wouldn't be magic. Once the magic wand is waved, the mystery is born. Now you see her, now you don't. I've personally always wondered how they saw those women in half and not make a mess. Suffice it to say, it wasn't a pretty picture with Jill.

And I wished she'd been shorter.

DOC HOLIDAY

I asked the desk clerk if Room 209 was still occupied, the one I'd shared with Special Ed on Friday night. Maybe he was still here and could provide some kind of explanation. The clerk checked his computer screen again. He shook his head and told me that the Room 209 "guest" had also checked out at 8:00 a.m.

But I couldn't leave town without seeing inside Room 211 for myself. None of this made any sense, so I told the clerk I'd left my camera in there and was trying to catch an 11 a.m. flight. Could I take a quick look inside?

He offered to check the Lost and Found in back, forcing me to play it cool and wait an agonizing few minutes. Apparently even shitty motels had a "policy," and for a delirious moment, I imagined that Megan from Beachfront Property and this guy had conspired to make my Spring Break all the more miserable.

I couldn't believe those guys checked out! (Everyone I knew was either "checking in" or checking out.) When the guy returned with a weary apology but no camera, I removed fifty bucks from my wallet and offered it to him.

"This isn't The Four Seasons, is it?" I said. "I'll just be a minute. Okay?"

WARFIELD

I made sure to keep the speed limit. If we were pulled over and a cop took a look inside the trunk, it was game over. But Early Man was impatient with my driving. He told me I should've rented a faster car. I told him he was an asshole. Special Ed giggled.

"Hey, you know what? We should really do this again next year," I said.

Early Man grinned "I'll e-mail you."

"Crazytown."

You know who said that.

DOC HOLIDAY

The two beds were stripped bare. No sheets or pillowcases in sight. Room 211 had been thoroughly cleaned. It was chilly because the air conditioner was cranked to the max, but there was a sharp stench of disinfectant. I wondered if the housekeeping woman had already been there. I didn't see any signs of blood. That was the good news.

I dialed Early Man's number again, but the call went straight to voicemail. I left a frantic message: "Early Man, it's me – Doc Holiday. Where are you guys? I'm in your room! What the Hell's going on? You left town before calling me? That girl I hooked up with Friday night? Jill? She's missing!" I hung up and dialed Special Ed's number. It went straight to voicemail. I left a similar message and then called Warfield's number. This call also went straight to voicemail. I left the same message.

I considered either calling the police or going directly to the station, at least to absolve myself of any suspicion they may've cultivated. I'd tell them the truth: Jill left my motel room in the wee hours yesterday morning, but I never heard from her again. It was the least I could do. Too many strange factors at play here, not the least of which was that Jill and the Boogeymen were missing. And everyone was looking for me.

I darted into the bathroom to pee and was assailed by another stinging reek of disinfectant. When I switched on the lights, a large, smiley face scrawled in toothpaste greeted me from the mirror: ☺

My skin crawled a country mile. What the Hell? I noticed that the tiles, sink, and toilet were shiny and sparking clean. This room had also been tidied up nice. Too nice. When my BlackBerry vibrated, it startled me and nearly tumbled out of my hand. It was a text message from Early Man.

EARLY MAN

I shut off my phone after sending the text to Doc Holiday.

DOC HOLIDAY

I read the text. Terse and haunting, six words I will never forget: "JUST REMEMBER: <u>YOU</u> FUCKED HER FIRST." I glanced back at the smiley face on the mirror:

My own terrified reflection even chilled me, as if it were a monstrously distorted image from a funhouse mirror. But that was it. The Breaking News and smoking gun, and straight from the mouth of the barrel.

The Boogeymen had killed Jill Cassady.

EARLY MAN

When I told the guys the message I texted, Warfield had no response, remaining focused on the road. He clearly still harbored serious reservations about our plan. Of the three of us, it was obvious he'd be the one forever haunted. Special Ed, on the other hand, he smiled so wide I thought he might crack open in two.

DOC HOLIDAY

I was awash in clammy perspiration, like my whole body was suffused with swamp-ass. Do I even respond to this text? I wondered if any response might implicate me, too. Maybe Early Man was tempting me to do so, baiting me, a bold move to play, a dangerous gamble - to actually text me those words. To put them out in the world, as it were, while Search and Rescue teams were doubtless gearing up in Canard Beach.

But he probably thought self-preservation was as important to me as it was to him and the others. He must've instinctually known I'd do the "right thing," which was to do nothing at all. He had to figure I wouldn't go to the police. Not now, not ever.

I was the last one seen leaving Barnacles with Jill on Friday night before she apparently vanished. Now these guys had vanished, too, and I was standing in the probable crime scene.

I deleted his text. It was time to get the Hell out of there, but not before parting the shower curtain, the one section of the motel room I hadn't yet thoroughly inspected. The bathtub tile glistened brightly - no blood or gore. Both the faucet and the shower nozzle were also polished clean. I crouched down to scrutinize the drain, which also appeared to have been scoured or scrubbed to a shiny shimmer.

Then I saw it: blood on the ceiling. Just a small blemish, maybe the size of a silver dollar. And if I didn't know before, if I wasn't completely sure, now I knew I had to do the right thing. No more fucking around. No more lollygagging. I had to do the right thing.

Because if I didn't I'd never be able to live with myself.
"Just remember: you fucked her first."
So I wiped the blood away.

WARFIELD

After the final deed was done, I'd be hitting the highway toward Miami. The others were going to split a cab to the airport in Fort Lauderdale. It was over. It really happened, but it was finally over.

Yet at the same time, it was really just beginning.

DOC HOLIDAY

After returning the key card to the desk clerk, I nearly dove into the back seat of another cab. I called another quick audible: I'd take a bus back to Boston rather than switch my flight. It seemed the less conspicuous move, so I told my cabbie to take me to the Peter Pan bus terminal. I hunched down in my seat and muscled through a series of shudders, as I spotted an anti-flu sign plastered to the sign of a passing bus: "IF YOU ARE SICK, GO HOME!" Sounded like a plan.

As I exited the belly of the Canard Beach beast, it was as if I were departing the Island of Misfit Toys, a sanctuary for the unwanted and defective. March Madness had wound down to the Final Four: The Boogeymen.

I thought about my selfish decision to switch hotels, thus separating myself from the Boogeymen. Had that decision cost Jill her life? Or made me complicit in some fashion, an unwitting accessory to whatever they did to her? And what did they do to her? I sure wished I'd conducted some kind of background check on my old camp friends.

"Will you tell me a ghost story?"

EARLY MAN

Special Ed and I shared a silent cab to the airport. I was scouring the Miami Herald for any updates on the missing Canard Beach coed. Nothing yet. Good news for us. But somewhere you just knew that chittering lunatic Nancy Grace was priming for a vigorous new hour of Righteous Indignation.

Tonight, Breaking News on missing college girl Jill Cassady: she's still missing. Later: Global Warming and why you really shouldn't give a shit.

The cabbie was Haitian and smelled like a camel's ass. Special Ed noticed, too.

"He stinks, don't he?" he whispered.

"They all do."

"Yeah. Why is that?"

"No one knows."

He shrugged. I present you with another one of life's quiet

mysteries: your cab driver smells like shit, speaks little English, and usually has no sense of direction. Other than that, you're all for illegal immigration.

Staring out the windows, we watched the new crop of bright-eyed and bushy-tailed college kids barnstorming into town for their week of Spring Break. Special Ed fidgeted anxiously, fighting to compose himself.

"Stay in character," I told him.

DOC HOLIDAY

After purchasing a bus ticket at the Peter Pan terminal, I emerged from the building and threw on my shades. My head on a swivel, eyes and ears peeled for police and sirens.

A few college boys were smoking cigarettes on the sidewalk. I approached them. After volunteering that I'd quit the habit five years before, I asked if I could bum one.

"Thought you said you quit," one boy said, as he handed me a Marlboro Light.

Yeah, well, I'm allergic to peanuts, too, but there was this one time, with this one girl, and...

SPECIAL ED

At the Fort Lauderdale airport, I got off at the United Airlines terminal. Early Man was flying Delta but I was surprised when he climbed out of the cab with me. He gently hugged me. It was nice. But the Forced Enjoyment Tour was ending, so it was also a little bittersweet.

When he adjusted his shades, I saw a few college girls in their reflections, milling about with their travel bags. Two uniformed cops were standing guard by the terminal entrance. I gestured to Early Man's swollen black eye and asked if that wasn't a concern or cause for suspicion. He casually dismissed it. "Dude, a guy on Spring Break with a black eye ain't unlike a girl on Spring Break, with a sore snatch: an occupational hazard."

LOL.

WARFIELD

I drove straight toward Miami, never looking back. That was the plan, going forward. Never look back. Of course, there was still

Doc Holiday to consider. There always would be. He was capable
of bringing down the whole house of cards. You couldn't blame
him for doing so, for doing the right thing. In fact, you'd like to
think that if you were in his shoes, you'd do the same. You'd go
to the police and tell them your story. But you're walking in
different shoes. Very different shoes. And there's blood on yours.

I was desperately curious as to what he would choose to
do, and that concern kept my mind occupied during the entire
drive to Miami. I fought countless, irrational urges to respond to
his texts and voice messages. But I couldn't go scratching that
surface. What could I possibly tell him? Certainly not the truth.

But he wasn't the only one I needed to worry about. How
would I know Early Man wouldn't someday text my wife those
photos of me with Jill? I couldn't trust him. None of us could trust
each other. We hardly knew each other anymore.

It was horrifying to believe we were leaving Canard Beach
with a dead girl in our wake. I couldn't believe it. I still can't. I'm
the one who assaulted her first and killed her later. Oh, God. What
the fuck did we do!? How did this happen?!

*"Sounds like you could use a little vacation, though, no? A
vacation away from the 'crazy.'"*

I hated Facebook.

DOC HOLIDAY

I was the first one to board the bus, clutched in a full-on tremble
and arming away perspiration. Rows of buses were parked beside
me, looming like dormant monsters, big green PETER PAN
lettering splashed across their sides.

Even though I was alone, I sequestered myself inside the
bathroom at the back. I called the other Boogeymen, but each call
went to voicemail again. Keeping my voice down, I left them a
uniform message: "Where the Hell are you guys? What
happened? Where is Jill? Call me." I splashed cold water onto my
face and stole a peek into the small mirror. What stared back at
me looked like Ass and Death, after thrown together into a
blender and stirred within a septic tank's fetid potpourri.

I came out of the bathroom and plopped down in a seat,
scouring out the long windows. Nearly expecting to see police
cars screaming up to the terminal at any moment. I had traveled to
Florida to reacquaint myself with three relative strangers, thinking

I was temporarily getting out of Dodge, only to find myself ass-deep in it. I'd thought there were no mysterious agendas in Canard Beach, and that you wouldn't find an ulterior motive for twenty miles. Boy, was I wrong.

I was in desperate need of peace and solitude. I had thinking to do, serious ruminations to explore. It wasn't going to happen on this bus. Maybe I would alert the Canard Beach Police Department upon my return to Boston. I'd have some quality distance at that point and be ensconced within a semblance of refuge. I had a 20-hour bus ride to noodle on the pros and cons of such an action.

A herd of college kids began to board in a listless procession, shouldering carry-on bags and nursing gruesome hangovers. Prattling on phones and stabbing at BlackBerries, their faces pinched pink, tight, and weird from too much sun.

I was grateful no one sat next to me as the bus departed out of Canard Beach. I stared out the window in a rather dazed, listless stupor. Moments later, a college boy en route to the bathroom stopped to curiously regard me. He appeared uncertain, before his Eureka Moment landed on his face with a giant grin. When it became obvious that he recognized me, I plummeted into a wormhole of dread: you're shitting me. But then I recognized him: Andy Starkovich, an American Literature student of mine.

"What are you doing here?" he asked.

"Family thing. Vacation. My cousins," I said. "Kinda last-minute."

"Oh. Cool beans. Well, still funny seeing you here," he said. Tell me about it. When he shambled off towards the bathroom, the notion that I'd be back teaching in three days chilled me.

A skinny girl plugged into her iPod was seated a few rows across from me. When she jumped to her feet to retrieve something from the overhead rack, I saw the words embroidered on her yellow T-shirt: "I SURVIVED SPRING BREAK." It felt like a sharp kick in the groin.

Because I was pretty sure I knew a girl who didn't.

WARFIELD

After checking into my hotel room in Miami, I ordered a cheeseburger and fries from Room Service and called Nikki back in Phoenix. She put our daughter on the phone for a minute and it was good to hear my little one's voice. My big one's voice, not so much.

I couldn't even begin to imagine what Nikki's reaction to my arrest on murder charges would look like. As I spoke with her, a dark idea floated into my head, before I swatted it away: in the history of jurisprudence, had anyone ever pleaded "Unhappily Married," instead of Insanity? But that could've set a really dangerous legal precedent.

"I'll be back at 11 tomorrow morning," I told her. "Day earlier than scheduled."

"Is everything all right?"

"Everything's good, yeah. Real good. It went well. Missed you guys."

She gave me a little hell about only calling her a few times, as I grabbed the remote from the coffee table. I apologized to her.

When we hung up, I never channel-surfed so nervously in my life, seeking Breaking News about the missing college girl in Canard Beach. A local newscast had something. A devastating chill shot through me, as I plated my burger and listened closely. A reporter said a "person of interest" had been detained who might have "evidence that could provide valuable information in the case."

Fuck! That was it. It was over. We were dead meat. I obviously knew who that "person of interest" was: Doc Holiday.

DOC HOLIDAY

I checked my BlackBerry for messages from the Boogeymen. None. The only e-mail I'd received had been from Classmates.com. It was a notification and advance warning of the upcoming high school class reunion the following November.

"LIFE HAPPENS. STAY IN TOUCH."

"RECONNECT WITH YOUR OLD HIGH SCHOOL CHUMS, WILLIAM!"

"DOES SHE REMEMBER YOU?"

I knew she did. Of course she did. But I also knew that you "don't ever tell anybody anything. If you do, you start missing everybody."

WARFIELD

I was pleasantly surprised to learn that my assumption had been wrong: the TV reporter said the "person of interest" was a student at Ohio State University. That must have been that shithead I had punched out at Barnacles. Police weren't yet officially confirming him as a suspect, which meant he probably was their guy. More important, it meant Doc Holiday had not gone to the police. At least not yet.

This might grant the rest of us more time to cover our tracks, now that we had a little distance. But this was temporary appeasement and not enough to prevent me from wondering when and how my inevitable apprehension would go down.

Someone in Canard Beach must have seen something, or one of us must have said something seemingly innocuous at the time, but in hindsight would prove incriminating. I wasn't impressed with our chances. The other shoe was bound to drop, and probably sooner than later. People like us just don't get away with murder anymore.

DOC HOLIDAY

When darkness had fallen hours later, the bus grew considerably chillier. Many passengers were dozing, open-mouthed and reclining in their seats. A few throaty snores filtered through the cool night air. I remained wide-awake during this strangely peaceful interlude, watching the highway racing by.

An SUV crowded with college kids zoomed up beside us in the next lane, probably homeward-bound, too. I slouched down in my seat, flinching from the sudden growl of angry thunder in the sky and the jarring flashes of lightning. And then came the torrential rains, peppering the roof of the bus in a yammering backbeat.

I closed my eyes and thought about the Boogeymen. And what they must have done to Jill.

"Here's to old friends and young girls."

I think we were somewhere in South Carolina when I began to cry.

WARFIELD

I took a long shower before hitting the sack, and started thinking about my daughter. If I were ever arrested for this crime, what would she think of her Daddy when old enough to know better?

I couldn't let that happen. I needed to bottle up the guilt and hope the seal took. I'd be fiercely bullish and promise myself to give it my all, in an effort to get away with what we had done. I would be a man. And what kind of man just caves and throws it all away like that? I had bills to pay, mouths to feed, a new baby. I wouldn't crack because I couldn't crack. I wouldn't put my wife and daughter out to pasture like that.

I'd privately take responsibility for my actions. I'd own it, and do my best to keep the secret buried inside me. I'd always been pretty good at keeping my emotions in check, but now I'd need the ultimate game face. As insane as it may sound, and I know it does, I owed it to my family.

So yes, I would follow Early Man's directive. When I returned to Phoenix, I'd change and cancel all my contact information: e-mails, Facebook, iPhone number. Our landline number was already unlisted. Other than activating an emergency dummy Facebook account, I'd disappear from every possible tangent connecting me to the Boogeymen.

When I finally climbed into bed and killed the lights, the pitch-dark sanctuary of a strange hotel room was a liberating reprieve. I was nearly invisible, untraceable. Too bad I couldn't stay there forever. I recalled never looking forward to those early summer mornings before busing off to Camp Hideaway. I was practically homesick before we even hit the road.

But now I was suffering some kind of reverse-homesickness, because I was afraid to return home in the morning. God knew what the AM would bring. Maybe another development in the Canard Beach investigation; a fresh new wrinkle or urgent message from either Early Man or Special Ed, telling me we needed to change our story. Whatever that even was. All I knew was that there was no happy ending. Just like there's no happy ending for those bulls that run in the streets of Pamplona.

Amusement comes at a price.

DOC HOLIDAY

In August of our last summer before college began, Reese, Lansky, and myself journeyed to see a Grateful Dead show in Saratoga, N.Y. After decamping in the parking lot of the Saratoga Performing Arts center, we raged all day long, eating lots of acid and 'shrooms and pounding enough beers to cripple an Australian rugby team.

The place was a demented circus, a teeming madhouse of decadence; not a functioning brain cell for miles. Lots of chemically imbalanced folk having the time of their lives, or whatever passed for them. Music blared: *"Come all you pretty women with your hair a hanging down/Open up your windows cause the Candyman's in town... "*

Some Deadheads were buck naked, and most were the kind of unsightly folks who really should've remained covered up. People were blowing bubbles, like sugared-up toddlers at a birthday party. An errant Frisbee toss bonked Lansky on the back of the head. The thick, cloying stench of patchouli oil freighted the air, rancid, annoying, and quietly overwhelming. Reese called it "Loser Smog."

It was a parade of mindless freaks, hawking wares and drugs. "Doses! Who needs doses?!" was the prevalent declamation of the day. Everyone was soaring high and mighty on dope, acid, and booze, and whatever else hadn't officially been invented yet.

I remember someone waving a flag bearing the legend **"DEAD SHOWS - TIME OUT FROM WHOEVER YOU ARE!"** The bumper sticker affixed to the Microbus parked across from us read **"LIVE, so the preacher won't have to lie at your funeral!"**

Shortly before the stadium gates opened, I was heading towards the woods to pee when I came across a crazed, raging Deadhead being restrained by his pals. He wore a STEAL YOUR FACE T-shirt, featuring that fabled, sniveling Dead skull beneath another legend: **"DEAD GIRLS NEVER SAY NO."**

"She's in my stadium!" he ranted, wild-eyed, furiously flailing about, a scary lunatic intensity about him, doubtless fueled by whatever illicit drugs he'd been ingesting since breakfast. I saw a few girls quickly escorting their pretty blonde friend away from this guy and his pals. "She's in my stadium!" he howled, nearly baying at the moon and stabbing a finger toward the blonde girl. "She's in my fucking stadium!"

His agony was ugly, oozing and immeasurable; an open wound in Reeboks. His friends were desperately trying to console him, offering him a cold beer, a cigarette, a blast from the nitrous tank – a Whippit for his worries. Maybe a flyer for a dating service. Anything, they figured, so as to offer emotional support. No mean feat, mind you, considering they were all goosed off their snots on an aggregate total of 21 hits of acid. Because love is madness. Sickening, isn't it? And hate is one of its virulent symptoms.

I stopped to regard this drama, the acid coursing through me momentarily spiking my curiosity anew. Watching it unfold, I tried to imagine its genesis, choosing to create a little extemporaneous fan fiction, even as my straining bladder beckoned for evacuation.

How did this guy's screws come loose? He goes to a concert with his friends, wanting to forget about life for a while, yet who does he run into? His ex-girlfriend, who broke his heart to pieces and snorted them out of his chest cavity. And his life. Now his heart was gone with nothing but jagged black rage and white jackass friends to replace it.

All day long, he was probably having a splendid time: dancing and laughing with his dopey chums, pie-eyed with intoxication beneath his wraparound shades. And then he spotted The Ex and unraveled on a dime. Total meltdown. His emotional wallpaper was shorn right off, rendering him a puddle of whimpering, pathetic ectoplasm. *She's in his stadium?!*

Because sometimes we fall so hard and so fast, we never get up again.

So he was forced to downgrade and gobble 3 hits of mind-walloping Windowpane with his pals. I was out of my gourd as I watched him, thoughts swirling through me like some kind of brain flatulence, loopy revelations piercing through my intoxication: *there's a reason the kid who was burned beyond recognition in the concert fire still continues to listen to the band's music. Maybe that's what love is.*

But when he suddenly caught me staring at him, a knowing smile swam up his face like palsy. "Real life is a motherfucker!!" he hollered at me. That was my cue to finally shove off, flush with an unsettling knowledge that this ghoulish fella would be haunting me all summer long.

Once inside the stadium, Reese, Lansky and I found a decent vista on the grass. We sprawled out on a large blanket and settled in, stretching our legs, removing binoculars, cigarettes, weed, and bottled water. Lansky was constantly re-adjusting his sweat-soaked yellow bandana. "How sick are our lives?!" he howled, a big smile dancing across his face. That was always his mantra whenever we were doing anything really cool together.

It was go time. More than 25,000 excitable Deadheads were jammed into the outdoor stadium, pleasure pilgrims awaiting supplication. This was one band that knew its audience. I imagined this was what Jonestown must've been like before the suicide hysteria and mass Kool-Aid consumption. When life was good.

A giant full moon shimmered in the dark sky. Never really got the appeal of the "full moon." It's just a bigger moon, no? Why all the excitement? But it was pretty cool on this deranged night, this shiny white eye in the dark face of the universe.

But I almost felt like a target under its weighty surveillance, probing and unflinching and flanked by what looked like encroaching, menacing thunderheads. They appeared to slowly crawl closer to us, creeping stealthily through the heavens, like alien ships readying for either an invasion or air strike. Then again, I was soaring on crazy amounts of acid.

A few songs later I was waiting in line at the concession stands, looking forward to another frosty round of beers and air-guitaring to "Scarlet Begonias" filtering out from beyond. The girl behind me had facial moles, with sparse, black hairs sprouting out of them. Hippie moles. Her glow stick necklace only served to illuminate them. Her T-shirt read **"SOME OF MY BEST FRIENDS ARE DEAD."** A white sticker was also affixed to her forehead, featuring the word **"Damaged."** If you didn't know any better, you'd think this was one truly bummed-out gal.

There were bathrooms flanked to either side, Deadheads shuffling in and out of them, bopping and shimmying to the music.

"She had rings on her fingers and bells on her shoes/And I knew without asking she was into the blues/She wore scarlet

begonias tucked into her curls/I knew right away she was not like other girls... "

And then a terribly familiar girl emerged from the bathroom. I didn't notice any rings on her fingers or bells on her shoes. And she certainly didn't look like she was into the blues. But I did know right away she was not like other girls.

It was Camden.

I hadn't seen her since high school graduation ceremony two months earlier. That Tears for Fears song "Everybody Wants to Rule the World" was playing on the car radio during the distressful ride up to the school. Not the most significant detail in the world, but one I don't think I'll ever forget.

"Welcome to your life/There's no turning back... "

I muscled through a double-take so strenuous, I nearly pinched a nerve. Camden? At a Grateful Dead show? In Saratoga, New York, no less? It didn't make sense. What the Hell was she doing here? She was a Bon Jovi fan. Did she lose a bet? And whom could she possibly be with? I watched her head back to her seats, unsure whether to go say hello. Or goodbye.

She was always in my stadium.

Knowing it was a wildly controversial decision, I gave up my place in line and followed her. A pursuit as dizzying as it was discreet, as I was careful to keep my distance, the whirlwind of pharmaceuticals crackling through me; the stage lights crashing and flashing, casting intermittent phosphorous glows upon the crowd a-swaying and a-braying in communal synchronicity.

"Well I ain't often right, but I've never been wrong/It seldom turns out the way it does in the song/Once in a while you get shown the light/In the strangest of places if you look at it right... "

I snaked through a sea of rollicking Deadheads and tracked her, but when she finally returned to her friends, I didn't recognize any of them. They were congregated on a large blanket, a collection of tangled limbs and cigarettes and sandals and bottled juices and thwarted ambition.

"Well there ain't nothing wrong with the way she moves/Scarlet begonias or a touch of the blues... "

I watched Camden plop down beside a Deadhead with a crushed nest of black curly hair, dirty feet and epicene features. He had around 54 ratty bandanas wrapped around his neck; over-bandana'd, you might say. But he may've been a little handsome, and now he was leaning into Camden and knifing his tongue into her mouth. Oh, boy!! I abruptly halted and nearly stumbled over three prostrate Deadheads.

When she removed her denim jacket, I saw a sleeve of colorful tattoos inked on her bare bicep. Alas, I realized the error of my stupored ways: it wasn't her. Camden had no tattoos. I was simultaneously relieved, disappointed, and embarrassed, which was one dangerous power trio when blasted silly on acid.

But as I headed back to the concession stands I suddenly shuffled to a halt and spun around, mad, swirling trouble on the brain: what if those were temporary tattoos on that girl's bicep? It was entirely and disturbingly possible. What if it really was Camden? It was, wasn't it? It was her. She was hiding in plain-view at a Dead show, using fake tattoos and strange new friends as creepy camouflage.

But there was no reason to shoot a wounded man - what would've been akin to a self-inflicted gunshot to the head - so instead of pursuing this mystery any further, I returned to the concession stands and bought three cold beers.

"I had to learn the hard way to let her pass by, let her pass by..."

The guys and I had planned to stay overnight in Saratoga, but it was pouring rain after the concert, thunder and lightning vomiting across the sky. We were too zapped on acid and too cheap to look for a motel, and had a hard enough time just finding our car. Reese and Lansky - rain-swept, crazed, and out of their fuckin' craniums - had argued over where they thought the car was parked. Each got it wrong about seven different times before we finally found it.

We headed home in the hammering rainfall. Damp, soggy clothes, heads full of acid and Dead tunes on the radio.

"Like I told you, what I said/Steal your face right off your head..."

We were oblivious to what should've been obvious: we were too polluted to bother looking for a motel, but not to drive home three hours in a fuckin' hurricane?

A scattering of Deadhead hitchhikers dotted the highway in a weary, listless procession; their toxic resiliency was boundless, shivering and soaked to the gills, many holding signs seeking to further their pilgrimage and hook a ride to the next town where the band would be playing. Some wore tie-dyes sporting leering skulls and skeletons - a seemingly melting frieze - that appeared more sinister in the rain as approaching headlights incrementally washed over them. Migratory, merry, and mindless, these folks were righteously devoted, all right, eternally enchanted and smitten with this band.

Reese was at the wheel, squinting through the rapid, repetitive squeal of windshield wipers. Lansky rode listless shotgun. I was in the back seat, chain-smoking, mesmerized by the sea of blinking red taillights up ahead seemingly winking at me through the blinding sheets of rain.

"Sick show, huh?" Lansky asked, finally removing his befouled bandana.

"The sickest," Reese replied.

We had a long commute ahead of us, and it didn't appear to be the best idea we ever had. We were reminded of this about an hour into the journey when a rapidly merging, rain-blurred 18-wheeler sliced out of the murky shadows like a rapacious monster, and almost sent us into the afterlife.

It was almost dawn when we returned to our hometown, stewing and slouching in quietude; completely spent, crushing fatigue having settled in. We'd managed to make a quick breakfast stop at a 24-hour McDonald's Drive-Thru and I was awash with relief that we'd beaten the rain and avoided the 18-wheelers. We were happy as Hell to be home, our brains still a trifle bouncy from the chemicals we'd ingested.

The streets were dead, the morning dew glittering from bright, green lawns, as yet unencumbered by daily newspapers or fresh dog shit. We were dropping off Lansky first. He lived on a quiet street nicknamed "Alimony Ave," which was lined with duplexes that housed divorced women exclusively.

I almost didn't recognize him without his bandana. Docile and feverish, he looked pickled, like a damaged puppet with his strings entangled and wires crossed. Reese used to joke that if you're prone to blackouts, you better have some reliable friends. The drugs had hijacked Lansky's immune system, every organ in his body now hostage to them. The toxins were leaving on their own time and not a moment sooner. That was their only ransom requirement: time. If some meta-scoreboard had been recording the results of the last 24 hours, it would read DEAD SHOW 1, LANSKY 0.

Before slowly extricating himself from the car, Reese gave him a sausage. He nibbled at it and guzzled the rest of his ice water. He was more than pleased. I think we all were. "Sick show, wasn't it?" Lansky softly said. Reese and I just smiled.

I would miss these guys.

Reese and I drove through the gloomy, overcast twilight, the long shadows seeming to guide us to the finish line. It had been a strange, interminable night, swirling with acid, malice, mushrooms and melancholy. And now it was bleeding into dawn with a ghost of blue sky creeping in, and a sliver of sunshine sneaking up the horizon like a cautious intruder. It seemed like we were the only people alive on the planet. The only other person we saw was a puffy-faced street cleaner, coasting by in that oddball robot machine. That must be a lonely job, I thought. Who applies for such a gig? That's a "morning person," all right. But were suburban streets really that dirty?

"Think that guy gets laid?" Reese asked me, eyeballing the guy in the rearview.

"I dunno."

"Are the streets that fuckin' dirty?"

I chuckled. "I was just thinking the same thing."

When we finally turned onto my street, all you could hear were the choppy PHUT-PHUT-PHUT sounds of front lawn sprinkler systems. As we drove toward Camden's house, I stole a glance at it, suddenly despairing and heartsick all over again. For a weird moment, I felt like crying. I really did. Because Camden was not like other girls. Reese gently honked his horn as we passed her house. "We maaade it, Camden," he said. I punched him in the arm, the jackass.

If high school was like a haunted funhouse ride, it had come grinding to a halt. Most were thrilled to get off and move on, but kids like me, we wanted more. More chills, more thrills, an additional chance to make up for lost time, things left unsaid, and bad decisions.

When we finally pulled up beside my house, I noticed Reese didn't look too sporty, either. Time's a funny thing, and during the course of our three-hour jaunt home, he'd grown a big zit in the middle of his forehead. Like a third eye or a battle scar. I hadn't even noticed it until now.

Everything was changing.

I waited until he drove off before planting down beside our own lawn sprinkler. Stretching out into a supine position on the wet grass, flat on my back, legs spread. The water sprayed onto me, cooling off my putrid stink. I smiled up at the coloring sky.

I'm pretty sure I haven't been happier since.

I looked forward to safely cocooning myself within the cozy refuge of my warm bed. My mother would come into my room, fraught with sleepless worry, but I would assure her that everything was fine. The guys and I had decided not to sleep over in Saratoga, that's all. Happy I was home safe, she'd kiss me atop the head and then return back to bed.

Dad was dead, just over a year now. He'd been sick for a while, but it's impossible to really prepare for the death of people you love. At least it was for me. Maybe being an only child made it that much harder. I was very close to him. You don't realize it at the time, but you end up paying a steep price for that. It's a price you would rather pay than not give a shit, either way, but also makes the end that much more painful. The ache cuts deeper, the bruising longer to heal. One day my father was gone from my life. Completely. Totally. It was so unlike him.

Don't think it won't happen to you, either.

"Real life is a motherfucker."

And maybe it was true. After all, there was cancer; death; war; paralysis; terrorism; and Steven Seagal movies.

And sometimes, she's in your fucking stadium.

"Welcome to your life/There's no turning back..."

We made it, Camden.

Sick show, huh?

WARFIELD

I couldn't sleep at all in Miami. There were so many questions. Where are you, Doc Holiday? What will you dream about tonight? What will I dream about? Do you know that we killed your girl? Do you know that she suffered terribly? Do you know that we left her in pieces? Do you know that I'm sorry? (And if you cheat on your wife with another girl, but that girl dies... does that still count as *cheating?*) Do you know that, according to legend, a man named Stanley Port-O-Potty was said to have built the first Port-O-Potty from the bones and cartilages of his slain mother, Bernice?

Thank-God for the Internet, right?

PART SEVEN

ZOMBIE CONFIDENTIAL

"What happens on Spring Break stays on Spring Break."

-- Bumper sticker

"In your head, in your head
Zombie, zombie, zombie... "

-- The Cranberries

DOC HOLIDAY

On TV, Criswell, from the seminally egregious Science Fiction classic "Plan 9 from Outer Space," was madly declaiming," *Greetings, my friend. We are all interested in the future, for that is where you and I are going to spend the rest of our lives. And remember my friend, future events such as these will affect you in the future. You are interested in the unknown, the mysterious, the unexplainable. That is why you are here. And now, for the first time, we are bringing to you the full story of what happened on the fateful day. We are giving you all the evidence, based only on the secret testimonies of the miserable souls who survived this terrifying ordeal. The incidents, the places, my friend we cannot keep this secret any longer . . . "*

I clicked off the TV. It was 3:41 a.m. Two days after my return from Canard Beach. I hadn't slept much since. During the previous 48 hours, I had constantly attempted to locate the other Boogeymen, but their respective contact information had disappeared. Cell phone numbers were disconnected and Facebook accounts deactivated; either that, or they'd chosen to "hide" me as a friend. Or "block" or "unfriend me." They definitely weren't "checking in" with me. They were completely gone.

I had spent all day channel-surfing, jumping back and forth between the major news stations: CNN – my go-to Tragedy Network - FOX News, MSNBC, NBC, CBS, ABC. The story was everywhere now. Headline news. An endless loop on TV and the Internet: college student Jill Cassady never showed up at the buses on the morning she was scheduled to fly back to school in North Carolina. It had been considered a "missing persons" case, but was now being investigated as a "suspicious death." No one had been arrested or named publicly as a suspect in what was now a criminal investigation. Jill's ex-boyfriend at North Carolina State had been questioned, but already cleared as a potential "person of interest." Volunteers were being sought for a search, 70 of them having registered thus far, copying and distributing flyers. They called it a "leaflet campaign."

There was talk of timelines and windows of opportunity. It was still possible that Jill was alive. There were theories and rumors and speculation; there always are, but it didn't look good. It never does.

Before finally drifting off to sleep earlier, I watched a reporter do a stand-up from Canard Beach, Florida.

"Dive teams searched a local pond last night, and scores of police officers from across the region scoured several square miles. They brought in helicopters and dogs to aid their search. Police say they weren't able to triangulate Jill Cassady's cell phone to locate her when she went missing."

Oh, boy. I thought about calling the police. If I was unable to locate the Boogeymen myself, the authorities surely could. But I was too frightened to call them.

SPECIAL ED
ABC, NBC, CBS, MSNBC. CNN. Fox News. Tru TV. "Dateline." "48 Hours Mystery." The 24-hour news cycle was in serious overdrive about the Canard Beach mystery. It was crazy to watch this reality show in which we played a part. Scary, too. I won't lie to you.

WARFIELD
Sean Hannity had Geraldo Rivera on his Fox News show. They discussed the Jill Cassady case in Canard Beach. It was a riveting, often feisty give-and-take. Geraldo couldn't say for sure that Jill Cassady was even dead, and Hannity thought he was nuts. (I was surprised he didn't think Democrats were responsible her for disappearance.) I wanted to change the channel, but I knew I shouldn't.

Nikki said she thought Hannity was "kind of cute." I was repulsed. I wanted to talk to her about getting new tits. But that was still on hold. We fucked the night before. I hoped it was better for her than it was for me. My fault. I was in the background. I had much bigger fish to fry at the moment. I still couldn't believe The Boogeymen made it safely out of Canard Beach.

It was going to be another strange, awful summer.

EARLY MAN
You could turn the TV volume off, and still get the skinny behind the story: our Fair Princess had been "full of bountiful promise.

America's Sweetheart.With a sassy 'zest for life.' National Honor Society member. All-State cheerleader. Hosted tea parties for the elderly. Spearheaded rescue efforts on Facebook to save stray dogs named *Jelly Bean* and *Shaggy* and *Help! I May Be Dead By* Christmas. Performed puppet shows at orphanages. Donated both time and money to countless charities. Never without a kind word to the less-advantaged. And an organ donor, to be sure! You just know she had a 'bright, exciting future ahead of her.'"

Because I don't know if you've heard, but apparently we're not supposed to believe that underachievers ever get murdered.

DOC HOLIDAY

On the first day of my American Literature class, I was pretty sure Andy Starkovich was regarding me rather strangely. I might've been looking at him differently, too. Of course, I was really paranoid, but couldn't help but wonder: did he know something?

I was the last one seen with Jill in Canard Beach after leaving Barnacles, so I feared there were eyewitnesses who saw us leave together. Either that or security tape or hotel surveillance video that implicated me. Jill's friends in Canard Beach had surely been questioned, as well as the Assholes From Ohio and the desk clerks from The Island Oasis and Beachfront Property. Maybe even from The Cabana Inn. Jill's parents had probably hired their own private detective and large reward money was being offered.

Once again, I thought seriously about calling the police. But I didn't.

EARLY MAN

When she wasn't undergoing another spooky makeover, Fox News's Greta Van Frankenstein never saw a piece of good news worth reporting. She was your "exclusive source" for the best in quality bad news when TV Trauma Queen, Nancy Grace, was on sick leave. If it bled, Greta led. She never covered a grisly crime scene that didn't make her moist. As far as I was concerned, these ladies owed The Boogeymen advertising money.

Tonight Greta was in Canard Beach, interviewing college kids on Spring Break. It was a parade of talking knuckleheads and unreliable narrators, their breathless sound bites seeking oxygen and airplay. They were searching for an audience because everyone wants to be part of a terrible story that isn't their own.

After yet another erectile dysfunction commercial, Jill Cassady's grief-stricken ex-boyfriend was interviewed from his hometown. He fought back tears as he pleaded for answers. But as I watched this poor bastard, I couldn't help but think about the unspoken fraternity of dudes who wouldn't be grieving for the Fair Princess.

Wasn't there some boy out there whose heart she'd once eaten alive? Someone who really wouldn't feel so bad that she was missing? Someone with a little monster in his blood? Someone who actually deemed her expendable? Surely, there was. Of course there was. There always is. And probably more than just one.

But who speaks for *that* loser jihad? Who interviews them on TV, and gets their version of events, their side of the story? Wouldn't that be "fair and balanced?" Who defends that heartsick fraternity, or sympathizes with its Fellowship of the Miserable?

No one, that's who. But The Boogeymen did. We fought the good fight. And someone's gotta do it. I was sure of that.

DOC HOLIDAY

Two weeks after Jill's disappearance, her distraught parents and sister were on the news, speaking at an emotional press conference. They were desperately pleading for answers about their missing daughter and talking about "closure." It was grueling to watch, and I wondered if the other Boogeymen were also tuning in. I was guilty by association, an accessory after the fact. I hadn't turned them in yet. I had serious knowledge to impart, but my self-preservation instincts wouldn't allow me to betray it.

I could only hope those guys would fuck up somehow and get arrested for Jill's murder. I counted on this to happen. It had to unfold that way. They were all dagger and no cloak. They'd never be able to keep such a secret.

SPECIAL ED

Mr. Cassady gave me the heebie-jeebies. This was Mr. CIA Man, the guy who was capable of melting us. Yikes. I changed the channel, wanting to find something more entertaining and uplifting. Maybe an authentic Reality show. LOL.

I caught the end of an interview with Chastity Bono, now known as Chaz Bono. I didn't get it. Why would any girl wanna make herself look more like a FAT GUY? LOL.

EARLY MAN

Our Fair Princess had an older sister named Meredith. She was also pleading with the public for answers about her missing sister. Meredith Cassady was pretty and blonde and big-chested. You'd hit that. She made good TV, and I knew no one was watching "American Idol" tonight.

DOC HOLIDAY

Two months passed since the Canard Beach business, and sleep was still not easy to come by. Jill Cassady was keeping me up nights. My thoughts would pinball every which way, in a restless trajectory of profound, heartsick dread. Have they found her body yet? Will I be implicated along with the others, when they do? If so, what will be my alibi?

Since returning from Canard Beach, I'd visit a local bookstore once a week and peruse the True Crime section. With all the "Insta-Books" published these days, I was achingly curious to see what kind of story had been assembled. What the theories were, who the suspects were. I expected to see some quickie, sensationalized account of What Might Have Happened In Canard Beach, but thus far, there was nothing but innocuous speculation and clinical conjecture from "FBI cybercrime supervisors" in a few "sensational" True Crime anthologies. But I had to keep up with the Joneses.

I learned what a "murder book" is: "a colloquial term used to describe the file on an open homicide investigation. During a suspected murder investigation, all collected information relative to solving the case, including crime scene photographs, notes or observations of responding officers and investigators, forensic reports, and suspect details, is compiled into a single file, otherwise known as a murder book."

I'd also been checking the TV listings every week to see when a newsmagazine was scheduled to do an "exclusive piece" on the Jill Cassady case. Like new salt in old wounds, every night there seemed to be something in the news about her.

I couldn't stop watching and reading and listening. Maybe I didn't have enough distance yet, and that's what I needed. I had to tune myself out from it. I tried to do everything I could to exorcise and eliminate her from my mind, or at least safely compartmentalize her within a distant part of its crawlspace.

But Jill remained very much inside me, despite my best efforts at detaching myself from all thoughts of what might have happened to her. She came in waves, agonizing flashes and intermittent glimpses that intruded upon my days, nights, and dreams. She wouldn't go away. She was a bell that was impossible to unring, and I couldn't help but feel I had failed her; I had cut and run, after all. I had "punted."

But I needed to make myself forget her, and could only hope that practice really did make perfect. That it wasn't some tired old cliché, or urban myth. And weren't perseverance, persistence, and attrition supposed to pay off for the good guys? Hadn't it been drummed into our brains since we were children, that if we worked hard enough at something, anything's possible? Okay, so maybe that was all bullshit.

I climbed out of bed and shuffled over to my laptop. I logged onto FINDJILLCASSADY.COM. This memoriam website featured news and updates about forthcoming candlelight vigils, prayer services, Search and Rescue funds, charity fund-raisers, and reward money. It was a busy place.

I stared at all the pretty pictures of Jill on display. She had such a nice smile, this Maserati now stuck in Internet traffic. She looked happy as she beamed from those Missing flyers, beneath the question: "WHAT DO YOU KNOW ABOUT THE DISAPPEARANCE OF JILL CASSADY?"

Visiting this website a few times every day was a wrenching exercise. Each time I did, I thought about calling the police. Occasionally I read the online Guest Book. There were many heartbreaking condolences and signatures and personal testimonials from all across the country.

But I had no interest in signing this Guest Book, either.

WARFIELD

Another online piece about Jill Cassady captured my interest. Since it was an unsolved crime and she was a frequent Facebook user, the police and FBI were theorizing that she was snatched from the Internet. Calling the Internet the "Lord of the Flies of the high-tech age," P.K. Kessler, author of *Cybercrimes & Misdemeanors*, said the Canard Beach case illustrates the dangers that lurked on the Web: *"I'm hoping that this case will make people think twice about what they do online, and what their actions can cause in the long run."*

But they had this one figured all wrong, because the Internet was utilized for a different purpose this time. Unlike the daughter of my salesman, Ricky Wender, Jill Cassady was never targeted online - the Boogeymen were. Early Man dangled the bait before us and we took it. We made that call and the ultimate responsibility was our own. If the Internet is a "weapon," I'd contend that weapons don't kill people, people do. If someone buys a fast car and drives it 100 MPH into a brick wall, it's neither the car's nor the wall's fault. The guy behind the wheel is accountable.

When the authorities and "digital detectives" recovered Jill's computer hard drive, and her ISP provided them logs of her e-mails and Facebook account activity, they wouldn't find our names associated with her. No so-called "cyber footprints" would belong to any of us. They say that Internet service providers store all sent e-mails, usually six to nine months. But none of us had ever e-mailed or Facebooked Jill, either, so no amount of "computer forensics" would implicate any of the Boogeymen.

The police would've traced her phone calls, text messages, and P2P communications. They would've studied her Internet and WAP usage and cell tower pings, but they wouldn't have found any signs of us. So unless some incriminating surveillance video from Canard Beach suddenly materialized, we were ghosts. We had chosen to live with our decision, and as long as none of us talked we were probably safe. We could attempt to move on with our lives, even if it slowly killed us. But did Doc Holiday feel the same way?

DOC HOLIDAY

Jill's Facebook page was still active. She actually had two pages now. One was a "Fan Page," of sorts, but obviously not the kind anyone would ever want for herself. It was called "FINDJILLCASSADY," a Missing Persons page created by the police, designed to share updates on the case. People were probably checking in to see if Jill had "checked in" alive anywhere.

There was certainly nothing I "liked" about any of this, so refused to click on the "LIKE" feature. But I imagined the other Boogeymen would "LIKE" the fact she was still missing.

EARLY MAN

The media was calling the Canard Beach mystery a "circumstantial case," since no body had been recovered yet. Who lives and who dies isn't always fair. You're either in the right place at the right time, or in the wrong one at the wrong time. It's Survival of the Luckiest, is it not? It's just plain dumb luck. In fact, your whole life is. Sometimes the truly expendable people live longest. Like Andy Dick. *That* fuckhead still breathes?

DOC HOLIDAY

As the months wore on and the seasons changed, I didn't change with them. I was still thinking about Jill and trying not to think about her family and friends. They must have been frightened and grieving, or pre-grieving. After several months with few tips, leads or suspects, they knew the score: she wasn't coming home alive.

Jill had disappeared from their lives. She wouldn't be graduating from college and returning to Virginia for the summer. No more hooking up with old friends. She'd never meet her pregnant sister's little girl, nor spend holidays with her family. She would never meet her future husband. Never have children. She would never have anything else of her own. Maybe the only scary part about having everything to live for is having that much more to lose.

While her body hadn't been discovered yet, her friends and family must have feared the worst, knowing it was just a matter of time before her remains were unearthed. Missing girls usually meet unhappy endings. It was just a terrible waiting game now, and that's never fun.

And from personal experience, I knew you could never really prepare for the death of someone you love.

"Goodbye Papa, pray please for me… "

EARLY MAN

I watched more and more talking heads bloviating on TV about the Canard Beach investigation. Roundtable discussions with defense lawyers, former cops, prosecutors, and professors of criminology. The networks were selling enough Jill Cassady soap to scrub the moon. But we were buying it, and I guess that's the point.

And this was just the beginning, too. If The Boogeymen were ever brought to trial on murder charges, those jury members would be ready for their close-ups 43 seconds after the verdict had been delivered. (This probably wouldn't be a "jury of my peers" either, because my "peers" were fucking sociopaths. So how do you figure?)

But suddenly anointed experts on "reasonable doubt," they'd go on TV and plead for our sympathy, describing for us the rigors of trial sequestration. Imagine their pain and torture: they sat in a courtroom for a couple of months. They listened to the evidence. They ate lunch. Listened to more evidence. Ate dinner. Slept in hotels… away from their families! Not that!! How arduous! Imagine such torment, suffering, and agony. Hotel living away from the family! Room Service! Such horror. Please. Isn't that what most of us call a *vacation?*

I mean, where were they staying, The Hotel Abu Ghraib? Were they waterboarded every morning or was the breakfast pastry at The Marriot just a bit stale? If they really didn't wanna be members of that jury, during voir dire they coulda uttered something either racist or homophobic, and they woulda been dismissed right away. End of story. But no… they didn't say anything like that because they wanted to honor their goofy "civic duty." Wanted to be part of the story, someone else's audience.

Fifteen minutes of fame wasn't enough time anymore. Now people wanted at least a week. We all want to be superstars, no matter how repellent the behavior it takes to warrant such status. So those jurors would write their shitty "tell-all" books and enjoy whoring themselves on the news magazine shows, because here's the thing: six days from now, they'd be painfully anonymous assholes again. Reduced to meek cries in the dark.

Yeah, I know. Sucks, doesn't it?

SPECIAL ED

I watched a lot of "AC 360" on CNN. Does this Anderson Cooper guy ever sleep?! He must be bionic. He's everywhere! The Forrest Gump of the media. Did anything newsworthy ever happen before he started working at CNN? LOL. That guy needs a vacation! A cigarette break. Or a clone. LOL. But I like him. He does good work. And super cool hair.

WARFIELD

No sleep since Canard Beach. Very little, anyway. It became a chore more than ever. Sometimes I'd wake in the middle of the night and stare down at Page while she slept. Sometimes I even cried for her, trying to imagine what a haunting existence it must be for the parents of a missing child. How would Nikki and I possibly hold up under the same circumstances? Probably not so well, since our child was perfectly safe and sound under our roof, and we still weren't talking about renewing our vows anytime soon.

I had done some online research and learned about those Parents of Murdered Children (P.O.M.C.) support groups. Sadly for Jill's mother and father, there were two empty seats just waiting for them in a P.O.M.C chapter somewhere in Virginia.

Most nights I spent locked in my office, logged onto Facebook. To me, that "checked-in" feature certainly seemed dangerous as a possible abduction tool. Imagine if you were looking to harm someone and knew their exact location, because of where they'd just "checked in?" But I was much more concerned with Doc Holiday. I always went right to his page and just stare at it. I was dying to know what he was thinking.

DOC HOLIDAY

I sometimes considered calling the Detective Tip Line in Florida, but only to inquire about the case, not divulge anything pertinent concerning it. News stories periodically reported leads in the investigation, but none of them proved to be "actionable." The police investigation was said to be "pretty much at a standstill."

Jill was a ghost now except for the online memoriam page and the memories close to her loved ones' hearts and minds. I wondered if closure was something the Cassadys still really wanted or needed. It might only cut a deeper wound, one that would take even longer to heal, if ever. If it were me, and my loved one had been killed, other than wanting her perpetrators to be brought to justice and maybe even executed, I'm not so sure I'd be snooping around for the gory details.

SPECIAL ED

When I was a little kid, my cousins and I would play KerPlunk, the game with the colored sticks and the marbles. You'd gently tug at the sticks, hoping you'd be the last one standing with marbles left remaining. Well, if I was that game, all my marbles had circled the drain. I was on empty. Out. Game over. Officially void of all things marble.

Ever since my return from Canard Beach, I'd been massively lonely. My "every day" was always filled with super anxiety. You might say I'd gone a little mental. I didn't like it in my head much but you can never really clear the history that's in your squash. There's no available "app" for that yet. But someday there will be.

Sometimes when walking outside in the rain, I wished I'd be struck by lightning. Mix it up a little. Maybe all my painful memories and appetites would be erased. Captain Rehab! I know that sounds kinda silly and Sci-Fi but it would've given me a fresh start. And that could've been nice, you know.

I suppose I'd grown up all weird and disappointing and *that's* very disappointing but this was my life. It wasn't rehearsal. So it would've been a shame to waste it by constantly feeling sorry for myself.

But do you remember "IT GIRL?" She was my supermarket lovely from months ago, who I attempted to call after learning her Club Card/phone number. Well, I never erased her number from my cell phone. I love technology sometimes. LOL. When I called her, I got her voice mail but at least it finally revealed her name to me: Kate.

I went to the supermarket one day and tried a little double-agent subterfuge: I used Kate's Club Card Number upon purchasing my delectable snacks, in the hopes, somehow, of obtaining her home address. But I didn't know how to proceed with this inquiry because I couldn't very well punch in her number, and then ask the cashier what my own home address was, could I? No, sir.

So yeah, my game still needed work. But practice makes perfect, and I now had six different girls' Club Card Numbers programmed into my cell phone. Someone's bound to sink her choppers into Special Ed's tender heart again. Right? Certain girls you follow on Twitter and Instagram, and others you follow in your car. LOL.

WARFIELD

One night when Nikki was out having dinner with a friend, I drank about five beers and read Page the "Jack and Jill" nursery rhyme. "Jack and Jill went up the hill to fetch a pail of water/Jack fell down and broke his crown/And Jill came tumbling after."

Jill. The very name caused me to grow uneasy. I stopped reading and just stared blankly at the pages. I couldn't help but ponder why Jack really went up that hill with Jill. Was it just to fetch a pail of water... or do something else with *her* pail? Was it a parable for date-rape? A teachable moment? Or was I losing my mind? Maybe both.

Page gave me a curious look. "What's wrong, Daddy?" she asked. Nothing, I said. Bed time, Boo-Boo. I kissed her goodnight and went into my office. Thinking about that downer nursery rhyme. I mean, "Jack falls down and breaks his crown? And Jill comes tumbling after?" That's just great. Did they die, too, like Humpty Dumpty?

Poor Page, I thought. Every clumsy nursery rhyme stranger she'd met in her young life had either fallen off a wall or down a fucking hill.

SPECIAL ED

While working morgue security, I usually waited until the witching hours before going online. I received this message on Facebook: "A WOMAN ON THE 'FACEBOOK' OF CHEATERS WANTS YOU. A married woman on the Facebook of CHEATERS is looking to sleep with you!"

That was followed by one from the Facebook "team," whoever they are: A message from the makers of *"What serial killer are you?"*

> *"This email was sent by What serial killer are you? Hello!*
>
> *We've added a new fun guessing game to our quizzes! We'd love if you checked it out. Here's a link for each quiz you've added to your profile:*
>
> • *What serial killer are you?"*

That's a "fun guessing game?" Who are you people?! First they tell me a married woman wants to sleep with me, and then ask what serial killer I am? That doesn't bode too well for that married woman, does it? LOL.

Here's an e- mail I got: *Edward, your neighbor is an escort Hi one of your neighbors is an escort! You can see her profile for free. Get instant access to over 21,500 Escorts in the USA and International!*
Catering to all lifestyles Straight, Gay, Lesbian, Shemales and BDSM.

But I didn't bother trying to see if my neighbor was really an escort. I was paranoid all the time because I had to be, always on constant edge. The doorbell would ring in my apartment, and I'd panic... before remembering it's just the pizza delivery guy. I imagined the other guys were super paranoid, too, and lived in a constant state of quiet terror. It was our new lifestyle choice, I guess.

Doc Holiday obviously presented the biggest problem for the rest of us. He was bad for business. Presumably, he was teaching back in Boston and keeping his own ass covered. I hoped that continued to be his thinking. I imagined Warfield was in Arizona, doing his grumpy married thing. I wondered how he was holding up and hoped he was hanging in there. Early Man, too. And really, what was the alternative?

The secret of where we disposed of Jill was safe with me, and I prayed it remained the same with the others. I had faith because I needed to have faith. We actually got away with murder. Who can say that? We can. In fact, that's about all the Boogeymen and Obama had in common: "Yes, we can!"

#GotAwayWithMurder.

WARFIELD

I remained frightfully worried about Doc Holiday. I needed to know what he was thinking and continued to monitor his Facebook page to see if he'd posted anything regarding the Canard Beach mystery. Maybe a link or Status Update. But he hadn't done a thing. Maybe he was smart, and that was good for us. Or maybe he was a slow burn and waiting for the right time to blow the whistle. I didn't know what would happen then.

I stared at his Facebook profile picture a few times every day: the white silhouette on the blue background, the same anonymous image the other Boogeymen now shared. But his facelessness really started to scare me.

DOC HOLIDAY

I ran into her in True Crime. By now my bookshelves were lined with True Crime books and others on forensic science, forensic pathology, and forensic anthropology. I learned everything I could about DNA, autopsy reports, and crime scene technology.

This included a lovely tutorial on decomposing flesh and its five major stages: fresh, bloat, decay, dry, and remains. Bugs and insects can be critical to forensic pathologists in their efforts to determine where someone was killed and establishing time since death, because they move in minutes afterwards. This is called "insect succession." And because corpses are rapidly infested with maggots before they embark on breeding patterns, they may ultimately prove to contain the DNA of a victim. Or a perpetrator.

EARLY MAN

FYI: it was far easier to get away with murder prior to 1996, the year they started "mito" testing. Typical mitochondrial DNA testing reveals hair in the hand of a homicide victim; shed pubic hairs in a sexual assault; hair in discarded crime scene masks or clothing; and skeletal remains in missing persons cases. This testing is used both to establish guilt and prove innocence. The post-'96 gang might deem this period the "good old days."

DOC HOLIDAY

Many of the True Crime books were about serial killers, unlike the Canard Beach perpetrators, but I felt the need to bone-up just the same. I wasn't particularly interested in the predictably "troubled" origins of these killers, nor their actual murders. But I was eager to know how they were apprehended. I did my homework and devoured the books pretty quickly, simultaneously repulsed by these monstrous crimes and morbidly fascinated by the oddest of details and minutiae attendant to them.

I discovered that Richard Ramirez, "The Night Stalker," was "attracted to yellow houses near freeways," where he would first kill the men, then rape the women. He even gouged out his share of eyeballs along the way. A witness later identified him by the AC/DC cap he'd left at a crime scene, but he was ultimately arrested for something as benign as driving a stolen car. Ramirez got married in a California prison seven years later to a magazine editor with an IQ of 152.

EARLY MAN
Trust me: that's the only way to meet smart chicks in Los Angeles. ☺

DOC HOLIDAY
Ramirez, on life: "I gave up on love and happiness a long time ago."

EARLY MAN
Thanks, Dicky. We *never* would've guessed.

DOC HOLIDAY
I learned that David Berkowitz, a.k.a. "Son of Sam," was 16 when he attended the Woodstock Festival in 1969. His reign of .44-caliber terror began in New York City seven summers later. Six people were killed. The female victims had long dark hair, so thousands of women subsequently either cut or dyed their hair to enhance their disguises. Blonde wigs flew off the shelves of beauty supply stores during that bad summer. Serial murder won't even halt commerce in New York City.

Berkowitz, on his victims: "I didn't want to hurt them, I only wanted to kill them."

EARLY MAN
How adooorable!

DOC HOLIDAY
I read that Ted Bundy, the "Elvis of serial killers," began his murderous rampage shortly after managing to win back his ex-girlfriend and successfully proposing to her. Only to then dump her. That sure gave "cold feet" a grisly new definition. Bundy told one of his many chroniclers that he "hit a wall in high school." His IQ was 125, which wasn't bad a bad score, if it also didn't nearly match his blood-alcohol levels on the nights of his murders.

I also learned he had a daughter. Born in 1982, she was conceived during a conjugal visit with the woman he married while in prison. Doing the math in my head, I figured his daughter would be about 28 now. Now there's a girl with baggage, I thought. Think about it: you're Ted Bundy's daughter. Oh, boy. Think she's got issues?

Bundy, on killing: "You learn what you need to kill and take care of the details. It's like changing a tire. The first time you're careful. By the thirtieth time, you can't remember where you left the lug wrench."

EARLY MAN
If I'm a betting man, I'd take a look inside that dead sorority girl's rectum.

DOC HOLIDAY
Jeffrey Dahmer literally had a skeleton in his closet. The police discovered a horrifying physiological bouillabaisse in his apartment: human heads, torsos, bleached skulls, hands, and sets of genitalia. The tools of his methodical removal-of-flesh trade included a claw hammer, handsaw, muriatic acid, Soilex, and a 57-gallon drum filled with acid. Three torsos were housed within it, in various stages of decomposition.

And not to be forgotten: the 3/8" drill, 1/16" drill bits, and the hypodermic needles – Dahmer's Take-Home Fun Zombie Kit. After drilling holes into several of his victims' heads, he would inject acid into them in an attempt to create the living dead. Because that way they'd "never leave him."

EARLY MAN
Who said romance isn't dead?

DOC HOLIDAY
An eclectic mix of Pop Culture was also discovered in Dahmer's apartment: a series of gay videos, the movies *The Exorcist II, Return of the Jedi,* and a single episode of *The Cosby Show.* The contents of his kitchen refrigerator, aside from the requisite human head, consisted of only condiments: ketchup and mustard. No shit. So Dahmer was an "ironic" cannibal, in that he actually found the taste of human flesh to be bland. I wasn't sure whether this factoid humanizes or de-humanizes him even more. Sometimes, truth really is stranger than fiction.

At his trial, when the judge asked him if he had any words to say to the families of his victims – these men whom he'd drugged, dismembered, eaten, and played zombie Doctor with – Dahmer softly uttered perhaps the understatement of his serial killer generation: "I'm sorry."

SPECIAL ED
Thanks, Jeffrey! Now ALL is forgiven. LOL.

DOC HOLIDAY
I was paging through a new True Crime "compendium," trying to see if The Boogeymen got a mention, when I saw her approach. She didn't appear to recognize me, but I wasn't sure if she'd gotten a good look. I couldn't even afford to be uncertain, so shuffled over to the Young Adult section.

I discreetly glanced over at this mysterious True Crime intruder. This time she caught my gaze, and even though I averted it, she nailed me. I was busted. It was serendipity, but I knew this was how these things happened. I'd done the research. Son of Sam? Busted because of a lousy traffic ticket. Ted Bundy? They ran a bad license plate on his car and after pulling him over, discovered the goods in the trunk: a crowbar, ski masks, an awl, handcuffs, an ice pick, and garbage bags. Clearly, he wasn't en route to a baby shower.

Jeffrey Dahmer? Busted because of a guy named Tracy Edwards, a.k.a, "The One Who Got Away," who proceeded to report Dahmer's ghastly intentions to the Milwaukee police. (Me? Busted after leaving my scarf behind at the scene of a snowman assassination). So if license plates, parking tickets, a stolen car, and some lucky bastard could lead to the arrests of these maniacs, you couldn't be too safe these days.

"Do I know you?" the suspicious girl asked me.

And even though I didn't notice any black rubber bracelets around her wrists, I said, "Um, no. I don't think so."

"What's your name?" She was either genuinely interested or playing Nancy Drew, but I just lurched out of the store, hoping she wouldn't follow. She didn't.

I had thought this was Ashley, Jill's college friend. Anything was possible. I bet if you'd told Son of Sam, in the throes of his New York State of Mindlessness, that a delinquent parking ticket would be his undoing, he would either have laughed or shot your fucking face off. I wasn't taking any chances.

SPECIAL ED

At work in the morgue one night, I was playing around on the computer when I discovered this website: WWW.FINDJILLCASSADY.COM. There were many well wishes and prayers and signatures on the Guest Book page.

One of them caught my eye: "MY THOUGHTS AND PRAYERS ARE WITH YOU AND YOUR FAMILY."

-- A Concerned Citizen
BOSTON, MA

This was super unsettling. Boston, Massachusetts? Now, maybe I was being paranoid again but was this Doc Holiday's message? I was convinced it was. I couldn't believe he would take a chance and write on Jill's memorial guest book. The guilt must've been gnawing off his brain or something. This was bad news. You had to wonder if he was gonna finally report us to the police. I started to fear we couldn't trust his silence any longer.

DOC HOLIDAY

On the Saturday night of Thanksgiving weekend, I decided to attend my high school reunion. Neither Reese nor Lansky were home for the holiday. I wasn't surprised. Since they'd gotten married and had kids, they'd become more like imaginary friends than real ones.

Sometimes I was even jealous of their lives, attempting to live vicariously through them. Imagining what it must be like to exist in a conventional narrative, coming home from work every night to a family. A wife and kids – a live audience. Dinners, homework, gentle scolds, bedtime readings, a wife's love and support and understanding. Family holidays and vacations and Little League games and block parties and ballet recitals and dogs and cats and goldfish and goldfish burials.

It might've been nice to temporarily exchange their all-inclusive lives for the bruising solitude of my own. Live inside someone else's skin for a while. Take a peek behind their curtain. They'd certainly be willing to exchange skins with me, since they probably envied my autonomy and independence. My life was one long, mostly disappointing bachelor party, but they'd think it was Xanadu. They'd like to take a peek behind my curtain, seize the opportunity to step out of the batter's box for a spell.

Which is the only reason I decided to attend the reunion. I desperately needed any kind of distraction and reprieve from the True Crime books and my infectious paranoia. If nothing else, it'd be an opportunity to air out my brain a little.

And, of course, I couldn't help but wonder whether a certain next-door neighbor would be attending.

The cocktail hour was held in the foyer of the Marriott hotel. Clusters of former classmates were making effusive small talk masquerading as genuine nostalgia. I joined the fray after sticking my nametag onto my black blazer, imagining the reaction I'd get if I crossed out my name and wrote TED BUNDY, instead.

If anything, high school reunions were excuses to see who'd had grown bloated and creepy since either high school, or the prior reunion. After getting a drink, I exchanged fleeting pleasantries with some old classmates. Everywhere you looked, ordinary people were trading rather extraordinarily boring stories. Did I have a story for them, I thought.

Many people busied themselves with comparing photos of their children. "Ketel One and soda, please?" was pretty much the extent of my rap, probably seeming to play in an endless loop. You know you've had a lot of drinks when the bartender – thrown by the velocity of your consumption - interjects, "Another Ketel One and soda, right?" – before you can even place the order.

Many of us had grown out of our high school caricatures, now reduced to battered composites of our former selves. Damaged goods with thinning hair, or jowls. Certain people were shocking developments and others were almost unrecognizable, some of them veritable imposters. It was nearly tantamount to a Halloween party where you had to unmask someone in order to decipher his identity. Nobody here really knew each other anymore, so if you were seeking confirmation, verification or the slaking of bibulous curiosity, the nametags came in handy.

Andy Garland had always been a skinny, dour, gloomy lad. He was a delicate balance, the kid who could've gone either way upon his arrival into adulthood: he'd either make a ton of money on Wall Street or plunge an icepick into his ex-wife's brain, and hydrate from it with a Krazy Straw. But tonight he was monstrously misshapen, like he'd been eating broken toys.

He felt the need to show me a picture of his new baby, before oddly oversharing how grateful he was because his wife had miscarried two times in previous years. Which was twice as much information as I needed.

At some point we got word that we could enter the ballroom, and everyone but me dispersed and shuffled through the double-doors. I remained behind and surveyed the row of tripod collages rooted at the back of the foyer, composed of old photos from our high school years; big, ambitous hair, carefree smiles, unbridled and unfettered optimism, and pimples.

The collage at the very end of the row consisted of photos of our deceased classmates. The Class Dismissed Collage. The deaths of former classmates are always hiccups in the Nostalgia Tour, and sadly, some of us had perished since high school graduation. Now their smiling senior yearbook pictures were blown up to the size of headshots. No one wants to miss a party.

Maybe someone always has to die, so the rest of us can count our blessings, I thought, before realizing the glaring omission on this posthumous gallery: Tracey Finn's picture.

Seemed like a terrible oversight unless The Collage Committee discriminated against suicides. But then I realized that, unlike the deceased others on display, Tracey died during high school. Hence the omission: she wasn't grandfathered in.

There was a decent spread of food inside the ballroom, along with a cash bar and a DJ. I heard Nirvana's old crowd-pleaser, "Smells Like Teen Spirit," one of those songs that put a stranglehold on your nostalgia. But not so much anymore; now it was mere background music. You may've remembered first hearing this song at a house party back in high school while inhaling your first Whippit, courtesy of an empty whipped cream bottle. Yet from now on the only thing you'll associate with it is the sight of Brian Baxter nearly finger-banging the cheese plate.

Then, amid the teeming throng of my former, nearly hypomanic classmates hitting and quitting conversations before moving onto the next target... I saw Camden.

Flanked by two old friends, she was standing by the double-doors as a groundswell of support threw itself at her as if, two months earlier, she'd discovered the cure for cancer. I didn't see any husband in sight. I recalled his name being Tucker, but it may as well have been "Whatever."

But Camden looked great, by far the prettiest belle of this goofy, swollen ball. I watched her say hello to some people, extending the requisite breezy smiles and fake hugs. I started to rehearse the conversation in my mind. She'd lived in my head for so long, practically taking up permanent residence, and maybe tonight was an opportunity to ask her how the accommodations were. *And can I get you anything?*

A little contact would be nice, so I would sequester her undivided attention for a few minutes, but not much longer, because I didn't want to come off as clingy and annoying. I'd say, "I have something terrible to tell you, but hope you'll forgive me." Momentarily concerned, she'd ask "What?" I'd smile and say, "You look amazing." She'd laugh. Wouldn't she?

After steeling myself – and hoping I wasn't too drunk to be breezy and charming and cool, or that my breath didn't smell like garbage – I started to approach her. Navigating through the meandering swirl of people, I nearly sideswiped Warren Olson and his mountain of noodle salad. But when Camden saw me approach, well, let's just say Mohammad Atta would've greeted me with more warmth. It was in her eyes: the wariness, the fear and queasy dread. It was a "tell."

In a frozen moment, I managed to say "Hey" to her, before pecking a cursory kiss on the side of her head, even as she slightly shrank away. She did. She shrank away.

Who shrinks away?

I darted out of the ballroom, feeling like Buckner exiting Fenway Park after a premature homecoming visit. I nearly collided with two former classmates - Hayworth and Fraini - who were leaving to meet their wives for Chinese food.

Seething and sucking ice from my empty cocktail, I repaired into the Men's Room and attempted to simmer down. What the Hell was Camden's problem? Yes, she'd been too cool for school, but no one's too cool for a school reunion. I mean, come on. And I thought I was obsessed with living in the past?

I had only seen her periodically over the past few years, usually at McCourt's Pub on those Wednesday nights before Thanksgiving – the local, traditional bacchanal. We always exchanged volleys of fleeting, friendly hellos; it was transitory but amiable, no harm, no foul. So unless she'd heard rumor that I'd been ass-raping small Laotian boys in my spare time, there could be no other explanation why her reception of me was so frigid.

All right, so I once decapitated her snowman. Guilty. And I self-poisoned myself with Peanut M&Ms just so I could hang out with her a bit longer. Guilty.

"Billy, you're crazy."

"Guilty."

But all of that was ancient history. I returned back into the ballroom and secured another drink, my mood so befouled that when I spotted Andy Garland showing baby photos to yet another unsuspecting target, I felt like reminding him that the evolution of his wife's uterus was of no interest to anyone. I certainly regretted coming to this reunion. It was supposed to be a fun, harmless, frivolous affair, but instead had only managed to summon the embittered ghosts of my creepy youth.

I was certainly curious to imagine what the Hell Camden and James Grybosh were possibly talking about. Why all the frothy repartee? You said four words to him in high school, and now you give a shit? Back in high school, Grybosh would follow you around like a comet, ultimately earning the nickname "Fire Marshall," because whenever he'd approach you at a party, you'd attempt to flee to the nearest exit.

But now Camden and Grybosh were getting along famously, catching up on old phantom times. She was engaging him like she genuinely cared – nodding, smiling, and laughing. How peachy and poignant. Because they shared such a rich, colorful history together, right? Please. She even guffawed. Yeah, she did. Who *guffaws?*

I wanted to open fire.

At least I shared a colorful history with her, even if it had been a black-and-blue one. To wit: we had something, even if was nothing. And at a high school reunion, that should serve as viable currency. But she still shrank away.

Glenn Flanagan took up the chatty cudgel from Grybosh, the same Glenn Flanagan who Camden also probably said four words to in high school: "Leave me alone, please." Or maybe even six words: "Leave me alone, you creepy shithead." Yet now they were annoyingly chummy and feasting on delusions of nostalgia.

In 11th grade, Glenn Flanagan heard of a new, cheaper way of getting high. Genius that he was, he stuck a bicycle pump into his rectum, because the "rush" of air was said to create a momentary high. True story. I couldn't make that up. But he didn't get high. What he got was small intestine damage and a legacy of scorn and infamy. So why wasn't she shrinking away from him?

I thought maybe I could wangle another moment with her, but the potential for adding insult to grievous mental injury was too great. No need to shoot a wounded man. She was far too busy and preoccupied anyway, her fan club boundless and impenetrable, pooling around her makeshift receiving line. Tipsy lemmings waiting to exchange revisionist histories.

Instead, I returned back into the foyer, oozing malice and melancholy. I'd had enough non-fun here. I removed my cell and called a taxi. Then I tore off my nametag, now wishing it had read TED BUNDY, if for no other reason than he would've had a better night.

I found myself actually jealous of Hayworth and Fraini and their Mai Tais, egg rolls and boneless spareribs; maybe even envious of their sleepy, predictable little married lives. Wives and Pu Pu Platters and sweet liquor drinks, and maybe a hot young, one-for-the-spank-bank nanny waiting patiently back at the house. What more could a guy want ten years after college?

Biding my time until my taxi arrived, something compelled me to return to the deceased classmates' collage. "Life changes. Stay in touch." Early Man had found a way to "stay in touch" with the Boogeymen, and now there was a missing college girl in Canard Beach who'd never get to "check in " at her first high school reunion. Maybe "staying in touch" is overrated. No one's ever thought of that? (And again: who guffaws?)

Emboldened by the confluence of vodka and dread, I was feeling bullish that Tracey Finn's picture absolutely deserved to be on the collage, even if they deemed it imperative that an asterisk be placed beside it.

The faces on the collage smiled down at me. As shitfaced as I was, I remained fervently lucid with a singular knowledge of which I felt obliged to impart to these ghosts.

"You guys didn't miss much."

WARFIELD

Nikki's parents came to the house to celebrate Page's birthday. They were a convenient diversion, and since Canard Beach they had proved to be a welcome distraction. If marriage consists of necessary evils, this was one I could live with. But I wasn't faring so well with the other one on my plate.

And presently on my office computer screen. I was online and staring at the latest troubling news about Jill Cassady's disappearance: the police had generated a composite photo. It was a work-in-progress, stemming from a few eyewitness accounts in Canard Beach.

I quickly e-mailed Early Man and Special Ed on their dummy Facebook accounts. Early Man's new screen name was DR. FRANKENSTEIN. Special Ed's was JOHN DOUGHY #2. Mine was MR. HYDE.

It was the first time any of us had made contact since Canard Beach.

SPECIAL ED

Early Man and I received a panicked e-mail from Warfield. Had we seen today's news? The police were creating a composite sketch of one of Jill Cassady's alleged abductors. It was described as a "rough, digital sketch." Yikes! I decided I would grow my hair back and give myself a self-made makeover. An identity change was necessary!

EARLY MAN

I attended another fund-raiser that my Good Samaritan sister was co-hosting. This one was a "tolerance" foundation, devoted to hate crime prevention. I didn't understand the concept of a "hate crime." Does it really matter whether you hated or dated the victim?

For example: would anyone really feel appreciably better if the kids who pummeled Matthew Shepard beyond human recognition told the jury they actually cared for his company? It's not bad enough they nearly shoved a chainsaw up his ass? Where's the confusion? What's unclear? You think they were actually *fond* of him?

I had become intolerant of all this "tolerance" for sale. It was a bit much. They had to go build a mosque near Ground Zero? That was so fuckin' necessary? It was like throwin' a Back-To-School Sale sponsored by the Columbine killers. Hey, while we're at it, why don't we make a stop at the guns 'n ammo emporium, so the D.C. snipers can do a little schmying? Maybe find Casey Anthony proper employment at a day care center? Or a new car with an extra big hatchback just in case she gets a hankering for a Girls Night Out?

And *I'm* the irresponsible one?

It was around midnight when I received the e-mail from Warfield, regarding the police composite sketch. Until now, three of us had remained elusive fugitives, lucky enough to have eluded and evaded the authorities every step of the way, while the fourth one remained a mytery.

But someone in Canard Beach had seen us, after all. Or was it Doc Holiday himelf who had anonymously provided the police with the composite sketch description? I didn't think so, and could only hope this was a false alarm. Special Ed and

Warfield asked me What do we do? But for once, their fearless Adventure Captain didn't have an answer for them.

DOC HOLIDAY
The composite photo splashed across the news and Internet was thrilling news. Unsettling, too, but the good news was this: the FBI was now involved in the investigation, and it looked like they were getting closer to nabbing the other Boogeymen. Of course they were. Good things happen to people who wait.

WARFIELD
Selfishly, I had to pray the sketch wouldn't look like me. That it wasn't me. I started to grow a beard. Nikki hates facial hair. This was going to be interesting.

EARLY MAN
Every few days, the white blank of the composite sketch filled in more and more. The features grew sharper, the edges smoothed out. It was starting to resemble an actual person. I could only watch and wait. Which was all any of us could do.

SPECIAL ED
The composite picture had hair! So it wasn't me. LOL.

WARFIELD
It definitely didn't look anything like me, but was still a close call. I decided to continue growing my beard.

EARLY MAN
When the police composite sketch was completely fleshed out, it resembled neither Special Ed, Warfield, or myself. I suppose I wasn't really surprised. In fact, the sketch resembled someone else entirely.

And introducing... from Boston, Massachusetts... Give it up for... The Head of the Snake! Cue the applause. ☺

DOC HOLIDAY

In the faculty lounge at the Community College, I stared up at the TV in quietly growing horror, as I struggled to ingest a mouthful of tuna fish that was starting to taste like ass. I fixed on the composite sketch displayed on CNN. I was pretty sure it resembled me, or certainly more so than it did the other Boogeymen.

But this made sickening sense. Of course it did. It was me who was talking to Jill most of the night at Barnacles. It was me who went back to my motel room with her. It was me her friends and the police were searching for in Canard Beach. It was me.

Now I definitely wasn't calling the police anytime soon. Unless I had no other choice. Because sometimes you get there a little too late.

WARFIELD

Maybe I'd been studying Facebook for too long, or maybe just going crazy, but the composite sketch almost resembled The Boogeymen's factory setting profile picture: the white silhouette with tousled hair. It was eerie. And still too close for comfort.

SPECIAL ED

What's that expression? "It's better to be wanted for murder than to not be wanted at all?"

WARFIELD

I started spending more and more time locked in my office at night after Nikki and Page were asleep. I'd log onto Facebook and go directly to Jill Cassady's page. I often cried for her, usually during my commutes to and from work. I became the colicky husband and father. I wasn't well at all, felt like there were barking dogs under my skin. I didn't know how much longer I could go on, not like this, not living this way, knowing what we did. What I did to her, and didn't do to save her.

Nikki practically begged me to shave the beard. She still had her needs and I had my wants, yet neither of us knew how to bridge that gap very well. "Hey, I stopped giving you a hard time about your hair, didn't I?" I scolded. She didn't understand why I'd grown so cantankerous and contentious. I loved my wife and wanted her to be happy, but I just didn't touch her all that much anymore. Our conversations were curt and my fuse was a lot shorter than hers ever was. I also didn't give a shit how she wore her hair anymore or if her parents voted for the Nazi Party in the next election.

I started drinking about six beers every night after work, instead of two. My marriage was still a robotic, rewind-and play existence, but with a dangerous glitch in the machine, always threatening to bubble to the surface and blow the whole thing into flames. My life had an unspeakable secret, one I fought daily to keep at bay. Good thing I didn't talk in my sleep, nor was stricken with Tourette's Syndrome. If so, good chance I'd be on Death Row by now.

On TV one day, President Obama was saying, "Don't fear the future." But the future is the only thing I could fear, so my eyes and ears would always be open. I needed to be vigilant and remain on personal "High Alert," if I didn't want to lose it all. If I didn't want Page to grow up knowing her father did a really bad thing.

DOC HOLIDAY

It was both disappointing and agonizing that the composite sketch never did provide a hard lead for the police or FBI. Nothing substantial panned out from it. In fact, a second composite was being drafted, and the thinking was that maybe there were two people responsible for Jill's abduction. Unfortunately, their theory fell one person short.

SPECIAL ED

No news was good news. As more time passed, there were fewer and fewer developments on the missing girl in Canard Beach. The media had moved on.

EARLY MAN

LGBT's slogan "It gets better," probably applied more to The Boogeymen than it did those gay, transgendered oddballs, because there's always a new villain to "steal" the headlines and grant you a hiatus or reprieve. A breather. Yesterday it was about you, but today it's about the psychopath in Ohio who decapitated his Special Needs son. Or cannibalized her baby's intestines. Or dismembered his wife and uploaded the pictures of her remains on Tinder. Or Zoosk. Or whatever the next fucking one is called.

Someone else is always wagging the dog and upping the stakes for the ravening news cycle. And the latest distraction was a school shooting in New Jersey. Some goofy bastard riddled his classmates with a semiautomatic weapon.

I watched some interviews in the wake of the massacre. Predictably, in describing the gunshots they'd heard, a few witnesses explained that, at first, they thought "the sounds came from a car backfiring."

Really?

Do cars backfire that often? So often, that you actually mistake gunfire for them? GUNFIRE? I don't think so. In fact, in your entire lifetime you've probably heard more live gunshots go off, than cars backfiring – or at least an equal amount.

Still other witnesses voiced a different take on things: "First, we thought the sounds came from firecrackers." You did? Really? Were you high? FIRECRACKERS? Why? Was the shooting on the 4th of July? Because if it wasn't, why would you think firecrackers were suddenly poppin' off in the middle of the day?

FYI: cars don't backfire that often and firecrackers don't pop off in the streets the other 364 days of the year, so stop showing up on TV newscasts, yearning for face time and scratching at your openings and pretending you're Sherlock Holmes.

Are we clear?

And other stunned, frightened locals voiced their outrage to the media, attempting to divine some sense from the inexplicable. Invariably shouting out what's become the latest indignant American epitaph: "How could this happen here?"

But let's face it: Rome may not have been built in a day, but all it took was ten minutes to fuck that shit up sideways. Like New York City on 9/11. It can happen here. And it does, doesn't it? "Here" is the new "There," in that no populace is impervious. No one's truly immune or ever really safe. They're either just lucky or unlucky.

After the news story ended, they went straight to a commercial for erectile dysfunction. The Fair Princess had become back page news. It was inevitable, because we don't live in a vacuum anymore. Our memories are shorter than our attention spans. Jill Cassady may have been a fabulously cool girl with white teeth, great hair, and a high, lovely ass, but even she couldn't compete with the rest of the big, bad world.

No one can.

DOC HOLIDAY

I thought about Jill Cassady waving at me in Barnacles as she joined up with her friends. I thought about us dancing; the smell of her perfume; the way her cocktail sloshed inside her glass the more she moved to the music. She was having a wonderful, carefree time in what's really the springtime of her life. She was in college and graduating in a few months. Loved her classes. Had lots of friends. She was happy and healthy and beautiful. The future was hers.

Except the Boogeymen – these terrible tourists - have crashed the Spring Break party that is her life. Wolves in sheep's clothing with axes to grind, they've found the handle they've been looking for.

"Are we still in character?" Early Man asks us, grinning madly. And sadly for Jill, her loved ones, and everyone she's ever known… they are.

I woke up from this nightmare, momentarily incapacitated. I had to shake it off and jump in the shower. I had classes to teach. During my morning commutes to the Community College, I tried not thinking about Jill's friends back home and in college, who would have to delete her name and number from their cell phones and e-mail address books. Essentially delete her from their lives. These things wouldn't be easy.

"Goodbye friend, it's hard to die… "

During the week I read essays and homework assignments, and on the weekends I laid pretty low. Dinner at my mother's house every Sunday; an occasional foray into Boston for drinks with a couple of fellow single teachers at the school. A few wanted to fix me up with some of their friends, yet I wasn't ready for any of that just yet. But perhaps Bundy's daughter and I would've gotten along just fine.

My life became a pretty pedestrian routine. I wondered if it would always be this way. If I was lucky, it would. Anonymity – that was the ticket. The composite sketch was the last straw. I no longer attempted to contact the other Boogeymen or find them online. If I'd been searching for them before, now I needed to hide myself.

The longer it took for Jill's body to be discovered was the distance I needed. I was guilty by association, but as long as she wasn't found I was also innocent by association. Naturally, I dreaded the notion there might be dangling loose ends. And if there weren't now, there might someday be an inculpatory thread that came loose and tightened the noose around my neck.

If the others were arrested, they'd surely claim I was equally complicit. If Jill was dead I couldn't bring her back, and I couldn't reasonably defend myself, either: I had fled Canard Beach nearly as fast as the others. How would I explain such behavior?

I recalled three words Early Man had written at the tail end of his online seduction: "safety in numbers." Now I was pretty sure what he meant: the more accomplices the merrier, because the blame could be spread thinner or parsed out. A fiendish democracy meant the net could be cast that much wider, possibly absolving or mitigating the others' murderous involvement. Maybe that's why Early Man's online invocation claimed he was "looking for an audience."

So until or unless my burden became too haunting to keep under wraps any longer, my lips were locked. Had to be. There was no way around it. I would play it by ear, that's all. This notion of such stubborn, even irresponsible inaction plagued me with an inordinate amount of guilt. There was no way around that, either.

Some days, it escalated and resurfaced, only to slightly taper off or plateau during others. But it was always there, noodling around. I sure needed to get my story straight if the inexplicable happened: I was arrested along with the others. It was a work in-progress. What would I tell the police? The truth or the fiction? Each was stranger than the other.

I had dreams where I would be driving to work in the morning, and glimpse a small plane aerial advertising above in the sky. But it wasn't skywriting ads for casinos, beer, banks, retail stores, or cell phone providers. What was skywritten was this: ☺

I'd pin the gas and race away, but it followed me, gliding along the vast blue sky in ostensibly gleeful pursuit - ☺ - as if tracking or targeting me like a drone. And when it suddenly broke out in a spasm of hysterical, jeering laughter, it sounded like my laughter. That's when I'd jerk awake, breathless and fighting to re-orient in the darkness. Oh, boy.

Other dreams featured seven or eight strange, dark planes soaring overhead, like an alien invasion. But they weren't advertising vodka, doughnuts, airlines, or Internet providers.

They were advertising this: "JUST REMEMBER: YOU FUCKED HER FIRST."

That's when I would wake up, mortified and flailing in the shadows, as if punching at phantoms. Before going to bed every night, I hoped I wouldn't suffer another disabling dream. Either way, when I woke up in the morning, the ominous reality would hit home again, the incontrovertible truth: there was a ghost in Canard Beach. Her name was Jill Cassady. Now dead and gone. Completely out of this life. Removed from it.

Just like me.

WARFIELD

On Christmas Eve, Nikki's parents arrived early to assist her with dinner. I was locked in my office, sucking on my third vodka-egg nog and Googling images of Jill Cassady. I had started to do this in recent weeks, always making to sure to clear my history on the off chance Nikki wanted to use my computer.

I started thinking about those last moments during our savage weekend in Canard Beach. Special Ed was in the bathroom getting busy with those tools. Early Man stood by the window, peering out from behind a curtain. His crazy wheels were spinning. "Beautiful night to bury a body," he said. We could hear Special Ed periodically groaning in disgust, the kinds of noises I never hope to hear again.

"Too bad chainsaws don't come with silencers," Early Man said, as if a noise reduction device was the key to solving our problems.

"What are we going to do with the body?" I asked.

He shrugged and exhaled smoke toward me. "I'm open to suggestions." Suggestions?! Body disposal wasn't exactly my bailiwick, thank you very much. I hadn't expected Human Sacrifice to be on our TO DO list. I was in software sales.

Yes, okay, the ocean was the obvious choice if you were playing this game. You chum the waters, play the percentages. Dump the parts in there and hope they become fish food before anyone's the wiser. Disposal would need to be done under the cover of darkness, which we had on our side. But the beach was too far from our motel, and we weren't sure we had that much time.

Early Man said something about a storage facility or a cemetery, but we didn't have time for any more "shopping." We were going to have to improvise now more than ever.

"Hey, how come you didn't invite us Boogeymen to your wedding?" he asked.

"We're really having this conversation right now?"

"It's just a question."

"Maybe 'cuz I preferred my wife's bridesmaids to survive the weekend."

When Special Ed had finally emerged from the bathroom, his doughy white body was spattered in gore. He looked like The Michelin Man after dismembering a rival mascot. Totally spent, if not considerably traumatized, he strained from the weight of the four garbage bags he was dragging.

Early Man looked staggered, the air deflated from his sinister balloon. "Shit," he said. "I bought the wrong fucking bags." And that's when I noticed for myself: Jill's parts were visible within those bags, because Early Man had mistakenly purchased *transparent* ones. Oops. Only then did Special Ed himself realize the error of Early Man's consumer ways. "Yikes," he said, and released his grip on them.

"Some Adventure Captain," I said to Early Man. "Maybe you should keep your day job." He muttered something about how that was his day job.

We needed to close this deal fast. Someone had to be responsible and accountable, so I immediately left for the CVS across the street. I bought the proper black Economy-sized garbage bags. The rest is history. And we were definitely on the wrong side of it.

But tonight was Christmas Eve, worlds away from the horrors of Canard Beach, yet not far enough. I drank a good deal of wine during dinner, attempting to tame the creatures in my head. I didn't talk much and ate even less. Nikki asked if I was okay, and I told her I was just a little tired. She kissed me and made some comment about how she "missed my face." Her father wasn't a fan of my beard, either, saying it looked "like a dog's ass."

I drank more wine and built a quick buzz, until I became so disoriented that the room started spinning around me; the dinner conversation overlapping, silverware clattering, Page giggling, my in-laws goo-gooing to her, Nikki, oblivious, throwing me a covert little air kiss.

Maybe I was tired of the lies and the guilt and the petty obfuscations since Canard Beach. Maybe my game face couldn't hold itself together anymore. Maybe I couldn't sustain being a "man" much longer. What kind of man does what I did in Canard Beach and then at holiday time, casually passes the mashed potatoes across the table?

Maybe the circuitry boards beneath my skin were on the fritz, the glitches in the robot about to cause an explosion. I could feel tears building in a slow but inexorable gathering, as Nikki announced she was going to bring in the coffee and rice pudding. I thought about Jill as I gently swiped a drop of gravy off Page's cheek. And Jill's severed head at the bottom of that transparent garbage bag, as I passed the carrot cake to my mother-in-law.

All charming Christmas thoughts, no? So, no, I wasn't well. Not me. And as Nikki brought in the coffee, the recent nightmare jumped to mind, the one I'm afraid I'll never get out of my head. It kept me home from work for two days, bed-ridden and crippled with trepidation:

I was online and clicking on the "Free Video Chat With Strangers" feature. But imagine my surprise when Jill Cassady's dull, ashen face filled the screen. Her head was attached to the scaly, coiled body of a Rattlesnake. It thrashed fiercely, the rattle of its tail hissing barbarously, as it sliced and snapped into the camera.

Jill was missing her left eye, the jagged raw socket starting to blacken and scab over. She was dead… yet she wasn't. (I was beginning to know the feeling). "What's a stranger but a friend waiting to happen?" she teased with a smile, blowing me a kiss.

She was daring me to go on living like this, *with* this. Challenging me to play this game for the rest of my life. Early

Man had "created an Event" on Facebook. Come as you are. So we did.

And now there was a dead college girl who wasn't home in Virginia for Christmas.

SPECIAL ED

I spent Christmas Eve home alone and on my computer. I was still much cooler online. But it was tough to play with Words With Friends when you didn't have any friends.

> #BahHumbug!

DOC HOLIDAY

On Christmas Eve, the roads were laden with black ice and nine inches of snow practically entombed the grounds, dirty and rock-hard, heaped high in banks alongside them. Ernest Hemingway, when asked why the chicken crossed the road, replied: "To die. In the snow. Alone."

It was that kind of weather, and not unlike how I was feeling. I was slowly driving home from the 7-Eleven because my mother had run out of some dessert ingredients. I'd offered to go procure them, and though she was dubious due to the dicey road conditions, I promised to drive carefully. The Pretenders' Christmas anthem, "2000 Miles" was playing on the car radio. *"2000 miles is very far through the snow/I'll think of you wherever you go..."*

Reese and Lansky were in town for this holiday and had left me messages. I would return their calls later, or maybe not, preoccupied as I was with thoughts of the Spring Break skeleton in my closet. Holidays without their daughter had to be particularly trying times for Mr. and Mrs. Cassady back in Virginia.

> *"Goodbye Papa, it's hard to die... "*

Yet if someone called the Cassadys on Christmas Day and told them what became of their daughter, would this be considered a Christmas gift? Would they be grateful for the closure, or would it just darken their holiday all the more, like finding poison under the tree?

As I carefully negotiated the car down my mother's street, I saw several cars parked alongside Camden's old house. It was dressed up nice with pretty, colorful Christmas lights. Inside it, chestnuts were doubtless roasting on an open fire. The Millers were obviously hosting the holiday festivities.

And despite not being invited to the party, I pulled over across the street and killed the engine. Fueled by bittersweet memories and probably more ill-advised judgment, I climbed out of the car and turned to face the house. I started treading slowly towards it. The front yard was flanked by a stand of listing, skeletal trees, their bony branches tentacled in icy dread; their spirits broken, like starving dinosaurs fossilized in the freeze. Hunchbacked and disfigured, as if crippled with Osteoporosis, the trees appeared to snarl and grimace from the savage wind chill. *It must suck to be a tree in winter,* I thought, before realizing that was probably the single most retarded thing that's ever crossed my mind.

I trudged on, lurching through the high drifts, knotting my scarf tighter around my neck. I stopped about halfway, and began gathering up clumps of snow. I started building a snowman. Fierce winds sliced at my face, chapping my cheeks raw and stinging my eyes. But I would build this snowman if it were the last thing I'd ever do.

Because Camden was still in my stadium.

It didn't matter that she was married to that Tucker guy. I was happy she was if for no other reason that it meant she was safe and sound. She deserved that. But building this snowman was a way of paying my respects to myself, of protecting the memory. I constructed it in fairly quick, haphazard fashion. He certainly wasn't going be the tallest snowman on record.

I was nearly finished when floodlights popped on, slicing through the darkness and exposing me in their glow. The front door opened and Camden emerged. She wore a red wool sweater, blue jeans, and Uggs boots. She had bulky gray earmuffs wrapped around her head. Most people look downright silly wearing earmuffs, but not Camden. She even wore them with a decidedly stylish verve. I noticed her hair looked different.

But it was her.

"Billy?" she asked, walking toward me, shaking out a shiver.

"Hey." It was the best I could do. I wanted to die right there in the snow.

"What… what are you doing?" she asked.

"I know."

Which didn't answer her question. She was right, of course: what the Hell was I doing? But she masked her incredulity, braced herself against the chill, and generously chose to change the subject. "How have you been?"

"Pretty good. You know. You?"

"I'm all right."

We gently embraced and pecked each other kisses. "Are you okay?" she asked.

"Yeah. Yeah, I'm, yeah. I'm okay."

She shook her head. "Billy," she said.

"What?"

She looked almost embarrassed. Maybe even scared. "What are you doing here?"

Sharon Tate couldn't have asked it better.

"Are you all right?" she asked.

"Yeah," I said.

Oh, no! I wanted to say. *Very much no. Want to hear it? Check it out: Once upon a time on The Internet, I reconnected with three old camp friends… And we went to Florida last March, during Spring Break… A real clash of civilizations, I tell you… A total descent into madness and extremism… And this girl I met – WE met — she kind of reminded me of you. But ended up being abducted by them… You see, sometimes it's bad luck to take children to the candy store… And one thing led to another… And she got all messed up… But enough about me. Am I nuts, or have YOU highlighted your hair?*

She continued to shiver as we both waited for something else to be said. I felt like a mighty jackass. What the Hell was I doing there?

"Sorry about this," I said, pointing at the snowman, already regretting this foolish snowman endeavor, just like I had the last one.

"I heard you're teaching English," she said, kindly changing the subject again. Very cool girl.

"I am."

"That's great."

"What are you doing? You're in Connecticut, right?"

She looked doubtful as to whether or not to divulge the following information.

"No. I'm divorced, Billy."

I was stunned. I hadn't gotten this memo. "Really. Sorry to hear that." It probably sounded like a lie even if it wasn't, because it wasn't as if I were eagerly waiting in the on-deck circle of her suitors.

"Thanks," she said. The conversation was already waning, but I wanted to keep it going. You always do.

"How're your folks?" I asked. Her mother was nicer than pie, her father meaner than Stalin.

"They're good, thanks. How's your mother?"

"Good. Good."

We shivered like mad, our breathy exhalations springing out of our heads like those cartoon thought bubbles. We were virtual strangers, but God she looked beautiful. Nothing was mentioned about her frosty reception of me at our high school reunion, other than her saying she was "out of it" that night. This rocky encounter, too, would be over in moments. It was too unorthodox and ass-freezing and discomfiting not to end abruptly. I wanted to give her my business card, but English teachers don't carry business cards. And she was a mother so it was doubtful she carried them, either.

The commingling of emotions nearly rendered me dizzy: I was thrilled to be chatting with Camden, even as a spasm of nausea took hold of me. I wasn't ready to say goodbye, either, because that's always harder than saying hello. Still, another part of me wanted to run screaming for the hills.

"Well, I better get back in," she said, securing a solid conversation waiver and deftly running with it. Points for her.

"All right," I said, hoping that, if she had 1-800 RESTRAINING ORDER on her speed-dial, she wouldn't hit it the second she went inside.

"So… this was weird," she said, a tight smile on her face. "Have a good Christmas, Billy. Happy New Year."

"Thanks. Merry Christmas, Camden. You, too."

We embraced again and I held on tight, pretty much for dear life. I think she did, too. I really do. I pecked her a kiss on the cheek, and this time she didn't shrink away.

But maybe she should have.

Camden was divorced now, her life stuck in neutral. Not the end of the world or anything, but I still felt sad for her. Psychopath Early Man had been right about one thing: sometimes even Maseratis have to sit in traffic. Camden had fallen down.

After we released, she gestured to my snowman. "You don't have to finish that. It's the thought that counts," she said.

"Even when you're not thinking?" I said. She chuckled and it warmed me. I wanted to say, Well, maybe when the snowman perishes, we can attend his funeral together. Because sometimes one person's loss is another person's gain. I certainly remembered how Camden and I were in united in cozy grief at Tracey Finn's funeral. And our post-mortem tonsil hockey when I drove her home from the after-party.

I could spend the rest of my life with Camden. I could've and would've, but never could and never would. As she plodded towards her house, I watched her go. I always did. But because Christmas was supposed to be about stocking stuffers and not stalking neighbors, when she turned around towards me, she looked seriously troubled. You couldn't blame her.

She approached me again, muscling through another shiver, her pretty blue eyes narrowed in suspicion. Maybe she wanted me to finally drop all pretenses, but the last thing I wanted was her pity. Not hers. Never hers.

"Billy, are you sure you're okay?" she asked.

Now that I finally had her undivided attention, I wanted to say I had something terrible to tell her, but hoped she'd forgive me. "Never better," I lied, as I stumbled toward a tree and snapped off two branches. A nest of icicles shattered apart and pieces of icy shrapnel bonked me on the head. I snatched a short icicle from off the ground and inspected it in my hands. Measuring it for maybe for too long, because she ogled me rather strangely.

"What is it?" she said.

"Nothing," I said, tossing the icicle.

She cracked an uneasy smile, even as the fine line between "Is he sweet?" or "Is he creepy?" was probably jousting for explication within her little freezing head.

I inserted the two branches - one on each side - into the snowman. They were his arms, jutting out, crooked and akimbo, as if to ask: *What the fuck? Or Can I HELP you, Mr.*

Emancipator Decapitator? Or Dude, YOU again?! Or Leave me alone, already! I was perfectly happy just being ground snow! I removed my scarf and draped it around his head. A finishing touch.

Charlie Brown's Redemption.

And then she said it, and I wished she hadn't. I really wished she hadn't. Because when she did my heart crushed like a grape all over again. Because the truth is stranger than the fiction.

"We should keep in touch," she suggested, the wind knocking her hair aswirl.

"Yeah?"

She shrugged. "Want my number?"

"How many glasses of rum and egg nog have you had?" She chuckled. Very cool. Hell, it was Christmas, the season of giving and all that, so if she was offering up Pity wrapped in a frilly Yuletide bow, who was I to discriminate? "Yeah, sure," I said, removing my BlackBerry as fast as humanly possible. She gave me her digits and I programmed them in.

"So call me sometime," she said, swiping wind-blown strands of hair from her face.

"Okay. I will," I said, and shot her a smile. "Is now a good time?"

She giggled. "Bye, Billy." She gingerly shuffled off, careful not to slip and tumble ass-over-elbows into the snow, and I wondered if she had New Year's Eve plans.

I watched her disappear into her house, wherein she killed the floodlights, leaving me dumbstruck and listing unsteadily, yet suddenly emboldened with promise and purpose. Maybe this snowman endeavor wasn't so foolish, after all. I had put my best foot forward, and certainly stepped on a few landmines along the way. But check me out: still walking.

I glanced at the snowman, as if waiting for him to chime in. Now blanketed in shadow, he looked timorous, his new scarf snapping and flapping in the wind. But I didn't need his approbation. He was just a fucking snowman.

"You're just a fucking snowman," I said to the fucking snowman. And then I realized I was actually *talking* to a fucking snowman. Not cool. But that was okay because what was cool was that I could call Camden sometime.

I finally shambled back inside my car. Blubbering from

the bruising chill, I took one last look at my snowman. He appeared to sneer at me, despite the smiling eyes and swishy smile. *Leave it alone,* it seemed to say. *Haven't you already done enough damage? Leave it the fuck alone.* Oh, boy. Not sure if you've ever taken a disturbing cue from the object of your unrequited love's snowman, but trust me: not recommended.

I jammed my keys in the ignition and started the car. Waiting for it to warm up, my eyes ticked over to Camden's bedroom window. Shaking out the chill in my bones.

The one that remains inside them to this day.

"Goodbye to you, my trusted friend/We've known each other since we were nine or ten... "

"Thanks for the ride," I said.

Have I told you she messed me up?

WARFIELD

After Christmas Eve dinner, I was alone in the kitchen washing dishes when Nikki came in. She wrapped her warm arms around me. It was a nice hug, and she held on tight. Occasionally, marriage held some surprises.

"I love you," she said, kissing me.

"I love you, too," I said.

In sickness and in health. And so many achy, unbroken desires.

I must not have sounded too convincing, because her eyes went dark with rue and a few tears slipped out of them. I still loved my wife. I just didn't care much for her anymore. She had to know that she was losing me, because she definitely was losing me. I was in the background and that's where I'd be staying. This wolf was staying behind with the rest of the pack. There was frankly no place else to hide. She had no idea that I also cried for me sometimes.

But I'd never expect you to.

SPECIAL ED

Let's face it: online was where I really belonged, and maybe if I had stayed on the outskirts of cyberspace instead of entering into it to "dare mighty things," Jill Cassady would be alive somewhere and drinking a soy latte or something.

Cyberspace accepted me for what I am. It's the only audience I needed. Judge and jury but hopefully not executioner. It would've been nice to clear my history and create a new one but I was just gonna try to keep sane in a world gone batshit mental. Besides, the neighborhood Ice Cream Man has made more people happy than you or I ever will.

I sure hoped some crazy person didn't decide to make it personal and travel to the Facebook headquarters in Palo Alto, California, or the MySpace offices in Santa Monica, California. He could detonate bombs at the entrances of both buildings, and remove them all as "friends." Sorry, Tom. Sorry, Facebook "team" – BOOM!

I put on some Christmas music and decided to drop into a few Singles chat rooms. Special Ed doesn't know a lot of things in this world, other than that a grilled cheese sandwich and cold glass of chocolate milk is his idea of perfect bliss... but here's one thing he does know: someone else is always out there.

#Won'tYouLoveMe?

DOC HOLIDAY

Joining my mother and me at Christmas dinner was my cousin Denise, her husband Jerry, and their three kids, of whom I'd privately dubbed "Good, Bad, and Otherwise."

Denise told us about her new part-time job working as a "Professional Organizer." Normally, I might've asked, "What the Hell is that? Because let's face it – what the Hell *is* that? But I didn't bother, because I couldn't be bothered. I picked at my food, mired in a distracted daze from my dizzying Camden encounter. Was I suddenly waiting in the on-deck circle of her suitors? Was I on the comeback trail?

I'd cut through the fat and chaff that was the maddeningly capricious single scene, and like any resilient soldier I'd sustained my share of wounds. The battering and the bruising, the dashed hopes, wounded ego, lonely hangovers, Suicide Sundays, the ones that got away, the ones that never came even close. The nearly surgical removal of promise. I was a little battle-scarred but unbowed, and there had always been Camden. And now there was Camden.

Yet I politely listened to Denise babble on, narrating her life for us with cheerful ebullience. She was the kind of girl who literally had 958 pictures of herself on Facebook beneath the self-important headline, "MY LIFE IN 2013." (So yeah, she was certainly organized.) As if to remind her new audience – *"Hey, I'M here, too! LIKE me!"*

After dessert, I went into my old bedroom and closed the door. I plopped onto my bed and scrolled down my BlackBerry contacts. I stopped at Camden's number, this fresh new addition. Like a cool new toy under the Christmas tree. I liked having it there. Proud of its ownership. It would remain there for cozy safekeeping. For a rainy day. It felt like a victory and in due time, I'd commit this number to memory. Just like I used to commit to memory the makes and models of all her boyfriends' cars.

I could call her sometime. Maybe meet up with her for a drink or a meal or coffee or a movie. Or maybe, when the time came, a road trip to look at the fall foliage. Dead leaves in orange bloom. A frothy good time. Whatever it takes. Valentine's Day was less than two months away, so maybe I'd buy her a heart-shaped box filled with her favorite chocolate confections: Peanut M&Ms. But this time I'd promise not to eat any myself.

Her birthday was on October 5th, and her birthdays always managed to depress me. I guess that's when you know you're really incurable. Yeah, if you weren't completely sure before, this was cold, clinical confirmation. If a fractious, turbulent history of decapitating her snowmen, eating peanuts to impress her, and memorizing the makes and models of all her boyfriends' cars left any doubt at all, being bummed out on her birthdays pretty much sealed the verdict. Every October 5th, I found myself wanting to make contact with her, if only to wish her a Happy Birthday. Now I could do that.

I could call her sometime and jumpstart this old, damaged dance all over again. At worst, we could be friends again. And what were strangers, but friends waiting to happen? Who knows what could happen from there? Maybe nothing or maybe everything. But it was worth a shot, right? Time's a funny thing.

But sometimes you get there a little too late.

SPECIAL ED

After leaving the chat rooms, I logged onto Jill's website and read some of the "Letters to the Family of Jill Cassady." I then clicked onto the Message Boards and read a bunch of those. Most of the comments were super rude, cruel, and insensitive. These trolls were hungry and calling Jill nasty names. "Whore." "Cockhound." "Sperm bank."

I couldn't believe they were talking shit about her! These cockroaches didn't even know her. She was just another girl on the Internet that didn't want to meet them. But that's all I had in common with this online lynch mob because I had dared a mighty thing. And they hadn't. They were just big, lazy cowards.

I really wanted to post warnings to these offenders: "Watch your mouth! Do you know who I am? Do you? DO YOU? Do you want to know, tough guys? Do you DARE to know? Do you dare to do a mighty thing and actually find out? I could probably find you, you know. I could show you some crazytown. Will you be so brave then?! Will you be so hateful then?! Get a digital life!"

But I couldn't write anything of this sort. I had to remain in the dark. That's where I'd always be, thinking of Jill Cassady. Vibing on her memory because her flavor had remained with Special Ed.

Ladies and Gentlemen of the Jury, I am All Things Marble! Void! KerPlunk! Game over! When is a hero really a hero?

That answer still eluded me.

DOC HOLIDAY

Charlie Brown was crying hysterically as he hovered over Lucy's newspaper obituary. "I warned you not to go out that night!" he wailed. "Didn't I?!"

I jerked awake, gasping, once again flailing in the darkness. It was after 2:00 a.m. on Christmas morning. I was back in my apartment and the screws were coming loose. I needed to talk to someone but there was nobody, so I climbed out of bed and went online. Cyberspace has no curfew, and there's always someone awake, "creeping while you're sleeping."

I logged onto a Chat Room devoted to Jill Cassady. I was the only one in it, other than someone named "Ashes2Ashes." I wasn't sure how to proceed, but maybe any kind of anonymous unburdening would prove to be cathartic.

"I'm looking for an audience," I wrote.

"??" she wrote.

I steeled myself and swiped away tears. It pained me to continue.

"I want to tell you a ghost story," I wrote.

EARLY MAN

SPECIAL ED

WARFIELD

DOC HOLIDAY

"I actually met Jill Cassady once," I wrote to Ashes2Ashes.

"For real?"

"Yeah."

"No way."

"I swear. It's true."

"OMG. Where?"

A bone-chilling thought coursed through me. I hesitated to respond, fearing this was a possible tourist trap. Wasn't it possible that "Ashes2Ashes" was Ashley, Jill's best friend? Due to my state of perpetual disquiet, I knew I was probably being paranoid and that it was highly doubtful. But the very notion of it spooked me, and I needed to choose my words carefully. I would never again underestimate the potential insidiousness of online correspondence. You couldn't blame me.

"It was a long time ago," I wrote. "I didn't really know her."

"I pray for her every day. And her family. I really do."

Before I could type back a response, another name joined the room.

SPECIAL ED: "BOO!"

I edged away from the screen, slack with dread.

"Hi, Special Ed," Ashes2Ashes wrote.

Another name popped into the room.

EARLY MAN: "Hello darkness, my old friend."

I literally jumped up from my chair.

"Hi, Early Man," Ashes2Ashes wrote. But they were obviously addressing me, and playing a little online chicken. I could only stare at the screen, shaken and stupefied. One more name joined the room.

WARFIELD: "Stop it, Doc Holiday! Go to bed."

They'd come looking for me.

"U guys know each other?" Ashes2Ashes wrote.

EARLY MAN: "We're The Boogeymen. ☺."

SPECIAL ED: "☺."

WARFIELD: "☺."

EARLY MAN: "Here's to old friends and new girls."

I muscled through a bout of sharpening horror at their jeering attempt at backchannel conversation. But before I could type back a response, Early Man vanished from the chat room. Followed by Special Ed. And Warfield. They were gone. Ghosts in my machine. It was just Ashes2Ashes and me again.

"I think you need a new audience," Ashes2Ashes wrote.

You and me both, baby.

EARLYMAN@AOL.COM
To WARFIELD@GMAIL.COM,
SPECIALED@AOL.COM
SUBJECT: DOC HOLIDAY!

What the fuck is he doing?!? This isn't clearing one's history. This is how Big Bad Wolves get their jaws caught in the door!

DOC HOLIDAY

I logged off from Ashes2Ashes, and once again plunged within a wormhole of punishing dread. Almost instinctually, I clicked onto Facebook.

My News Feed immediately informed me of the following:

CRAWLSPACE
Early Man has checked in at Crawlspace
CRAWLSPACE
Warfield has checked in at Crawlspace
CRAWLSPACE
Special Ed has checked in at Crawlspace

There they were, hiding in plain view in cyberspace. They had turned the tables, because they were looking for me now. They had a created a "location," but were using their original names again. And their profile pictures were the same as mine, the factory settings: faceless white silhouettes against light blue backgrounds. Chilled, I stabbed the power button on the computer and shut it down.

I climbed into bed and drew the blankets up to my face, as if hiding from the scary monsters. I started to scroll through my BlackBerry contacts, stopping at Camden's number. It was clear to me that securing it had been a Pyrrhic victory. I couldn't desire her to be my audience, nor ever ask her to be. Any kind of intimacy would be too dangerous. I had a terrible secret I could never betray, and it was parked in my brain like an 18-wheeler.

Even Charlie Brown wouldn't have been surprised at this bittersweet development. It couldn't have been such a revelation. Disappointing? Yes. But truly enlightening? No. Because let's face it – the carpool crush never ends well. Never. It's not built to end happily ever after; it's ill-designed for such resolution.

So the lunatic irony is that Charlie Brown would essentially have to politely tell Lucy to fuck-off. She was now finally holding down the football that was her heart long enough for him to make a serious advance. Giving it up to her old, devoted, heartsick chum… but he wasn't having it. He, who was never never supposed to give up, would be forced to call it a day.

Thanks, but no thanks. I knew you when, baby. Loved you then. You, in your boyfriends' cars, always moving. Me, suspended in arrested development. You in my crosshairs. Me, barely in your rear-view. Maybe if you had stopped moving – stopped lifting the football away from the kicking tee — and I had kept on moving, everything would've turned out different. But no connection was made, no contact. I just landed flat on my ass. And you moved on. You wanted to explore the world. Whereas I stayed down, flat on my ass.

And sometimes we fall so hard and so fast, we never get up again.

You had roads to travel. Adventures to be had. You wanted your space. I tried giving it to you. I got the memo, after all: you needed your space.

But now I need mine.

I have to stay in character.

Pressing the Delete button wasn't easy to do. Just like it couldn't have been easy for Jill Cassady's friends or Tracey Finn's to do after their respective losses. I erased Camden's number from my contacts. And my life. I wouldn't commit it to memory. Because I could never call her. Not now, not ever. Not forever. I would leave it alone.

I started to softly cry. SPOILER: there really is no such thing as Santa Claus. They say a lot of people kill themselves around Christmas time. It's probably because they slip out of character. I imagine that's a mighty plunge and frightening freefall. Because it's not always such a wonderful life.

And no one wants to die alone in the snow.

My Death in 2013.

I knew I would never see Camden again. Or Jill. And I would miss knowing them.

You knew the girl.

AOL NEWS --
"BACKED-UP TOILETS LEAD TO DISCOVERY OF SKELETON IN SEPTIC TANK."

Excavation of this unconventional grave has begun to recover the skeleton, determine the cause and manner of death, and ultimately, the identification of the victim.

Unidentified Human Remains
File #: 4920-88
Date remains found: 1/18/2014
Location: Near Canard Beach, Florida
GENDER: Female
HEIGHT: 5'4"-5'8"
WEIGHT: 120-140 lbs.

ADDITIONAL INFORMATION:
This woman was the victim of a vicious attack and was
found in a septic tank just outside the Canard Beach
area.

CONTACT INFORMATION: If you have any
information to this case or to this person's identity,
please contact the Office of the Chief Medical Examiner
at 305-455-4824.

PART EIGHT

SICK DAY

"But Oz never did give nothing to the Tin Man
That he didn't, didn't already have… "

-- America

"I'll put on the creepy mask, if you'll grant me some
forgetfulness… "

-- Warren Zevon

DOC HOLIDAY

The day they found Jill's body was the longest one of my life. I plunged headlong even further into my wormhole. The story was all over the TV and Internet. Breaking News: her horrible coming-out party. Jill Cassady was all the buzz.

A week later, I was alone at my desk in my Creative Writing classroom, reading a newspaper story about the case and sipping a coffee. Class wasn't starting for another hour.

I heard the dry squeal of sneaker treads on linoleum. And then three students walked into the room, bundled up from the bruising chill in dark hooded parkas and knit caps. Startled, I realized they weren't students, after all. It was the Boogeymen: Early Man, Special Ed, and Warfield. They'd come to Boston to pay me a house call.

Chilled, I watched them plop down in desks in the front row, like eager students coveting knowledge. They had finally come looking for me. Now that Jill's body had finally been found, they'd come to sever the final loose end, once and for all. It made sinister, yet logical sense.

"Jesus. What do you want?" I asked, rising from my desk, frightened to pieces.

"We want to tell you a ghost story," Early Man said.

The Boogeymen smiled, and I knew this was, at worst, a threat. A warning and reminder that I best keep my lips locked about Canard Beach. They shoved up from the desks and creeped out of my classroom, those same dry sneaker squeals now trailing them like whispers.

From the window, I watched them departing the icy school grounds, three dark figures jaunting through the snow. The spoils of my nightmare having come home to roost. They suddenly stopped, turned around, and waved gloved hands at me. I jerked myself away from the window so fast I collided with an empty desk. And then, locking their hands safely together like young campers abiding with the mandate of a field trip's 'buddy system,' they turned and shuffled away.

I waited until they had vanished from sight before scrambling out of the classroom. I paid a quick visit to the English Department secretary and told her I was feeling under the weather. I had to go home. Chalk it up to a Sick Day.

When I returned back to my apartment, I stood by the windows, shaken and shivering. Haunted to pieces and scouring about for signs of the Boogeymen.Would they follow me home, too?

"We want to tell you a ghost story."

It's when I decided to finally take a look at my old, battered Camp Hideaway scrapbook. I opened to the first page, but instead of seeing old, faded photos of myself and the other Boogeymen - frivolous shots and mementos of summer camp fun and frolic – I came across old, yellowed news clippings from *The Cornish Tattler and the Portland Press Herald.* News accounts concerning the Bethany Joseph murder at Camp Hideaway. A few featured grainy photos of her smiling hangman and killer: Toby Danforth, the camp handyman's son with the steel plate in his head.

Turning another page, I was unnerved to see more press clippings about the Joseph murder, torn and dog-eared, from the *Bangor Daily News, Cornish Tattler, Lewiston Sun Journal,* and the Falmouth Forecaster. I flipped another page: more clippings, these from the *Boothbay Register, Gorham Times*, and the *Lincoln County News.* All of them were stories about the "grisly and unspeakable murder" of the Camp Wildwood girl.

A chill tickled me, for this was sure a trifle unsettling. I turned more pages, faster and faster, but every single page was haphazardly taped with similar news stories about the murdered Joseph girl.

Jesus, I thought. If I didn't know any better, I'd think this old thing was a "murder book."

EARLY MAN

"Greetings, my friend. We are all interested in the future, for that is where you and I are going to spend the rest of our lives...

WARFIELD

"And remember my friend, future events such as these will affect you in the future. You are interested in the unknown, the mysterious, the unexplainable. That is why

you are here . . ."

SPECIAL ED
"And now, for the first time, we are bringing to you the full story of what happened on the fateful day . . ."

EARLY MAN
"We are giving you all the evidence, based only on the secret testimonies of the miserable souls who survived this terrifying ordeal . . ."

DOC HOLIDAY
At the very back of the scrapbook was the only photograph, sandwiched upside down between the last two pages. Hiding in plain view. After swiping away the veneer of grime that had settled upon this photo, what I noticed first was its background: a Jolly-Roger-type pirate ship, with a skull-and-crossbones flag waving overhead.

Yes, here was that $2-for a photo of The Boogeymen at the PlayTown amusement park in Portland, Maine. But something was very wrong with this picture.

Something was really, terribly wrong.

EARLY MAN
"The incidents, the places, my friend we cannot keep this secret any longer... "

WARFIELD

SPECIAL ED

EARLY MAN

DOC HOLIDAY
I was alone in it.

PART EIGHT

PEOPLE YOU MAY KNOW

"'Cause they're waiting for me
They're looking for me
Every single night
They're driving me insane
These men inside my brain… "

-- Cheap Trick

DOC HOLIDAY

Over the course of the next several weeks, I became a total recluse, cocooned in bed all day and reading more True Crime books. Keeping up with the Joneses (and the Jim Joneses). Black, abominable observations and thoughts would jump to mind and stubbornly nest there: Andrea Yates actually cooked breakfast for her five children before drowning them in the bathtub. What was that all about? Why waste the eggs?

I couldn't believe that within weeks of dumping his pregnant wife's dead body into the San Francisco Bay on Christmas Eve, Scotty Peterson ordered The Spice Channel. He bought himself some porn. Imagine such wicked selfishness: okay, sure, it's nice to occasionally give yourself a Christmas present. But *two?*

Lee Harvey Oswald tried reconciling with his estranged wife on the night of November 21st, 1963. But she wasn't interested in patching things up. He was out of magic bullets, so he left the house in a dark, miserable funk. And the next day, JFK's brains went airborn in downtown Dallas.

I read that eight out of 10 people are interested in murder, and one is a liar. That didn't leave much wiggle room. I learned about Serialkillersink.com and Darkvomit.com, two websites devoted to selling murderabilia, serial killer art, and other True Crime Collectibles. For those yearning to own John Wayne Gacy letterhead or a "Ted Bundy was a one night stand" T-shirt, this was the place for you. MurderAuction.com is a similar website. Its slogan: "Every man has to have a hobby."

I suppose that much is hard to argue, and my new hobby was spending days and nights online, voraciously searching and investigating for new developments on the Jill Cassady case. It was the only thing that made me feel worthy or alive, this proactive online research and detective work I allotted for myself.

Other than that, I stewed in my own reclusive slop. No phone calls, no e-mails, and no visitors other than takeout delivery guys. I didn't eat much and showered and shaved pretty infrequently. I told my mother I had the flu. The Elephant Man had sharper social skills.

It wasn't the lifestyle choice I ever wanted for myself: the brooding, eccentric recluse. The tortured, hipster doofus who takes permanent furlough from his life. There's no romance in that despite the rapturous mythos to the contrary. I remembered The Unabomber, that lunatic Luddite freak, Ted Kaczynski. Former assistant professor of mathematics (further proof that too much math is good for nobody). He lived in a remote cabin in the woods of Montana. Rebel without electricity. He wrote furious screeds and manifestos, when he wasn't sending deadly letter bombs in the mail.

And that's no way to carry yourself.

Henry David Thoreau also notoriously holed himself up in the middle of the woods, so he could write his famous book, *Walden*, and refuse to pay taxes. Rebel without a W-2. But what's been conveniently omitted from the highfalutin' literary folklore is this little-known fact: his mother would periodically come visit and bring him cookies. True story. Hank Thoreau had his Mommy bring him fucking Oreos.

And that's no way to carry yourself, either.

Or Christopher McCandless, bozo 'hero' of the novel, *Into the Wild.* Frozen Tundra Boy. Rebel without a warm jacket. Made famous for embarking on a solo, "Odyssean" adventure into the Alaskan wilderness to "find himself," because his parents were too affluent and didn't get along so well.

Or something like that.

He decided to become a recluse - "one with with nature" - until nature decided to gobble him up until he was none with nature. And none with everything and done with everyone who ever loved him. Because he froze his testicles off in an abandoned school bus. Apparently he never received the newsflash that he wasn't being a noble pioneer or intrepid iconoclast. No, what he was being was a really stubborn douchebag.

In fact, the bumper affixed to the back of that shitty old bus should've read "LIVE, so the preacher won't have to lie at your funeral!" McCandless went in search of an audience with himself, only to die alone with a face full of icicles. Doesn't exactly sound like the most fun-loving of narcissists. Because let's face it: freezing and starving to death in a school bus in the middle of nowhere is no way to carry yourself.

The moral of the story: any asshole can drop out of society.

The tricky part is hanging in.

And that's what I planned to do: attempt to socialize and acclimate and test-drive my new attitude adjustment. So when Reese and Lansky came to Boston for a wedding in April, I agreed to meet them at a bar called Mad Hatter's. I knew this audience and needed the practice. Since they were my oldest friends, the usual suspects, what better place to start? I showered and shaved and threw on a clean shirt. You might say I got into character.

At Mad Hatter's, Reese, Lansky and myself were a few beers deep, and the waiter had just taken away the carcass of moldering chicken nachos. "Are you guys 'checked in' here?" I taunted, but was surprised to hear they were now Facebook haters. No longer could they stomach all those hideously mundane Status Updates. "Having a bowl of hot tomato soup. YUM!" Even they were too civilized to comment "WHO GIVES A SHIT?!"

We were drinking, laughing, and reminiscing, boozy recollections about former boozy recollections. The Nostalgia Tour. But I didn't tell them I saw Camden on Christmas Eve, or that she's still #1 on my Watch List.

My person of interest.

Because there's a girl out there in the great wide world who's perfectly capable of ruining your life. There just is. Somewhere. Could be anywhere, really. The worst part? Never knowing when she'll strike. But there's no question about it: she will. It's as certain as death and taxes.

I also didn't tell them I wouldn't be returning to Wilton Community College to teach the next semester, or that I'd recently taken a few Sick Days. I was in no condition to teach at the moment, not when there was so much I was still learning about myself. If Missing Chick Lit became part of next year's English department curriculum, I wouldn't know about it.

But omissions aside, we were having a good time together. I'd missed these guys and maybe they'd missed me. We had come full circle despite taking various detours along the way. As they say, "If it wasn't for the last minute, nothing would ever get done." And lately for me, every minute felt like it could be the last one.

Eventually they asked me about Canard Beach. They'd received my postcards from there back in March and wanted to hear everything about my Spring Break festivities. The "gory details," as it were. The March Madness.

"You went with your camp friends?" Reese asked, finding that hard to believe. He used to say that if you're prone to blackouts, you better have some reliable friends.

He has no idea.

Yet they wanted to live vicariously through me, doubtless trying to imagine or re-imagine what it must be like to nail a smokin-hot college girl, pickled-drunk on Jello shots and poor judgment. When they asked about the talent in Canard Beach, I hoped they wouldn't mention anything about the girl from N.C. State who was murdered to pieces down there.

But they never mentioned it, only interested in whether I got laid or not. Did I give it the old college try? Trying to ignore the dangling glob of sour cream perched on Lansky's chin, I said the only reason I went to Florida was because I wanted a change of scenery. Naturally, the guys groaned in abject disappointment. Married guys always groan in abject disappointment.

"Still didn't answer the question," Lansky pressed on. "Get any pussy or not?"

"Come on, guys. Curiosity killed the cat," I said.

"Yeah, but satisfaction brought it back," Lansky said.

"In a bodybag," I said, and probably a little too curtly, because the guys exchanged a look.

The conversation moved to the Red Sox and Celtics. This banter was far less spirited and somewhat of a downgrade; Reese and Lansky's Canard Beach enthusiasm was forced to play second fiddle to teams that had actually won World Series and championship titles in recent years. It wasn't the same. Nothing was anymore.

We said our goodbyes in the parking lot about two hours later. Reese and Lansky had no idea who they'd been drinking with. I was a complete mystery to them. But their ignorance was my bliss and would always have to be that way. If they knew what was good for them, they wouldn't go peeking behind my curtain. Ever.

That was maybe the moment I should have informed them I'd recently been diagnosed with a serious mental illness.

"Dissociative identity disorder is characterized by the presence of two or more distinct or split identities or personality

states that continually have power over the person's behavior. With dissociative identity disorder, there's also an inability to recall key personal information that is too far-reaching to be explained as mere forgetfulness."

Thanks to the series of medical tests, screenings, exams, and mental health evaluations I voluntarily underwent, I essentially conducted a background check on myself. And wasn't thrilled to discover what was lurking behind the curtain.

Crazy, right? My cousin Denise had 958 pictures of herself on Facebook, yet I had fucking "dissociative identity disorder?" But it may have explained why the truths were stranger than the fictions.

I could tell my friends I refused to take my medication very often, nor undergo the psychotherapy and hypnosis sessions prescribed for me. A mind is a terrible thing to waste, and I didn't like the side effects, particularly the loneliness. It made me feel less alive, less in the moment. And that's no way to carry yourself.

I could tell them that in Canard Beach, I played host to three distinct personalities – or "alters" – because there's no such thing as a perfect crime. Just a perfect alibi. I had three of them, these disappeared suspects in the war on terror inside my head. And I didn't want to kill these darlings.

I could tell them that I was just an English teacher who decided to take a vacation after hearing my students discussing their Spring Break plans. Canard Beach, Florida sounded quite nice. Sure, I was a little too old for Spring Break, but was sorely due a time-out from whoever I was. A holiday away from myself.

I deserved some space away from the tapestry of the same old routine: work, work, work, an occasional date, more work, holidays, work, solitude, the usual setbacks and disappointments, nothing monumental nor tragic, but colored with such stifling, crippling monotony, as to not make any difference. The winters too long, the summers too short, spring and fall being the biggest seasonal teases of them all. The change of seasons is overrated, if you don't ski and decapitating snowmen isn't your other favorite hobby.

The Internet was my only outlet. It's so easy to get lost out there in the infinite fantasia that is cyberspace. It's a lot of mental masturbation, but the Internet never sleeps, which means giddy fun for insomniacs. It's a vacation right at your fingertips, an interactive orgy of anonymity, where you can check your empathy and game face at the door. Where you can change your narrative, and become someone else for a while.

And because two's company, three's a crowd, but four's a party, I e-mailed my old camp friends: The Boogeymen. "Spring Break Risk Factor: There is always safety in numbers. Don't travel alone and try to travel in threes." I informed them of my vacation idea, and surprise, surprise: they agreed to meet me. I bought a plane ticket to Florida.

Once I arrived in Canard Beach, I hit the closest bar. The other Boogeymen were staying at their own motel and were supposed to meet me there. It was Karaoke Night, with clusters of boozy, bawdy college kids singing songs and searching for an audience. A girl and a boy were onstage, singing a duet to the old 70's sobfest, *"Seasons in the Sun."*

"Goodbye to you
My trusted friend
We've known each other since we were nine or ten
Together we've climbed hills and trees... "

I met a pretty college girl from Virginia. "So what's your screen name?" I asked. I told her mine, which was a lie. She was wearing snug shorts, a T-shirt and flip-flops. Her skin was browned from maybe too much sun, yet this only made her teeth that much whiter. There were no flies in her ointment, other than the "beauty mark" on her cheek. It could've had its own property deed. I'll never understand why they're called beauty marks and not, say, Little Ugly Bumps. But maybe that's just irony.

She was breezy and engaging and pleasant. The flirtation began. She was accessible and smelled like juniper berries. "Do you really smell like that?" I teased. Of course not, she giggled. Ah, so we had something in common: I wasn't the only one in the room who was lying through his teeth.

She was already fairly hammered so I was staked to a healthy head start. My bullets were chambered. The Boogeymen kept calling and texting me, but I ignored them. The girl and me hung out all night, draining tequila shots and trading easy smiles. I'd never been much of a closer but I could open like a bastard, and I was doing it again, charming her with my wit and humor and wallet. She was taking candy from this stranger. I was Willy Wonka, if the chocolate factory hosted free tours for sweet-toothed hot chicks maybe about to die.

I thought I spotted one of my students amid the jostling, beer-faced crowd. Was that Andy Starkovich from my American Literature class? I couldn't be sure. It just might have been, and that would be embarrassing. Undeterred, I continued to ply my girl with an equal amount of drinks and laudations.

When last call sounded, I honeyed her back to my motel room. It was gonna be a textbook take-down, like shooting fish in a barrel. We started to fool around, sloppy kissing and amateur maneuvering and clumsy groping, but fevered enough. My erection was begging to find some vessel for purchase, release, and resolution. I didn't discriminate, though I did deem handjobs consolation prizes for quitters and asexual folk. But hopefully we'd fuck like drunken Vikings. Maybe have breakfast in the morning if she decided to stay the night. Might be nice to finally attend a Continental Breakfast, like a gentleman. Muffins and coffee, maybe some kind of fun biscuit. And then she'd leave forever. And I would, too. No one gets hurt.

"I don't usually do this," she said, a mid-kiss disclaimer.

"Me neither," I said, jamming my liquored tongue back into her mouth.

But when I moved in for the kill, she grew shy and shoved me away. A change of heart: she didn't wanna fuck. Had no interest in making it interactive with me. And then she tried calling her friend before realizing her cell battery had died. She was unable to even text or Tweet. If she could only yodel, she surely would've given that a whirl.

I thought we were just role-playing. I chuckled, standing mock-guard by the door like a sentry, arms folded across my chest. It was just a touch of drunken foreplay. I was baiting the hook. Sometimes the little fishy says she wants to leave the barrel, but only because she wants you to sharpen your aim before you stick it inside her. She wants you to fine-tune it, to earn it. She wants to feel worthy of your imminent sexual assault.

"Come on," I pleaded with her, my fever spiking high and hard.

"No!" she said, steadfast and defiant. But if "no" doesn't

necessarily mean "yes," it sure as Hell means "maybe." And that I could work with. So I moved for her again, but she shrank away. Dead serious. She really wanted to split. I grew enraged at her improvisation. Even though I'd only known her for a few boozy hours, it just seemed so out of her character. Why so passive-aggressive? She agreed to come back to my room, so what did she expect we were going to do? Play a mean game of Scrabble? She was selling sex, but my money was no good here? I didn't get it: she sure *smelled* consensual.

Trying everything, generous suitor that I was, I told her I was perfectly capable of talking like a white African-American, if that's what she was into.

"I gotta go, I really gotta go," she insisted, re-adjusting the bra beneath her shirt.

"Go where, *yo?"*

"None of your business, okay?"

"Whatever, *G."*

"What the hell's wrong with you?!"

I shrugged. "Forget it, *dawg."*

She shot me a venomous scowl and reinforced her urgent desire to bounce by blasting me some shit about my age. She made it painful and personal. I had to be at least 33, she said. So what the Hell was I doing on Spring Break? It was fuckin' pathetic and weird, she said, me down in Canard Beach preying on college girls. Shouldn't I pick up someone my own age, or pick on someone my own size?

Come on, no one's perfect, I said. And then informed her that John Wayne used to ride small horses so he'd look that much bigger in the saddle. But she didn't know John Wayne from Lil Wayne, and when she went racing for the door it got physical. She managed to land a few innocuous blows on me, before I was able to wrestle her down onto the bed.

Fueled by my intoxication and hideous embarrassment, I found myself throttling her neck. Restraining her, because she was my mark, she was here, and now I was gonna hit it. Oddly empowering, it was – me on top, making the decisions. Her beneath me, wildly flailing, limbs thrashing, gasping and choking and crying.

And unless *she* was Ted Bundy's daughter, this was not her father's Spring Break.

Finally, she stopped resisting, having finally acquiesced, relented and submitted to my advances. Perseverance, persistence, and attrition finally paid off. Well, not really. Because she was dead. Tongue slack in her shiny lipsticked mouth, wide-eyed with her final wonder. No!! Jesus, no! NO!!!!! Frantic, I checked her vital signs, her pulse, whatever part of her I deemed "vital." But no sale. She was all gone.

Sometimes I just get there a little too late.

And that's when I summoned the three other Boogeymen from their motel. They came over and disassembled and disposed of the body, because I was incapable of handling that myself. I was just an English teacher at a fake college. I didn't do dismemberment. Was it a coincidence that an Ace Hardware store was conveniently located two blocks from my motel? Maybe not. And maybe that's what Fate is.

During my cab ride to the Peter Pan bus station the following night, I did a little online research. I learned that because her cell phone was dead and its battery removed, the police would be unable to triangulate it and locate her whereabouts.

I also learned that a college girl missing during Spring Break wouldn't be cause for the police to activate an Amber Alert, because only minors fit those criteria. *("Children and minors who go missing are more sensitive to Amber Alert activation than young adults or teenagers.")* The police would reason that a missing college girl on Spring Break might simply be getting lucky in lust somewhere, and it'd be too early in the game to surmise that she'd been kidnapped or under threat of serious harm. Or death.

Eventually the local authorities would check her bank account and credit cards for transactions, but it might take a few days to secure this information unless or until they contacted the FBI.

"What do you know about the disappearance of Jill Cassady?"

Everything.

But because you can't go crying wolf when you're a member of the pack, I took a bus back to Boston. Staring out the window, the shimmering orb of moon nearly felt like a Hellish searchlight attempting to expose the secrets of my malignant Spreak Break vacation.

It wasn't my night, that's all. It just wasn't my night. Sometimes it's like shooting fish in a barrel. Other times there's either no fish, or your gun is empty.

You know how it is.

So I killed a girl.

But I never raped her.

I misunderstood her.

Her death was an accident.

Maybe her life was.

I am the head of this snake.

We are The Boogeymen.

And we're not for the squeamish.

All four different Facebook accounts shared the same passwords. Because I hosted a party. Come as you are. And we took a vacation in Crazytown. And along came a spider. I had unwittingly created a little fan fiction, crafting three different counterfeit lives into a mental murder mystery. An amoral history of which I could never clear.

But a college girl did die in Canard Beach. There's no question about that. That truth is stranger than any fiction. And I still wonder how many people loved her. Truly loved her. Back home, back at school, out there in the world…

How many were there?

I wonder how many people still miss her. Truly miss her.

How many are you?

So I don't tell Reese and Lansky everything. In fact, I really don't tell them anything. I'd finally cultivated a mystery about myself, and I certainly couldn't betray it now. I'm pretty sure that would've been TMI.

Maybe in a terribly despairing moment that communiqué comes later, perhaps even within the body of a Facebook Status Update. *"Now that I finally have your undivided attention, I have something terrible to tell you, but hope you'll forgive me: I killed a girl on Spring Break. LOL!"*

For now, I just watch my friends drive off. It was good to see them again. I know this audience.

And you write what you know.

facebook

Timeline

About

Photos

Friends

EPILOGUE

CRAWLSPACE.C☺M

"I walk 47 miles of barbed wire
I use a cobra for a necktie
I got a brand new house on the roadside
Made from rattlesnake hide
I got a brand new chimney made on top
Made out of human skulls
Now come on take a walk with me
And tell me, who do you love… "

-- Bo Diddley

DOC HOLIDAY

A month later, I was home boning up on my sickness online. *"In order to deal with situations that are emotional beyond the control of a person, that person may create alternate personalities or "alters" to deal with those situations. At least two of these identities or personality states recurrently take control of the person's behavior... Inability to recall important personal information that is too extensive to be explained by ordinary forgetfulness... There are also highly distinct memory variations, which fluctuate with the person's split personality."*

CNN had reported all day long that the Canard Beach police were looking for the presence of blood in "field tests, but further lab results were pending." And that was a bummer. There was no more room in the wormhole; it was at full capacity. I couldn't brave these headwinds of madness any longer. I was Humpty Dumpty about to take a great fall. It didn't end well for him, either. He basically just died. He fell apart and crumbled to pieces. No one could help him. (Certainly not Jack or Jill, who clearly had problems of their own). The End.

To compartmentalize is to be human. Otherwise, wouldn't we all go crazy? Yet I couldn't live with this anymore: the agony and sleepless nights. The lies and nightmares. The punishing guilt and vexatious shame. I wasn't interested in living out a sentence of unabating dread, paranoia, and disquietude. Here's a dirty little secret: getting away with murder is fucking exhausting.

So I'd finally take responsibility and be accountable for my actions. I owed the closure to Jill's family and friends, and planned on turning myself in to the police.

Twenty-four hours later, my leering mug shot would be splashed all over the Internet and TV, and on newspaper front pages. Like James Dean for a day. ("ENGLISH TEACHER ARRESTED FOR ANTI-SOCIAL NETWORK CRIME.") A Wikipedia page would surely follow. I'd be another uniquely American story, defined as Free Enterprise at the cost of others.

I'd probably be smiling, too, because most of your quality madmen and overnight sensations love to smile in their mug shots. It's like some kind of editorial sick joke: we love you to death. There's always that creepy juxtaposition or tableau: the serial killer with the impish twinkle, or smirking homicidal martyr, visions of monstrous jihad dancing inside his head. David Berkowitz could've sold cupcakes on a street corner with his beatific smile.

Beneath my photo would be the salty tabloid bromide: *"Loved her to pieces. But left her in pieces."*

Steal Your Facebook right off your head.

EARLYMAN@AOL.COM
To WARFIELD@GMAIL.COM,
SPECIALED@AOL.COM
SUBJECT: DOC HOLIDAY!!

WHAT?! We got away with it and he wants to blow the mystery now?! Never. No way. Never happen.We need to cut the head off this snake.

WARFIELD@GMAIL.COM
To EARLYMAN@AOL.COM,
SPECIALED@AOL.COM

Can we please NOT talk about snakes?

SPECIALED@AOL.COM,
WARFIELD@GMAIL.COM
To EARLYMAN@AOL.COM

We could always blind him.

EARLYMAN@AOL.COM
To WARFIELD@GMAILCOM,
SPECIALED@AOL.COM

I say we dismember him.

WARFIELD@GMAIL.COM
TO EARLYMAN@AOL.COM,
SPECIALED@AOL.COM

Or snap his fucking neck.

EARLYMAN@AOL.COM
To WARFIELD@GMAIL.COM,
SPECIALED@AOL.COM

Whatever we decide, he needs to die. In the snow.
Alone.

EARLY MAN
"Billy, you're crazy."
"Guilty."

SPECIAL ED
"Billy, you're crazy."
"Guilty."

WARFIELD
"Billy, you're crazy."
"Guilty."

DOC HOLIDAY
A few days later I bought the weapon and the bullets on the
Internet. It was time to say goodbye, but there had been a change
of plans. I didn't want to go to prison for the rest of my life.
Who's got that kind of energy?

SPECIALED@AOL.COM
To EARLYMAN@AOL.COM,
WARFIELD@GMAIL.COM

Wow. We did it. He's a goner! Mission accomplished, huh? Hey, I'm gonna miss Billy. And miss you guys, too.

WARFIELD@GMAIL.COM
To EARLYMAN@AOL.COM,
SPECIALED@AOL.COM

Yeah, man. I will, too.

EARLYMAN@AOL.COM
To SPECIALED@AOL.COM,
WARFIELD@GMAIL.COM

Ditto. But show me a handsome corpse and I'll show you someone who didn't live up to his potential.

Our mancation is over, boys. What are friends but strangers waiting to happen?

So let's all sing it together now. One last time...

"Goodbye to you, my trusted friend.
We've known each other since we were nine or ten..."

SPECIALED@AOL.COM
To EARLYMAN@AOL.COM,
WARFIELD@GMAIL.COM

"Together we climbed hills and trees

Learned of love and ABCs..."

**WARFIELD@GMAIL.COM
To EARLYMAN@AOL.COM,
SPECIALED@AOL.COM**

"Goodbye my friend, it's hard to die..."

DOC HOLIDAY

When the moment finally came for me to link out rather than link in, I wondered if stone-deaf Mrs. Dubin next door would even hear the gunshots. Maybe she'd just think they were firecrackers.

I guess you're always leaving someone behind or someone's leaving you behind. I would certainly miss my dear mother. And miss teaching my students Poe's The Tell-Tale Heart next semester. Could've been interesting.

"Through a dream landscape, a girl flees in terror and is alone amid crumbling castles, antique dungeons, and ghosts. She nearly escapes her terrible persecutors, who seek her out of lust and greed, but is caught; escapes again and is caught; escapes once more and is caught... "

But I had enough Gothic elements in my own life, thank you very much. The voices in my head were different ones, new ghosts in my machine, espousing peachy admonitions and desperate pleas: "Do the right thing." And they weren't wrong.

There may be two sides to every story, but there were four sides to mine. It was time to clear my history, but not before putting my account on the record in the hopes of keeping it off the record. (And if you must know, certain motherfuckers self-publish for a reason.)

Because sometimes *you* make The Girl Next Door go away.

EARLY MAN

WARFIELD

SPECIAL ED

EARLY MAN

"Give me your tired, your poor,
Your huddled masses
Yearning to breathe free,
The wretched refuse
Of your teeming shore… "

The Boogeymen will never be reached for comment.
Sweet dreams, Oprah. Wherever you are.

This one's for you.

DOC HOLIDAY

They say that sometimes the arsonist returns to the scene of his crime because he gets a charge out of the aftermath, so I went online before ending my life. And because Facebook is nothing if not forgiving of the past, I discovered that I had a Friend Request: "CAMDEN MILLER WANTS TO ADD YOU AS A FRIEND. CONFIRM or IGNORE."

   "Finally she may break free altogether and be married to the virtuous lover who has all along worked to save her."

   She was smiling in her profile picture. A homesick ghost. We finally had something in common. I put the weapon down on my desk. Was this Fate?

   When in Rome.

   You gotta love Rome.

EARLYMAN@AOL.COM
To SPECIALED@AOL.COM,
WARFIELD@GMAIL.COM

SUBJECT: CAMDEN MILLER???????????????

Whoa! Who the hell is this? Is that the same chick he used to write those letters to during camp Rest Period?

SPECIALED@AOL.COM
To EARLYMAN@AOL.COM,
WARFIELD@GMAIL.COM

Yeah, it's gotta be her. This can't be good, can it?

WARFIELD@GMAIL.COM
To EARLYMAN@AOL.COM,
SPECIALED@AOL.COM

Jesus! What if he tells HER what we did? What do we do?!

EARLYMAN@AOL.COM
To WARFIELD@GMAIL.COM,
SPECIALED@AOL.COM

I say we put her down like Old Yeller.

WARFIELD@GMAIL.COM
To EARLYMAN@AOL.COM,
SPECIALED@AOL.COM

You want to kill a THIRD girl?!

**EARLYMAN@AOL.COM
To SPECIALED@AOL.COM,
WARFIELD@GMAIL.COM**

Bethany Joseph doesn't count. We were minors then.

**SPECIALED@AOL.COM
To EARLYMAN@AOL.COM,
WARFIELD@GMAIL.COM**

LOL?

DOC HOLIDAY

Maybe it was finally time to properly bury the past instead of continuing to exhume it. Maybe Camden was coming over to my side of the ball. Maybe she was going to save me. Maybe she was going to extend my moment.

Because this is a story about a girl.

So I clicked the CONFIRM button. Perfect timing, too, because she had just written to me in Facebook Messenger's chat window:

"Hey, Billy. I thought you were going to call me." XOXO

"I'm not for you," I wrote back. XOXO

"What do you mean?" XOXO

"Sometimes you just get there a little too late." XOXO

"What are you talking about?" XOXO

"You're not in Kansas anymore." XOXO.

"???" XOXO.

"You can find everything you ever wanted to know on Wikipedia, except for two things: the cure for cancer. And why she never loved me." XOXO

"What are you TALKING about, Billy? Let's get drinks soon." XOXO

"Only if you're feeling vulnerable." XOXO

"Haha!" XOXO

SPECIALED@AOL.COM
To EARLYMAN@AOL.COM,
WARFIELD@GMAIL.COM

Wait. I'm confused. What is he doing?!

WARFIELD@GMAIL.COM
To EARLYMAN@AOL.COM,
SPECIALED@AOL.COM

I don't know!

DOC HOLIDAY

Camden was looking to find a friend. So she could vent over cocktails and tell me everything that went wrong with her ex-husband, Tucker. "But we're still best friends," she'd promise. An unnecessary disclaimer. No one gives a shit. No one's interested. Seriously. Fuck Tucker. Fuck ALL of them. And by the way: there's no way you're still best friends with the ex. "Friends," maybe. But "best" friends?

Stop it.

Yet I'd sit there, pretending to be a good listener, nodding and drinking, and curious as to whether Facebook was as equally forgiving of the future as the past, and maybe I'm sneaking peeks at her cell phone, wondering if her battery is either dead or dying, and she'd be blissfully oblivious as to where she really was in my head: my apartment, where we're making love or hate or whatever it's called and her egg is running and she's not shrinking away and she's either coming or going, meaning I'm either falling for her again or striking back – stay tuned! - and she's screaming and screaming because I can be her bad boy, too, and this is my life and there's no turning back and life is a battle cry and I get like this when I don't take my meds, which I haven't, because no one wants to die alone in the snow, and I love you Mom, and I miss you Dad and "don't ever tell anybody anything. If you do, you start missing everybody," and that's no

way to carry yourself. And love is madness - sickening, isn't it?
        "Billy, you're crazy."
        "Guilty."
        I'm the Boogie Man. That's what I am. And I'm staying in
character. Every day until I'm dead and buried deep within the
black bosom of the Earth. Maybe someone always has to die, so
the rest of us can count our blessings. And FYI: have you ever
considered that a really sharp icicle might be the perfect murder
weapon, since it melts and leaves behind no evidence? And what
doesn't kill you doesn't make you stronger – it makes you lucky.
And sometimes a ghost story is a love story in disguise. And
Camden is howling and screaming and thrashing and Mrs. Dubin
next door prob'ly thinking a human sacrifice is underway, and
really, maybe, not being far from the truth...

EARLYMAN@AOL.COM
To WARFIELD@GMAIL,
SPECIALED@AOL.COM

I think I know what he's doing.

WARFIELD@GMAIL.COM
To EARLYMAN@AOL.COM,
SPECIALED@AOL.COM

WHAT?!

EARLYMAN@AOL.COM
To WARFIELD@GMAIL,
SPECIALED@AOL.COM

He's looking for an audience…

DOC HOLIDAY

"Okay. We'll make a plan," I finally wrote back to Camden. "But I can't make any promises I'll be on my best behavior." XOXO.

And we won't.

Doc Holiday has checked in at Crawlspace.

ACKNOWLEDGEMENTS

I'd like to thank my own personal "audience," of whom generously helped me slog through this ghoulish journey into the literary fucking abyss: Scott Rosenberg, Josh Appelbaum, and Andre` Nemec. Editor, Clair Lamb. And Langley Perer of Mosaic Media Group. And I'd probably be remiss if I didn't issue some special, demented thanks to Bret Easton Ellis, George A. Romero, Ted Bundy, Jim Morrison, Pete Townshend. And, of course, to my mother, who could've institutionalized me when she had the chance. And lastly, there's Henry Black. To all of the above: thanks for playing...

-- Phil Rosenberg